MALE FOR SALE

Author Bari Bacco

Darling Nicola

Love 🖊 x

Forward

Based on a true story of an attempted Royal blackmail plot in the UK, 'MALE FOR SALE' is fiction and not necessarily based on fact.
Some of this story has been created for dramatic purpose.

Names and most places have been changed to comply and protect innocent parties, and the victim's anonymity.
Any similarities to people or places, that have the same name, are purely coincidental and unintentional, although some names of places are used in fantasy scenarios.

Known as *'The Firm'*, this sensational attempt rocked Buckingham Palace, who sent in MI5 and MI6 to investigate, which resulted in being World News.

Not since 1891 had there been an attempt to Blackmail a member of the Royal family, when the Duke of Clarence son of King Edward VII consulted a solicitor, to pay off £200 to a prostitute he had visited, in return for indiscreet letters he had written to her.

Warning

This book contains Expletives, and description of Explicit and Erotic sex acts with both sexes.

Synopsis

Rogan Ford Is Male For Sale — Cougars, Sugar Daddies, Socialites, Celebrities, the Rich, Powerful and Influential. It was all the same to him as long as they paid!

"You Pay, I Play!" Rogan Ford.

"They've been laid, I've been paid." Rogan Ford.

Roaming the party scene of London's glitterati and in millionaire playgrounds around the world whilst networking amongst *'Movers and Shakers',* bisexual Gigolo handsome hunk Rogan seeks out clients who will pay for his extravagant lifestyle in return for *'pleasure par excellence'.* Feeling comfortable and confident both in luxurious *'Five Star'* hotels and socialite parties with the rich and famous, and diversely in the deviant salacious underworld of Bondage and Transvestite nightclubs, Rogan like a chameleon plays out his changing role, but always with champagne, cocaine and sex just at arms length.

Introduced by his cockney friend Eddy; to Hugo a wealthy man who is the *'Executive Manager'* of *'Ranley', an* exclusive store in Mayfair owned by a member of the Royal family, the friends plot and hatch a devious plan of intrigue to extract explicit and inappropriate information from Hugo, that incriminate and target the Royal for blackmail, which sensationally rocks the Royal Family establishment.

Scenarios

The scenarios in this book lead up to the inconceivable attempt to blackmail a member of The Royal Family.

The future 3 years on...

"We're gonna take the Royals to the fucking cleaners!"
Rogan Ford.

Present day. ITV News

A television newscaster delivers an explosive top story of the day.

"Good morning I am Marcus Holby, we have a breaking news story. Buckingham Palace has been rocked by the news of an attempted royal blackmail plot! Two men have been arrested and are helping police with their enquiries, we are going straight over to our royal correspondent Amelia Pancarty who is outside Buckingham Palace."

"Good morning Amelia, do you have any more details to this astonishing story of who the men are, and who were they trying to blackmail?"

"Marcus, all I can tell you is, two men were arrested last night in a top hotel in Mayfair London, after the police had a tip off. Buckingham Palace press office has declined to comment."

"The Queen must be very upset and angry, mustn't she Amelia."

"As I said Marcus, the Palace has declined to comment."

"Thank you Amelia."
The newsreader continues talking to the viewers.

"We will keep you updated throughout the day, as this story unfolds and develops..."

3 Years previous...
Friday night Mauies Club

"Sorry fellas your outfits are not suitable, you're not coming in." The 'Picker' had spoken – his word was final.
The two drunken laddish guys wearing traffic cones on their heads were rejected and escorted from the queue by two burly club bouncers.

It was Eddy's 25th birthday, and he had never been into the exclusive glitzy Mauies Club in Chelsea before, as it was difficult to get past the *'Picker'* and doormen, who had a strict door policy for entrance and vetted all of the people, eager to get into the famous club, frequented by celebrities and VIPs. This was the club of the moment to go and be seen! The *'Picker,'* a camp looking young man with pink glitter lipstick and matching pink glitter eye shadow, wearing a pink sequin tailcoat suit with giant pink feathers adorning his shoulders, pink sequin top hat and pink sequin thigh length boots, sat on a high pink stool in front of the door entrance, which had a giant shocking pink 'M' letter above the entrance that lit up and spanned the height of the building.
Clutching a clipboard that had a VIP guest list attached, the *Picker* looked down at it every-time a person reached the front of the fifty strong queuing, and gave their name. Many of them would lean over the top of the clipboard and point out their name listed.
As the list was in alphabetical order, they would often point to a name in the section, that was a similar spelling and lie, saying *'Your office have misspelt it!'*
The *Picker* was wise to this trick, but his thoughts were *'If you're not good-looking, than you're not coming in! If you are good looking, who cares about the list!'*

He was the Pink Queen of Mauies, It was all down to him, who got in?

Eddy at 5ft 10" in height, had a slim perfect package sexy physique.

Many girls referred to him as a 'Pocket Rocket'. Eddy would respond by grabbing their hand and pushing it into his pocket, so they could feel his rocket!

He was wearing a black kid leather bomber jacket, by designers Dolce and Gabanna, which he had bought several days before from a shoplifter he knew, who stole it from Harrods Menswear department.

The shoplifter offered it to him for cash deal of £300, which Eddy could not resist, as the retail price swing ticket for £1,900 was still on it.

Underneath he wore a white T-shirt and white skinny jeans which he thought would give him a cool jet-set hipster look, and look complete with the £250 black Prada shades he had bought from another shoplifter a month ago for £50.

He had tried several times to get into Mauies, but had been refused entry.

On one occasion the streetwise cockney was stopped at the door by the security, because he was drunk and high on drugs, and on another, refused due to a friend who was with him, swearing at the doormen, who had informed him the dress code for entry did not allow 'Trainers' he was wearing, even if they were designed by DSQUARED2.

This time his friend International porno model Roberta Spetzini who was a member, had invited him to celebrate his birthday as a treat.

Roberta had long blonde hair, and 36 DD implant breasts, that she called her Barbie boobs, and an hour glass figure to match, making her irresistible to man and beast.

As soon as she walked up to the red rope barrier in front of the entrance, a doorman unhooked it from the metal stand and ushered her through with Eddy in tow, to be checked off by the 'Picker'.

As she walked past them, she sashayed swaying her hips side-to-side.

One of the doormen pursed his lips and screwed his face with a look of pain, lust and desire, enjoying a vision in his head of stripping Roberta of her dress and imagining her naked.

"I'd like to give her one!" He said to the other doorman, who made the same expression salivating at the same thought. Since his other attempts of stepping into the exclusive nightclub, the doormen and Picker employees had changed, so Eddy's previous attempts to enter the club would not be registered, although Roberta was his guarantee and the key to Mauies front door, as the doorman were transfixed feasting their gaze on her enormous breast and long legs.

As she stood giving her name to the *'Picker', the doormen* admired her pert bum, bursting through her short tight white virginal dress, and the top of her thigh revealed through a long slit up to her waist, which left little to the imagination, taking the focus off Eddy who slipped by. Inside the club, Latin American dance music was playing, and as soon as Roberta stepped inside, she raised her arms above her head, bent slightly sticking out her bum, and began to 'Twerk' *(Shaking her bum side to side in fast repetitive movement)* in time to the rhythm. Roberta was an attention seeker and loved to make a grand entrance sexing up the crowd.

Eddy went behind Roberta who was taking centre stage of the dance floor and grabbed each side of her hips as he pumped his crotch forwards and backwards, imitating anal Intercourse.

After their exhibition of sexy dance moves, they made their way to a table booth.

Rogan a frequent Mauies member, had watched them taking center position on the dance floor, and went across to their table carrying an ice bucket with a bottle of champagne chilling inside.

Without asking permission he sat down on the pink leather sofa alongside Eddy, and placed the ice bucket down on the table in front of them

"You two need a drink to cool down after that hot performance, you turned me on! Will you join me for some Champagne?"

"Ta mate, lovely, it's my twenty fifth birthday today, that will go down well."

"Mmm' I like a boy who goes down well." Rogan said laughing as he reached and removed the Prada sunglasses Eddy was still wearing.

"Lets see what's behind those shades."

Eddy winked and blew a kiss in the air at Rogan.

"That's better, I can see the windows of your soul, and I'm about to climb in!"

Rogan placed his hand suggestively on the inside of Eddy's thigh, and gave it a squeeze.

"Blimey! 'ang on, you 'aint poured me a glass of bubbly yet!"
Eddy grabbed his hand from going any higher.

"I didn't give you permission to enter by the back door."

"I was going for the front door and looking for your knocker! I'll check out your back door later?"

They both laughed.

Eddy had high hollow cheeks that led to his large voluptuous lips, surrounding a large mouth that dominated his face, giving him great androgynous sex appeal.

His voice was deeper than expected, and he spoke with a cocky cockney accent, that was intriguing, confusing the attraction of him as 'A bit of rough'.

As he moved his head, his long light brown hair parted in the middle, split his floppy long fringe, to fall as curtains across his eyes, which he repeatedly pushed to either side as he spoke.

The waiter arrived at the table, and Rogan took command, *"Could you bring some champagne flutes?"*

As the waiter walked away Rogan grabbed the champagne bottle by the neck, and lifted it out of the ice bucket *"Lets have a drink whilst we're waiting."*

Roberta leaned across Eddy, pursed her plump filler lips, kissed the palm of her hand and blew a kiss at Rogan.

"What's your name sexy?" Rogan said as he kissed Eddy on the cheek. Before he could answer, Roberta leaned across. *"Roberta."*

Rogan laughed, *"Amazing he said that without moving his lips!"*

Eddy outstretched his palm in front of Roberta's face, as a signal not to speak. *"Speak to the hand! My name is Eddy, the diva is Roberta."*

"Those lips should be around something long." Rogan said suggestively as he leaned across Eddy, teasing Roberta, and sliding the bottleneck gently down across her lips, until the opening reached her open mouth.

As he poured some of the champagne into her mouth, she threw her head backwards in order not to spill it down her dress.

Deliberately pouring it fast, so that the drink overflowed out of her mouth, and ran down her neck onto her breasts, he stood up, stuck out his tongue and bent across Eddy, suggesting that he was about to lick the top of her cleavage.

"You cheeky gobbler." Said Eddy with a broad smile, as he put his forefinger into Rogan's mouth.

"Be careful, I might gobble you up next!"

The waiter reappeared at the table with three champagne flutes.

Taking the lead again Rogan told the waiter to bring three Tequila shots.

"You're a wild geezer, I love you." Eddy said as he downed some more champagne.

Rogan knew a lot of the club members, as he went there several times a week.

Good-looking girls and guys wearing the latest designs in fashionable clothes wondered up to their table and stopped there, to chat with Rogan and an introduction to the hot couple.

Handing out his own glass of champagne for them to sip, Rogan acted with an air of superiority blessing the selected few.

Eddy was impressed with his charismatic style and realized Rogan's popularity would secure his VIP entry to the club for the future, without relying on Roberta to flaunt her breasts when she was back in town! He would be able to name drop *"I'm meeting Rogan here."* Rogan must become his friend.

Step into the World of Rogan Ford
Champagne, Cocaine, Sex.

Present day...
The Mostyn
Pimlico London SW1

In his flat within a private block, set in the smart residential area of Pimlico London, 32-year-old handsome Gigolo Rogan Ford undressed in his bedroom and pulled down his white designer Calvin Klein briefs, stepped out and kicked them across the floor as he walked naked into his *'state of art'* wet room, complete with a built in sound system that would play his favourite sound tracks, he had previously set.

Pressing the sound button, James Brown's Sex Machine boomed out. Rogan wriggled his snake hips to the beat and sang along, 'Get up, *get on up, get up, get on up, stay on the scene, get on up, like a sex machine'*.

Turning the temperature dial tap, the warm water 'rain effect' shower beat down onto his muscular tanned shoulders, mixing with his expensive Jo Malone exotic shower gel, and enhancing the aroma of the Lime, Basil and Mandarin cream he had applied to his chest. Forming white soapy foam lather, it continued its way down across his six-pack.

His bronzed muscles glistened, as the suds slithered by and gathered in his black pubic hair, reminding him of the 48 year old divorcee client, who last night had spread yogurt over his abdomen, and then licked it off.

Reaching down to his pubic hair, he scooped some of the suds to wash around his penis and testicles.

His soapy penis felt good in his hand, as it slipped back and forth in his grip.

Rogan smiled proudly of his long thick throbbing 'Lick Stick', the name he, (like most men do) had given to his penis and often joked about with his friends.

It had been good to him, and had provided more than just a meal ticket, as he was living in a luxurious flat, and although rented, was very expensive and indirectly paid for by his clients.

The water temperature suddenly turned hotter *'I must get that fixed'* he thought, but the action sent his blood rushing around his body exciting and arousing him as he got a semi erection, and for a moment he was tempted to masturbate, but thought that would be a waste, as he was booked for action again that night, and wanted to give his best performance.

As he stepped out of the wet-room shower, which was en-suite to his bedroom, he grabbed a Ralph Lauren white fluffy bath towel embroidered on a corner with the designers logo in navy blue, of a Polo player mounted on a horse taking a swipe with his mallet at a wooden ball. Wrapping the towel around his shoulders to mop some of the water still running down his shoulders, he took a second towel to rub down his toned muscular thighs, buttocks and the thrill seeker between his legs.

The bedroom was fitted with floor to ceiling honey colour beech wood wardrobes, edged with black ebony and black glass handles, which spanned the length of the wall facing his Super-King size bed. This was his inner sanctum, and not for the clients he would escort or sexually service, arranged by the agency *'Pleasure Par Excellence'* that he belonged to, or clients who had booked him through his personal website.

He had been sleeping with both men and women, sometimes both together, for money since his early twenties, which would conjure connotations of him being a 'Rent Boy', although he preferred to say he was a 'Gigolo'. There wasn't much difference, no matter what title.

Sometimes clients just wanted to lie in bed next to him cuddling without sex, and others wanting a sensual massage or to massage him.

Several nights a week, he would visit clients in their homes, hotels, and other places of their choice.

Clients had requested his sexual services in all kinds of fantasy scenarios; membership to the '*Mile High Club*', back seat bonks in Bentleys dressed as a chauffeur, and rolling in the hay of Horse stables, dressed in riding britches, - but not for very long!

His strangest request was to impersonate the 'James Bond' style actor, wearing a black polo neck sweater and trousers in the TV advert for Cadburys Milk Tray, who climbed up a mansion wall and entered a bedroom window, to secretly deliver a box of chocolates to a sleeping woman in her bedroom.

Rogan did not have a head for heights, and would only deliver the chocolates from inside the house.

The woman pretended to be asleep, as he placed the chocolate box next to her on a bedside table, and unlike the actor in the advert, he stripped off naked and slipped under the woman's bed covers, caressing her body.

On the bedside table was an open 'Hermes' handbag containing a roll of money secured by an elastic band, for him to take as the fee for his mysterious services, and then to leave as mysteriously as he had arrived - without a goodbye!

The kinkiest booking that left him wondering to the identity of his client, happened when he visited Cliveden House Hotel Berkshire.

Rogan had Googled the hotel on his laptop and discovered it had been the scene of the 60s Scandal 'Profumo Affair', when the married up and coming Conservative Secretary of State for War, John Profumo embarked on an illicit affair with Christine Keeler, the Mistress of a Russian Spy.

Cliveden Hotel near Windsor is nine miles from one of The Queen's other residences' Windsor Castle.

The booking seemed even more exciting; *'Would the client be a spy wearing a black patch over one eye, holding a gun to him as they demanded he performed sexual acts?'*

As always when visiting a client at a hotel, his name was listed as an expected visitor at the reception desk. He had been told to ask for Room 69, which he found amusing that the client had gone to the trouble of going to the extreme detail, of choosing the room number that had sexual connotations *'Soixante-neuf'*, known as the sex position when two people simultaneously perform oral sex on each other.

The receptionist ushered Rogan through to go up to the room.

The front door was ajar and Rogan intrepidly entered.

Sitting on the bed was a giant yellow furry Bunny wearing a gold crown!

Rogan could not contain himself and burst out laughing.

The person in the Bunny costume stood up and hugged Rogan around his waist, and placed their head on his shoulder.

As the Bunny did not say anything, Rogan burst out laughing and jokingly asked, *"Would you like a Carrot? I've got a big one!"*

The Bunny jumped up and down, displaying excitement, and then jumped onto the bed and continued jumping up and down, before bouncing off into Rogan's arms.

Rogan took off his denim jeans jacket and T-shirt, as the Bunny still silent, motioned for him to also undo and take off his jeans, as they were unable to do it, with the bunny costume gloves.

Wearing just his pants, the Bunny pulled him onto the bed and kneeled with his back to Rogan with his bum raised, and pointing to the seat of the costume, adorned with a white round bobble tail.

Rogan fumbled through the fur and found a slit leading to the bunny's anus.

Before Rogan could examine any further, the bunny turned around and mauled at Rogan's underpants, indicating for him to take them off.

Over the years Rogan had performed in many sexy fantasies his clients had organized, but he had never fucked a bunny, and found the idea bizarre and funny, making it difficult to be sexy and get a hard-on.

The bunny put their head towards Rogan's penis, pushing their tongue through a slit in the mouth, wanting to give him oral sex.

Rogan had to close his eyes and think of another sexy encounter, as the image of a bunny sucking him, would have been too funny to maintain an erection.

Holding onto the bunny's ears, he pulled their head towards him, so that every time they retracted, he would maximize his pleasure by forcing them to take his thrusts.

As he was about to ejaculate he pulled the ears so hard, they tore off, which made him laugh out loud and loose his erection for a short while!

Stuffing his payment into his jeans pocket, he could not resist laughing as he said in a squeaky voice, the closing line of Disney's Looney Tunes Cartoon Character 'Bugs Bunny' – *"That's all folks!"*

He never found out if the person inside the costume was male or female or a foreign spy?

As Windsor Castle was so close, he romanced with the idea of the person inside the costume, was a member of the Royal Family?

Rogan was well suited to being a professional Gigolo and Companion, which satisfied his insatiable sex drive and paid him well.

Being bisexual he serviced Cougars, Sugar Daddies and sometimes Celebrities; it was all the same to him, as long as they paid.

As he walked naked across the white shag carpet, his feet sunk into the luxurious plush pile tickling his toes, and giving him the feeling of comfort that he had achieved a high standard of life.

Opening a drawer built into the run of wardrobes, he pulled out a pair of white briefs bought on the Internet from an American designer of kinky male underwear that focused on maximizing the size of a penis by way of being styled with an uplifting pouch, that projected the penis and testicles forward to increase and enhance a more attractive bulge. Stepping into them, he pulled them up and gazed in a full-length mirror at the sudden increase of his bulge, trapped and looking for a way out.

Laughing, he mumbled *'Budgie Smugglers' (The name given to tight fitting Speedos, sometimes also called 'Lolly Bags'). 'Not right, too tight'*.

Pulling them down again, he stepped out and threw them onto his bed, which was covered with a big black fur throw that trailed onto the floor next to some magazines he had been reading in bed; GQ, Mens Health, Esquire and Attitude. Reaching into the drawer again, he selected another pair of white trunks emblazoned with gold initials 'E.A' on the waistband, for designer Emporio Armani.

His pants now on, changed his look from 'Sleazy to Sophisticated and sexy', more apt and appealing to the rich client booked for his services.

As he looked at his reflection with admiration and vanity, pointing at his image in the mirror, he grabbed his bulge with his other hand and said out loud, "W*hat you see is what you get! – You Pay, I play!"*

His laptop that was on a bedside table rang to inform him of a Skype call coming through. Recognizing the on screen name was his friend Eddy, he answered the call by switching the camera on, and stood sideways at hip level to the built in camera, and to jokingly shock Eddy as he showed off his huge bulge, on the screen.

"Wow! I'd know that dick of death anywhere." Said Eddy laughing.

Rogan turned towards the Laptop screen pulled down his pants and pushed his cock towards the built in camera.

"Wanna nosh?" He said laughing

"Hi you Gay Tart, 'asn't it fallen off yet?" Eddy said still laughing at Rogan's bold remarks and image.

"Not yet buddy, but when it does, I'll post it to you and you can shove it up your arse!"

"You out tonight? Or are you keeping your junk in your pants?"

"Yep, I've got some Rich Bitch to fuck at her hotel on Park Lane, but we can meet first for a drink at 'Mauies Bar' if you like?

"Great, what time?" Eddy replied keenly.

"Eight is good." Replied Rogan once again as he pushed his semi erect penis towards the camera.

"Your eight inches is also good!"

Eddy responded by pressing his thick sensual lips against the screen, spreading them as if they were about to swallow the whole laptop.

"See you later Big Boy."

Eddy now a member at Mauies, sat at the bar having a drink, as he waited for Rogan to arrive.

"Alright darlin." Rogan said affectionately and deliberately dropping the 'g' off the end of 'darling', to imitate Eddy's cockney accent, as he grabbed Eddy from behind, causing Eddy to swing around on the stool, knocking his knee into Rogan's crotch.

"Sorry mate." Eddy said laughing at the comical blow, as he covered his mouth with his hand

"Fuck! You knocked me right in the goolies! What are you trying to do, kill the goose that lays the punters?" Rogan snapped.

"It's not my fault you've got a big pecker stuffed down your trousers!"

Eddy jumped off the stool and placed his hand on Rogan's crotch, giving it a shake. *"Ah diddums, shall I kiss it better?"* The two still laughing sat on the stools.

Eddy passed a Cocktail glass to Rogan. *" 'ear, I already got you your favourite cocktail, a Black Russian."* Eddy confirmed the ingredients. *"Coffee Kahlua, Vodka, Coke and one piece of ice! I popped into that swanky store Ranley in Mayfair today, to see an old friend of mine I've known for a while; Hugo, 'ees the manager, 'E picked me up last year in the 'City Of Quebec pub', we call 'The Elephants Graveyard' back of Marble Arch.*

Rogan interrupted and repeated. *"Elephants Graveyard?"*

"Yea! It's where all the old gay codgers go, 'oo are on their last legs looking to get some cock!"

I was standing at the bar, all the rent boys call 'The Meat Rack' and Hugo offered me an'undred to go back with 'im. I said you're 'aving a laugh, aren't you! I don't cross the road for less than two fifty! And don't get into bed for less than a monkey, you've 'ad that! 'E paid up!" Eddy laughed.

You've got to meet 'im, 'ees a right laugh, really camp, knows all the celebs and Royal tarts, some of the stories 'e tells, are

'ilarious, 'ees tongue spits out one liners quicker than a machine gun, and can be as cruel as a viper!" Eddy said in-between taking gulps of his favourite Peroni beer, which he was drinking straight from the bottle through a piece of lime, wedged into the bottleneck.

"'E's invited me around tonight, wanna come, 'ees a good contact, right diamond geezer, lovely gaff near Marble Arch, plenty of wonga." Eddy said with a wink, as he rubbed his thumb repeatedly across the inside tip of his index finger and middle finger, as a gesture sign for lots of money.

"I already told you this afternoon, I've got to bang a rich old bird first, Myra Stanwick, she only booked me for two hours though. I've checked her out, she's American and married to a Movie Mogul. I've also checked him out on the Internet and 'Celebrity Bulletin,' and his flying in from Palm Springs Florida tonight! It will be exciting fucking against the clock! "

"Oh yea! I forgot, I should have realized, your shirt open down to yer tits, enough to flash your pecs, wasn't a come on for me! What's Celebrity Bulletin about then?" Eddy quizzed.

"It's a monthly bulletin sheet which I subscribe to on the Internet, that tells you information of all the Celebs and people in the entertainment business, the dates of when they are arriving in London, and what hotels they are staying in. I give some of the desk clerks in the top hotels a hundred quid a month, to give my business card to any of their clients on the bulletin sheet, who want some escort company, and a tip on results. They can book me direct on my website, that way I don't have to pay any commission to my agency."

Well, why don't we meet afterwards, and go for a laugh." Eddy said, eagerly.

"Okay, Fuck it's nearly nine! I'm supposed to be there now!" Rogan said looking at his watch, as he downed his Black Russian, slammed the glass down onto the bar and jumped up from the barstool.

"Maybe she'll start without you?" Eddy said laughing.

"Meet you back here about eleven thirty? It'll be Wham Bam! Thank-you Mam! As I give her a quick one, a poke in her mouth, grab her money, piss off, and leave her in heaven licking the cum off her lips, before Mr Hollywood gets to town!" Rogan said with a wink as he laughed *and grabbed Eddy's head, pulling him closer to kiss him, on the cheek.*
Rogan and Eddy's friendship blossomed striking up an affinity.

There was no real sexual chemistry between the two, but occasionally when Rogan got asked for another guy to take part in his clients' fantasies, he brought Eddy into the equation.

They both enjoyed mix and match threesomes together, with both women and men who were paying, and went on the town several nights a week clubbing and seeking out parties, living off cocaine and looking to mix with all kinds of influential people.

'Danté Suite' The Marmion Hotel

Rogan walked confidently into 'The Marmion Hotel' Park Lane Mayfair, wearing his dark navy blue suit by designer Armani looking impeccable, and a navy white spotted classic design silk necktie, he had bought a few weeks before, along with a 'Mr Pink' white shirt, from Gentlemen's outfitters Turnbull and Asser of Jermyn Street St James. He had put the tie on in the taxi after leaving Mauies Bar, as he had to look *'sartorial chic'* and an open neck shirt would not give a good impression to the hotel receptionist.

His love for fashion was important to his look when mixing with affluent people and potentially benefactors of his lifestyle.

His meticulous metrosexual checklist of vanities consisted of a 'Top to Toe' weekly grooming regime, with visits to the salon 'HERO' in Fulham, where Chinese stylist Cheng looked after him to maintain his looks that made him money.

His eyebrows were plucked to give clean arch shapes, and every month tinted a darker brown to his hair, along with his eyelashes, to bring more attention to his sunken eyes. Cheng also manicured Rogan and had once applied clear nail varnish, but Rogan thought he looked effeminate, and had it removed as it was not the image he portrayed, and preferred to stick with an 'American' manicure of just being buffed with a shine, and cuticles cut to show off his half-moons.

At the salon, his favourite exotic relaxation therapy was to firstly soak his feet in a tank of tiny Garra Rufa (Doctor Fish) nibbling away at the dead skin surrounding his toes, and then to soak in another tank blend of Peppermint Essential Oil, Lavender Essential Oil, Sweet Almond Oil and Sea Salt, ending with foot reflexology and a pedicure.

Sun bed sessions, kept his bronzed all over body image looking attractive, and of a man looking internationally 'Jet-

Set' and well travelled, following the sun, to the Worlds hot spots and Millionaire playgrounds.

His hair was cut close to the sides and short on top, except for some strands falling onto his forehead, giving a 'Boyish' appearance.

Some hair grew on his back, shoulders and chest, which he also had removed every fortnight at the salon, being 'Manscaped' along with the painful removal of hair from his 'Sack and Crack'.

Cheng always laughed and got sadistic pleasure from Rogan's screams, as he removed the wax strip from his testicles.

It was important that his body was smooth for clients to run their hands across, and Rogan was taking no chances of aging too quickly. Wanting to keep his body and face young forever, he used 'Augustinus Bader' anti-aging body cream at £130 a jar, along with the occasional Botox injection on the lines of his frowning forehead.

His body was for sale; everything in his shop had to be presented to the peak of perfection.

Every three months he went to his dentist to have a top up of Laser whitening for his teeth. The dentist had warned him, it was too often, but Rogan was obsessive that his teeth sparkled with a Californian smile.

At the LA Gym, he pumped iron, lifting weights, believing the weights were the only way to pump muscle, and were no comparison for the workout machines used by novices.

A ripped six-pack was appealing and always-turned clients on, as it signified potency in bed.

At the Marmion reception desk he gave his name and his client's name, and that she was expecting his visit.

The French receptionist picked up the hotels internal telephone and pressed some buttons, which rang through to the suite.

"Madame Stanwick, your guest is at reception. Yes certainly."

Myra Stanwick asked for him to be sent up to her suite.

"Please take the lift signed 'Dante Suite' at the far end of the hall Mr Rogan." The receptionist said with a friendly smile.
"Thank you." Rogan shook the receptionist hand, and discreetly passed him a folded fifty-pound note tip.

As he walked to the exclusive lift that only went to the 'Danté Suite' where his client was staying, the receptionist watched him enter the lift, and as the sliding door closed, turned and gave a knowing smile to the concierge, who acknowledged with a return smile and a nod.
The receptionist and concierge who had been trained to be discreet of the hotels guests and their sometime unusual requests, had seen the handsome fit and well dressed young man in the hotel before, and knew of the reason for visiting the middle aged woman staying in the most expensive suite in the hotel, was not to discuss the décor?

Rogan pressed a buzzer on the painted turquoise door that had 'Danté Suite' written in gold on a plaque above.
He had serviced clients before at the Marmion hotel, sometimes men, sometimes women, sometimes both husband and wife together, but never visited the iconic 'Danté Suite'.
Many famous illustrious people had stayed in the expensive suite; Film Stars, Arab Princes, Billionaires and the woman he was now about to fulfill with her desire of pleasures.

The door opened, a sexy woman in her mid 50s wearing a Versace Baroque style bathrobe, which was tied loosely and slipping off her shoulders, greeted Rogan.
"Hi honey, my oh my, what a big boy you arrre!" She said in a Southern American drool accent, as she took his hand pulling him into the suite.
Rogan laughed at her forward remark and eagerness. She was ready for action.
"Have you got X-ray eyes?" Rogan joked referring to her welcoming comment.

"I was talking about your height, not what's in your pants honey! But whilst we are on the subject, I don't just look in the windows when I go fashion shopping, I like to try them on!"
"Let's go!" She said laughing.
"Where?"
"Around the world, and don't stop until we reach Paradise!"
Myra had a great figure for her age and was hot.
"I've got some champagne on ice." She said as she threw back her head, and swished her long red hair to one side behind an ear, revealing her diamond earrings that flashed as they caught the spotlights, and oozed wealth. *"It's in the bedroom."*
Not letting go of his hand, she led him through from the hall. Muted colours of woven summer flowers adorned the silk fabric curtains at the window, with swags, tails and tiebacks in canary yellow. The sumptuous décor was befitting of the Super Queen size bed, also flanked by the flower fabric on the padded headboard.
A bottle of champagne in a silver bucket full of ice and two champagne flutes also chilling, had been placed on a table.
"Would you open the bottle and lower the lights to dim." Myra said, as she sat on the side of the bed, with the lower part of her robe open enough to look seductive, as she posed her long legs slightly apart.
After he had dimmed the lights and walked back to the bed, Rogan gave a broad smile, noticing Myra's robe had opened a little more, revealing that she was not wearing panties. Myra caught his eye and coyly crossed her legs, pretending to be embarrassed. Her seduction had been delivered. Towering over her, he reached for the champagne, opened it and set the flutes ready to be filled.
"You're even better looking in person, than the photo on your website." Myra purred as she took the filled glass Rogan handed her.

After a sip Myra placed her glass back onto the table and stood up, *"That's a very nice tie to wrap around your wrists."*

She said suggesting putting Rogan in bondage, as she started to unravel it.

Rogan held his arms out limply, submissive to Myra's control as she took his champagne flute from his hand and placed it on the table.

After removing his tie, she unbuttoned his white shirt down to his navel, revealing his firm muscular body, and gave a sigh as she ran her hand across the contours.

Her long Venus-red fingernails began to dig into his flesh. She was a *Man-eater!*

Not taking any chances of having claw marks scarring his body, which would spoil the perfect product he regularly sold to his clients, he grabbed her hand tightly, so that she got the message not to dig deep, and then pulled at the lapels of his jacket, pulling it back off his shoulders, and letting it fall to the floor.

Myra enjoyed control of her beautiful man who was at her disposal, and stared constantly into his eyes.

Without looking down she reached for his belt, undid the clasp and slid it out through the trouser loops.

Rogan smiled as she fumbled, having difficulty to find the top button of his trouser waistband, and reached down to unfasten it for her.

Under her command, Myra held his wrists and pushed his arms behind his back. Whilst still standing infront she fumbled with a feeble attempt of bondage, by trying to tie Rogans wrist together with his silk tie. Turnbull and Asser took pride they sell ties for every occasion, be it formal or casual, but had never mentioned in their promotional literature; Bondage!

Although the tie was only wrapped around his wrists, which would be easy for Rogan to break free, he played along with the scene.

Giving him a kiss on his lips, and still in a quiet sultry voice, she said breathlessly and in a patronizing manner, *"Good boy."* And began to slowly unzip his fly.

Rogan began to breathe heavily and was aroused. *"I'm going to enjoy this."*

No matter how many times he had sex with women or men, he still got excited at the thought he was at their disposal for whatever their sexual needs, and to please them, either in his control or in theirs. He was sadomasochistic and could easily adapt to any role-play.

Looking down, and then directly back into Rogan's eyes, Myra slid her hand further down to the top of his white pants, teasing the elastic waistband, as she gently tugged it towards her and then releasing it to snap back, which she repeated several more times.

She wasn't wasting time, conscious that her husband would now be on the plane, and crossing the Atlantic on his way to landing at Heathrow.

Seated on the edge of the bed, she was at eye level with his erect penis bulging in his pants, and gently bit the top of the Waistband, holding it in her teeth whilst looking up at his facial expression of ecstasy, with his eyes closed, as he secumbed to the predictable pleasure he was expecting, and about to receive.

Tugging them down a little further with her teeth, some of his black pubic hairs were revealed poking out of the top, and brushed against her nostrils. The natural smell of his manly body sweat was increased by his high testosterone level and excited her to continuously lick the cotton material of his pants until they were transparent, revealing the head of his penis.

Breaking his hands free from his own loosely wrapped tie, he gently grabbed her shoulders, as they both slid onto the bed in an embrace with him on top.

Sitting up he undid the laces of his shoes, pulling them off along with his socks, and then stood up to let his now undone trousers slip to the floor, and allow him to step out. Myra gazed at her irresistible sex toy before her in his white pants. His penis bulging stiffly erect, ready to serve as he lowered himself on top of her.

Oral sex, Penetration, bondage, left Myra in paradise with the taste of Rogan's sperm on her lips.

She got laid he got paid in £50 notes, and was £1,500 richer!

Mauies Club

Eddy stayed at the bar drinking until just after eleven thirty, when Rogan came rushing in, and called out across the now crowded bar.

"Eddy come on, I've got a black cab outside, or is it too late?"

"Na! 'ee won't mind, it's Saturday, 'ee won't go back into his coffin til Sunday night!" Eddy jumped off the bar stool and carried on his conversation as the two pushed through the crowd

"How was the old bird?"

"Loaded! She booked me at my online price of a thousand, but I offered a lot more! And I mean a lot more than the usual in and out. Occasionally I convinced her I was enjoying it, and gave a few moans and groans, and got another five hundred out of her! They always think they're going to get the full works for the price on the internet, but I tease them with sex they have never dreamed of, so they don't' realize the clock and till are clicking up more money for overtime!" Rogan made a sound, imitating a mechanical clock timer. *"Beep-Beep."*

Eddy laughed. *"You milk them!"*

"No they milk me, the difference is I enjoy it! Anyway, I did let her off the VAT!" Rogan laughed as he climbed into the cab that was waiting at Mauies entrance.

An attractive black girl with bright pink hair and matching lipstick, being helped by Eddy, climbed into the cab and sat down next to Rogan.

Eddy followed and closed the door behind him, and then pulled down the seat opposite the pair to sit on.

Rogan beamed a smile, *"And who is this sexy fascinating creature?"* His eyes focused on her bulging breasts.

"Ain't she a one off? We met tonight!" Eddy said as he stroked Candy's knee.

"I'm Candy Floss honey, and who are you!" said Candy outstretching her hand to shake.

Rogan took her hand and kissed the back of it. *"I shall call you Princess Candy. I'm Rogan but you can call me Prince Charlie."*

"Oooh honey I'd like to snort you up!" Candy was quick to reply, referring to Rogan's humorous made up name, commonly known in circles as slang reference for cocaine. She ran her hand along Rogan's inside leg, stopping short of his crotch.

"The best way to snort a line, is along a dick before it rises to full attention!" She said as she squeezed his thigh.

Rogan felt his cock twitch, ready for command.

"You wouldn't be able to finish it on me, my dick goes up quicker than London Bridge!"

"The bets on" Candy said laughing.

"Count me in", added Eddy who was also laughing. *"My conks like an 'Oover, I could do with a line."*

The young cab driver turned in his seat to face the threesome.

"When you lot have decided whose doing the cleaning, (Referring to Eddy's Hoover remark) *can one of you tell me where we're going?"*

"Sorry mate, take us to 32 Sussex Gardens, just off Hyde Park Square – Ta." Eddy replied.

The Ride is on!

As the black cab pulled up at Sussex Gardens, Rogan's eyes widened, at the imposing private block of flats, and a smile stopped him short of licking his lips, as he recognized the signs of money.

"This looks very nice."

"Told ya 'ees got plenty of Wonga."

Rogan paid the fare, and the three stepped out of the cab making their way up the wide steps, that led to the double doors at the front entrance, flanked by spiral topiary trees in silver troughs spaced between tall Corinthian stone columns.

Inside the reception hall, they strolled across the black and white marble floor to the concierge wearing a double-breasted bottle green uniform suit, with gold braiding on the lapels and six gold buttons on the front, defining the shape. He was engrossed watching a 'Soap series' on a small television placed at one end of the counter, and had not noticed the three visitors.

"Allo Peter wot yer watching, Porno's?" Eddy said laughing and unable to hold back his cheeky character, although he had rememberd not to call him 'Pete', after Hugo had pulled him up on one occasion, and said not to be too familiar with him, as he was too nosey about the residence and their private business.

 As he looked up, he instantly recognized the familiar face.

"Hello Eddy seeing Mr Walford are you?"

"Yea."

The concierge picked up the telephone receiver and pressed code numbers on a display screen to make the call to Hugo.

"Hello Mr Walford, I have Eddy and two other people here at the front desk, shall I send them up?" The concierge handed the receiver to Eddy *"He wants' to speak to you".*

"Allo Hugo, yea! I've two friends wiv me, they're gooduns, you'll luv 'em." He said laughing down the handset, and then passed it back to the concierge.

As they walked towards the lift, Candy's designer *'Louboutin'* stilettos echoed on the marble floor, sounding like rapid machine-gun fire. With each step, glimpses of *Louboutin's* signature design of red soles reflected, giving a clue to her personality and the style of a seductive - *'Femme Fatale',* *stepping* through the blood of her victims.

Stopping on the fifth floor, they walked along the hallway and were greeted by Hugo standing in the hall by his open door.

His portly figure dressed in a flowing black kaftan, edged with gold braiding around the neck and sleeves.

One of his arms was reaching above his balding head and holding on to the doorframe in a seductive pose, with a Black Russian *'Sobranie'* cigarette smoldering between his fingertips. In his other hand a crystal *'Baccarat'* glass flute filled with champagne.

Eddy leaned forward and kissed Hugo on the lips and took the champagne glass from him to take a sip. *"Allo daddykins, these are my friends Rogan and Princess Candy."*

Candy giggled at her new title given by Rogan, and offered her hand to shake. Hugo pulled her outstretched hand towards him, bypassing shaking and pressed his cheek next to each side of hers, as he made the sound of a theatrical kiss. *"mwah-mwah. "Oh maybe I should have curtseyed, forgive me Princess."* He chuckled, and then grabbed and lifted the hem of his Kaftan, as he bobbed in a curtsey.

"And you are Rogan." Hugo said as he brushed the side of his thinning hair making sure it was in place, assuming he would look more appealing.

"I've heard so much about you from Eddy, but he never mentioned you were the mythological Adonis god of beauty and desire." Hugo beamed wrapping his arm around Rogan's waist as he led him, Eddy and Candy inside to his flat.

Eddy turned towards Rogan as they entered the flat. *"That's Hugo's normal greeting, champers all the way!"*

"Champagne! My kind of man!"

Eddy and Candy followed Hugo, who was now holding onto Rogan's arm.
"I feel like I'm holding onto a rocket."
"No they're my guns," Rogan replied referring to his biceps.
"My rocket is hidden, but always ready to launch!"
Hugo laughed. *"Hope you give me a ticket for take off?"*
His kaftan was too long for him, as it was a size for a taller person, and as he was 5ft 4" the extra length created a train trailing majestically behind him, giving him a superiority air to his procession along the hallway. Candy accidently stepped on to the train, which pulled back the neckline of the kaftan, causing a jolt on Hugo's neck that made him croak, and bringing the procession to a sudden halt. Looking back at Candy, Hugo said laughing, *"Darling are you with the Mafia? Are you an assassin?"*
Candy laughed, *"Sorry, you're fabulous."*
"Yes!" Hugo agreed smugly.
Walking on, Rogan stopped to gaze at the gold-framed oil paintings, by Rome's most famed artist in 1600, 'Caravaggio'. Many depicting male nudes in pose that cut the line between art and provocation.
"All fakes darling." Hugo said laughing.
Running his hand gently along the walls, Rogan admired the expensive quality of the black-flocked wallpaper, which added to the drama of the imposing red lacquered Japanese double doors, embossed with giant hand painted gold crane birds on them, beaming at the end of the hall.
Hugo grabbed the huge gold dragon door handles, and dramatically threw the doors open wide, for his procession to be greeted by his ornate living room.
Rogan's eye was immediately drawn to the huge ornate Jacobian with Gothic influences stone fireplace, carved with semi naked figures, columns and berries that reached the ceiling and dominated the room.

"Wow! This is magnificent!" Said Rogan, as he run his hand once again over the carvings.

Hugo took his champagne flute back from Eddy, who had been holding onto it. *"I bought it at a seventeenth century manor house auction sale in the Cotswolds. Unfortunately for the owners, although they had titles, they had no money and were forced to sell off their home."*

Hugo waved his hand above his head in a regal manner. *"As they say, All Mink and No Knickers dear!"*

Eddy sat next to Candy, opposite Hugo and Rogan sitting on a matching black velvet velour three-seater sofa, and reached for the bottle of champagne sitting in the silver cooler on the coffee table.

"Oh all this divine beauty around me, has made me forget to get the glasses." Hugo chuckled referring to his guests, as he squeezed Rogan's knee.

"Eddy darling, you know where they are, be a luv and get some for our guests."

Eddy jumped up and walked over to open the cocktail cabinet.

"Which ones?" He asked Hugo, as he opened the doors and gazed at the range of Crystal glasses.

"Well not the tumblers, get the Baccarat flutes on the top shelf." Hugo leaned forward, and then giggled as he lifted his hand to his mouth, to mask whispered words to Candy. *"He would prefer the tumblers; drinks like a fish darling!"*

Candy laughed, *"I've been known to swig Jagermeister straight from the bottle at a party where we were playing 'Spin the Bottle', and every time it stopped, you had to take a swig and remove a piece of clothing. I kept loosing and got very drunk. That was the night my new boyfriend I picked up at the party, discovered I'm transgender. He didn't mind, as he was bisexual, and said with me he could have two for the price of one! So when we got home, I fucked him!"*

Hugo, Rogan and Eddy all laughed at Candy's funny story.

Eddy brought the champagne flutes to the coffee table, and placed them in a row for Hugo to fill from a bottle of Dom Perignon.

Hugo was struggling to remove the champagne cork. *"Rogan can you wrench this flaming stopper out? I'm not used to such resistance!"* Rogan took the bottle and eased the cork, which shot out with a pop sound across the room.

"Oh you've popped your cork, I hope you haven't peaked too early?" Hugo said with a wry smile and pursed lips, as he jokingly looked down at Rogan's crotch.

Eddy took a cocaine wrap from his pocket, and opened it. *"Alright to chop some lines on the coffee table Hugs?"* (His nickname for Hugo)

"Of course." replied Hugo as he raised his glass above his head, as a salute to carry on.

Eddy knelt down by the coffee table to chop the lines of cocaine.

"Whilst you're down there?" Rogan said laughing and spreading his legs provocatively wide as he slumped back into the soft sofa cushions.

"Oh you naughty boy!" Hugo said laughing as he slapped Rogan's muscular leg, and leaving his hand resting on the inside of his thigh.

"Hugo, Can we put some music on?" Said Candy jumping up.

"Of course darling, press the play button on the contraption." Referring to his computer.

"Eddy's play list is programmed with funky sounds on Spotty Dick, for when he comes here to dance the Seven Veils, trying to seduce me!"

"Ha!Ha! Spotty Dick! I think you mean the Spotify music-streaming channel? And as for a dance of the Seven Veils, in your dreams! You don't need much seducing, you old letch." Eddy hit back.

Rogan passed a rolled up fifty pound note to Hugo, from the payment his rich client had paid earlier, to use as a snort tube for the cocaine, laid out in four rows on the glass coffee table.

It wasn't unusual for Rogan to have fifty pound notes in his wallet, as terms of payment for his services, were cash only, which also suited all of his clients who would pay cash with the large currency, so there could never be a record on their private bank accounts, which their partners may see and investigate, learning of their association with a male prostitute, who preferred to be called a Gigolo.

Hugo rejected the note and passed it back, as he reached forward to the table, and picked up an ornate mother of pearl box, adorned with a gilded gold mermaid perched on top, and flicked the lid open to take out some small gold metal straw tubes.

"I prefer this, you don't know how many noses the note has been up before?" Taking out three more he passed them to his guests.

Rogan went next, as Candy and Eddy looked on eagerly waiting for their turn.

"What line of business are you in Rogan?" asked Hugo, as he pinched his nostrils with his forefinger and thumb, for a final sniff of the cocaine stuck in a nostril, to venture into his blood stream, and give the high he desired.

"Entertainment."

"Are you an actor, singer or something else?"

"It's more like Home Entertainment."

"Don't tell me you're a Television Engineer?" Hugo quizzed and belly laughed.

"No! I'm an engineer of sex entertainment."

"In that case if you don't mend televisions, you can press my buttons instead!"

Candy, who was dancing behind the sofa that Rogan and Hugo were sitting on, reached her outstretched arms around the two, clasped their shoulders and leaned between them, as she kissed each in turn on the cheek.

"You two seem to of hit it off?"

"I knew they would – made for each other." Eddy chipped in and winked at Rogan, as he looked up from cutting another round of lines, whilst he knelt beside the coffee table.

"You look like you're praying down there darling." Said Hugo.

"Yeah! I'm praying for another line!" Eddy joked.

"Top up time." Rogan reached for the Champagne bottle, and poured the last drop into Hugo's glass.

"There's plenty more in the Champagne fridge." Hugo said, giving permission for Rogan to help himself.

Rogan was pleased, that Hugo was welcoming him to be familiar in his home.

"Uh! Champagne fridge?" Rogan said raising an eyebrow in a puzzled expression.

"Yes you'll find it." Hugo commanded in an Imperialistic manner, as he sat up and moved to the edge of the sofa seat waving his hand nonchalantly, pointing the way to the kitchen, and then sinking back again into the cushions, and inhaling another exotic 'Sobrane' Cocktail Cigarette wrapped in purple paper.

Rogan walked into the ultra modern monochrome colour themed kitchen, dominated by a huge black marble top island in the middle, with six white leather stools running the length of one side. All of the walls were shiny black, with shiny white flush cupboards; no door handles could be seen. His eyes scanned the walls for the fridge, but there were no clues of what lay behind the hidden cupboard doors.

Suddenly he noticed an iridescent colour changing light on a small screen set into one of the hidden doors. He had seen this before in *'Interiors'* magazine, which he had subscribed, to keep up with the luxury lifestyle he craved, and for others to pay.

As he lifted his hand to press the hidden door panel, which he thought would respond on a rebound, it suddenly opened without touch, reacting by a hidden sensor.

Inside the giant fridge to one side, it was full of groceries, many with labels of Harrods, Fortnum and Mason and M&S stores, and on the other side, an internal glass panel door with a temperature monitor at the top, which was set to keep the champagne stocked and bottles of wine at the right temperature setting.

He grabbed two bottles of Champagne; one label read Bollinger the other a gold label Louis Roederer Cristal. Walking back into the living room he held the two bottles up to Hugo. *"I brought two in, one for Candy and Eddy, and one for us."*

Knowing the Bolinger cost £45 and the Cristal £180, he handed the Bolinger to Candy who had no idea of the hierarchy of champagne and giggled at her gift. Eddy was so stoned on coke he would drink anything, even Lambrini at £3 a bottle, often consumed on 'Hen Night Out parties'.

Rogan started to unwind the wire, by turning each section that secured the cork in the top of the champagne.

"It's seven and a half twists - you know. I would need eight and half twists around my cork." And winked at Hugo.

Hugo laughed out loud at Rogan's boasting remark, inferring the size of his penis.

As he spun around to the music, Rogan placed the bottle between his legs at his crotch, enticing Candy who was still dancing, to wiggle and twerk her bum against it in a suggestive manner, whilst he pushed his hips forward, prodding her with it.

Hugo seeking his opportunity, as Candy turned to dance with Eddy, got up from the sofa and then knelt down in front of Rogan, pulling on the champagne cork of the bottle between his teeth.

Simulating masturbation with his hand around the bottle, he gave the cork a turn and a hard yank, as Rogan pulled back with the bottle securely trapped between his strong thighs. All of Rogan's shaking the bottle about, shot the cork across the room, and a white bubbling fountain of champagne gushed, shooting its load into Hugo's face.

Hugo tried to catch some of the champagne that was spilling and opened his mouth as he sucked on the bottle, but could not swallow so much as it spilt from the sides of his lips, onto the Chinese silk carpet.

"You'll have to do better than that, to satisfy me!" Rogan said in a dominant sadistic manner.

"Yes sir" came a weak masochistic reply from Hugo who was drunk, and still trying to catch the Champagne drips, as he licked the sides of the bottle.

Eddy who was standing alongside Rogan and laughing at Hugo's bizarre antics, bent down and grabbed the neck of the bottle whilst it was still in Hugo's mouth, and then put his hand on the back of Hugo's head forcing him in a lock-hold, to continue guzzling the champagne from the bottle.

"Go on, give it a good suck!" He said roaring with laughter.

"I'd rather have the real thing." Hugo said pulling his head back off the bottleneck for a breath, as he looked up at Rogan's crotch.

Rogan reached down under Hugo's arm, to help him stand up, and then pulled him so that they both slumped, onto the sofa, laughing at their game.

Candy was also drunk and stoned on the cocaine, but was still dancing around the room, occasionally stopping to pick up an ornament from the side tables to admire. As she passed in front of the sofa she deliberately collapsed onto Rogan's lap, and then lay backwards across Hugo's lap.

"You've got great tits." Rogan said as he hovered the champagne bottle over her revealing bulging breasts.

Candy grabbed the sides of her breasts and pushed them close together. *"They should be, I've had them done twice the first lot looked like lemons and I had them replaced with Melons!"* Rogan tilted the bottle slightly teasing Candy with the threat to pour some champagne onto her cleavage, a fetish he enjoyed doing to women with big breasts in his company.

Candy caught his eye, pouted and blew a kiss, as a come on to his mischievous action. *"I dare you! Come on break out the booze"* she said giggling.

He poured a small amount of champagne onto her cleavage. *"You'll have to lick that up, you naughty boy."* Candy said suggestively as she pulled his head towards her cleavage, and then rolled sideways on Hugo's lap, and at the same time pulling his head down onto Hugo's crotch.

"Keep licking!" Candy said laughing as she jumped up, leaving Rogan staring between Hugo's legs.

"Ooh darling we've only just met, did I say dinner is served?"

Hugo was about to be taken for a ride, and not in a taxi?

Monday...
'Ranley' Luxury goods Store
Mayfair

Late afternoon, and just a few well-heeled people were still browsing at the objet d'art and silverware in the exclusive store 'Ranley' in London's Mayfair, owned by a member of the Royal Family, 30 year old Viscount Alexander Ranley, the son of the Earl and Countess of Ranley.

Sitting at his ornate gold inlay French style Louis XIV reception desk, well groomed 57 year old Hugo the executive sales manager, looked at his £15,700 Jaeger-LeCoultre watch admiring it's beauty as he stroked the glass face and checked the time, and then sighed as there was still an hour to closing.

Walking boldly through the store towards him, a smart stylish woman wearing a navy fitted coat and white fur stole thrown over one shoulder, and on the other shoulder, dangling from a gold chain a Hermés 'Birkin' handbag.

As she was clutching a huge box, she struggled with her shoulder movements, to balance both the stole and bag from slipping off.

Hugo jumped up from his seat to greet her, and took the box to place on his desk.

"Good afternoon Contessa Lemosvitch, how can I help you today?" Hugo asked oozing his charm.

"I am sorry dis does not vork with my décor." She replied in her Russian accent.

Ranley's policy of sales to their clients was to allow them to have goods on approval of two weeks before payment. If returned, there was no charge. All of their clients were extremely wealthy and some billionaires, so their custom was very valuable, as many of them would spend £200,000 on the blink of an eye.

Turning on his charming smile, Hugo lifted a hand painted vintage Lotus Jardinière out of the box, which had been cast in 1722. *"What a shame Contessa, it is so beautiful and the only one of a kind."*

"So am I, but it did not stop my last husband running off with the maid!"

Hugo laughed at her personal background of marital problems, she revealed.

"Ze colours of the gold hand painted dragon fish, shwimming amongst the sea grasses are not bright enough, and do not compliment ze gold leaf table, it vas standing on in my hall, ze Count said I must return it."

Hugo tried to reason with her, explaining the dull colours reflect the influence of the age, but she was not accepting his knowledge and was only concerned of its colours not matching her decor.

This was a disappointing blow to his commission that he would have received for the £52,500 price tag, as in his mind he had already spent it on a holiday to Miami, where the boys are fit on *'Muscle Beach'* and have a price.

Always courteous, he escorted her to the door, and assured her, there would be no charges on her account.

As he was dealing with the paperwork at his desk, out of the corner of his eye, he saw a man walking sharply towards the front door, and brazenly holding an expensive £39,000 humidor, made in walnut, with inlays of oak, mahogany and maple. The design interpreted a miniature form of the White House, and used for keeping cigars dry at the right humidity. Although portly and still quick on his feet, Hugo Jumped up from his seat behind his desk, and raced towards the thief trying to apprehend him by grabbing the back of his coat, but the thief broke free causing Hugo to fall backwards onto a display table, and accidently knock a French Lalique bowl, that fell and shattered on the marble floor.

Lifting himself up from the floor, he ran to the door, only to see the thief speeding off in an accomplice's car.

At the back of the store several of the staff were chatting to each other and had not noticed the thief, until their attention was drawn to the crashing noise of the glass bowl, and then ran to Hugo's aid.

Hugo was angry with all of his sales team, *"If you paid more attention to the customers in the store, instead of gossiping, this may not have happened!"* He bellowed at the staff in a stern manner.

Brushing his tailcoat down, he stooped to pick up his red carnation flower that had fallen, which were delivered daily by a florist, for the male sales assistants to wear as a buttonhole.

All of the male staff was required to wear black tailcoats, waistcoats, grey pin striped trousers; black laced shoes, white shirt and a navy blue tie that bore a gold embroidered monogrammed 'R' for Ranley in the centre.

The directors of Ranley had instructed the male staff, of their tie, which was not to be tied in the common four-in-hand knot, as the bulbous Windsor knot.

Although made popular by the late Duke of Windsor, the directors regarded the style of the Windsor knot to be 'Spivey', as City boys, working at the Stock Exchange, wear it?

Female staff wore a white blouse, navy jacket, skirt, black tights and black shoes; their heels must not exceed six inches and definitely no flats, as stated in their employment contract and which one snobby director described as *'Very Council'*.

They too had the gold embroidered monogrammed 'R' on the breast pocket of their jacket.

The clientele that patronized Ranley were Royalty, celebrities and the super-rich from all corners and millionaires playgrounds from around the world, as the store specialized in exclusive sourced collective pieces of decorative and eclectic objet d'art, befitting of palatial homes.

Russian bejeweled Faberge eggs and silver photo frames sat alongside Warhol and Old Master paintings, Tiffany candlesticks, Italian Renaissance lanterns, French ornate mirrors and Japanese lacquered furniture.

Sitting at his desk Hugo telephoned the police, to report the theft, and arranged for them to interview him.

As he put the telephone receiver down and was about to release the staff of their days' work, he saw a young man enter the store and went to greet him.

"Hello Rogan, you look smart. (Rogan was wearing a tie) what are you doing around here?" Hugo said, changing his expression from surprise to a broad smile.

"I was just around the corner, at the Marmion Hotel for a business meeting, (Myra's husband had jetted off again?) *and remembered you telling me you worked here."*

"Oh that's nice, you thought of seeing me, how flattering." Hugo said as he touched Rogan's shoulder affectionately.

The staff of two young women and two young men, walked past Hugo, who glanced at his watch to check closing time.

"Good night Hugo"- "night"- "night" several of the staff said individually, as they gave an acknowledging smile to Rogan, and slipped past the pair, who were standing half blocking the front door.

"Night.' replied Hugo to the whole group, who had checked closing time and not waited for Hugo to officially close shop.

"Sonia, I expect you on time tomorrow, you've been late twice this week. You know the rules, three strikes and your out!"

"Yes Hugo, I won't let you down."

Hugo was showing his position of power to impress Rogan, which was a different side to the camp, witty and lecherous man who was mauling him the night before.

"I've got to close up now, and have to wait for the police, as we had an incident here today, which I have to give a statement, but if you want to pop around to my flat later, about eight, we can have a drink and a chat."

"Lovely, do you wanna a line (referring to cocaine) *before I go, and I will come round later."*

Hugo gave a nodding approval as he put a key into the door and locked it, so they would not be disturbed.

Rogan took out a wrap of paper, folded into the shape of a small envelope containing the cocaine.

Hugo noted it was a pink lottery number form that had been cut in half as a container for the drug.

"Did your numbers come up?" Hugo said laughing, as Rogan chopped up two thick lines using a credit card, and then passed a rolled up fifty-pound note to Hugo to snort through.

"Fifty pounds! Lucky boy, your numbers did come up! Haven't got one of my straws, so I'll take my chances."

They both walked to the front door and as Hugo unlocked the door for Rogan to leave, Rogan kissed him on his cheek whilst giving him a squeeze on his bum, and in a cockney accent imitating his friend Eddy, said in a cheeky manner, *"Looking for a bit of funny business Mister?"*

Hugo pursed his lips *"You sound like a bit of rough! Can't wait to see a LOT more of you later?"*

"I can resist anything except for temptation."

Oscar Wilde.

The Anniversary

Over the coming months, Rogan and Hugo built up a close relationship.

(Most relationships are about 'Give and Take', this was one sided; Hugo gave and Rogan would take! Although in bed it was reversed?)

Hugo liked having a sexy good-looking young man on his arm, as a showpiece, and the pleasure of a firm body in his bed.

In return, Rogan enjoyed Hugo's generosity, his witty humour and caring ways, which he never received from his father, who had left his mother when Rogan was at an early age.

Although Hugo did not give Rogan money, he often treated him, buying him designer clothes and jewellery, and taking him to the best restaurants in town. Hugo was on Rogan's hook!

Through business relations, Hugo was often invited to VIP A-Lister cocktail parties, and invited Rogan to be his companion.

As a social climber, Rogan was always pleased of the opportunity, which enabled him to network the room, taking the opportunity and advantage of being able to circulate such affluent and influential business people.

Whilst chatting with them, he would discreetly pass his calling card to both women and men, who may take up an illicit booking with him, for their private company and sexual needs.

Many of Rogan's rich clients, either women or men were visitors from other countries without their partners, and would return back to their homes, with their sexual affairs kept secret and relationships in tact.

Although on the other side of the room, Hugo was aware of Rogan touting for business and accepted this was his lifestyle and vocation.

From their first meeting, Rogan had been upfront and told Hugo of his business affairs, providing sex for payment, often described as living off immoral earnings.

Whilst in bed together, sometimes Hugo would ask Rogan to tell him of his sexual exploits, which would excite him.

Rogan was pleased to tell his stories, and would embellish them, tantalizing Hugo to climax quickly, giving Rogan an early night.

Rogan and Hugo sat next to each other on the sofa in Hugo's drawing room.

"More Champagne?"

"I've still got some."

"Oh shut up, get it down you." Hugo topped up Rogan's glass. *"Drink up, I've booked a table for dinner at Scotts restaurant in Mount Street Mayfair for our Anniversary. Can you believe it, we've known each other for three months already!" Have you been there before?"*

"No, but I've had it on my list of restaurants to try." Rogan said as he drank the last drop of champagne from his glass.

"Its seafood, is that okay?"

"Great!"

"Last time I was dining there, Prince William and Harry were sitting in a corner booth, they both smiled at me as I walked past, they obviously recognized me from Ranley, when they came in looking around to buy a Christmas present for grannie." Hugo boasted.

"Grannie?" Rogan puzzled.

"The Queen dear!" Hugo laughed.

"Of course" Rogan said laughing, *"It was very thoughtful of them to buy you a present!"*

"Oh you're quick tonight! I better get my super-bitch script out, I can tell you're getting to be a handful!"

"You can find that out later."

"Talking of presents."

Hugo took a parcel from behind a cushion he was lying on, and handed it to Rogan who instantly recognized where it had been bought, by the aquamarine blue wrapping paper, the brand colour of the famous exclusive Tiffany & Co Store in Bond Street Mayfair.

"I got you an anniversary present."

"You shouldn't have!" Rogan said excitedly as he unwrapped the square parcel.

"Tiffany's Table Manners Book for Teenagers." Rogan read out aloud.

"Huh?" Rogan was confused of how to react to the strange gift. Was it an insult to his eating habits?

Disappointed he felt like repeating. *"You shouldn't have."* And mean it! But used an excuse as he placed it down onto the coffee table. *"Unfortunately I'm not a teenager anymore, even in your dreams?"*

Hugo laughed at Rogan's reaction to the present he teased him with, and took another Tiffany parcel he had hidden behind his back, and handed it to him.

Rogan's eyes lit up again, and hoped the contents were not another unwanted gift.

This was more like it! He thought as he opened the small black leather box, inscribed with the name of Tiffany's in gold on the lid.

"That's stunning!" Rogan was pleased with the silver ring designed with two 'T's head to head surrounding the band, and slipped it onto his finger as he gave Hugo a kiss.

"Happy Anniversary, your present is coming later?"

The internal house phone was ringing in the hall, interrupting Hugo before his comeback with another jibe. Hugo went to answer it. *"Okay Peter, tell the driver we are coming down."*

Scotts Restaurant

As Hugo and Rogan entered the exclusive restaurant patronized by celebrities, the Maitre d' approached them. *"Good evening sir"*, the Maitre d' said with a welcoming smile. Hugo took charge. *"Hello we have a reservation for 9. 15, in the name of Walford, - for two."*

The Maitre d' gestured with his hand, *"Yes sir, please come through, I have a very nice table for you, would you like to have a drink at the bar first?"*

Hugo turned towards Rogan, *"What would you like to do?"*

"Yes, let's have a drink at the bar, if that's okay." He said looking at the Maitre d'.

The Maitre d' smiled, *"Certainly Sir."* As he showed them to the bar, *"please let me know when you are ready for your table."*

The brown leather stools were high, and Hugo grabbed the bar for support as he lifted himself onto the seat.

"You okay?" said Rogan being attentive.

"I knew I should have worn my stilettos!" Hugo said laughing.

Rogan laughed at Hugo's quick wit, which was never far behind in any conversation.

The young barman approached them. *"Can I get you a drink Sirs?"*

Hugo turned to Rogan, *"What would you like?"*

"Large Whisky please."

"Do you have a preference Sir?" the barman enquired.

"What do you have?"

Turning sideways, the young barman pointed to a range of bottles lined up on the shelf behind him. The bottles were backlit showing off the golden colour of their contents. *"A whole range Sir, Dalmore King Alexander the third, single malt, Glenmorangie, Johnnie Walker blue label 1805."*

"Do you have Laphroaig?"

The barman moved along the whisky range looking at the labels and selected a bottle from the shelf.

Yes Sir, I have this one it is ten years old, and will be very peaty."

"*Perfect*" Rogan flicked his hand as a hip gesture of acceptance.

"*Would you like a mixer on the side and ice?*"

"*No thankyou, I like it straight up, I think mixers take away the true flavours of any drink, and only one cube of ice please.*"

"*I agree.*" The barman laughed and turned towards Hugo.

"*And you Sir?*"

"*I'm easy, Vodka and Coke with ice.*"

"*Any particular Vodka?*"

"*What ever you recommend.*" Hugo said smiling at the handsome barman.

Turning towards Rogan, Hugo grabbed Rogan's arm.

'*You are both a good boy and a naughty boy. Good, because you did not choose the most expensive whisky Dalmore King Alexander the third, at one hundred and fifty pounds a bottle, and a naughty boy, telling that young barman you like it straight up, I thought you were saving that for me?*"

Rogan winked and poked Hugo in the chest "*That all depends if YOU are a good boy.*" At the same time he turned in his seat to look at the other diners, and then back to Hugo, as he beamed with excitement.

"*Don't look now, Rod Stewart and his wife Penny Lancaster are sitting directly opposite.*"

Hugo could not resist and glanced at them, "*All the celebrities come here it's the place to be seen!*"

Rogan put his head closer to Hugo and began to sing, "*Do you think I'm sexy, do you want my body?*"

Hugo laughed, "*You can sing that tonight as my lullaby, but I can assure you, it won't send me to sleep.*"

"*You need something in your mouth.*" Rogan said as he took two big olives from a dish on the bar and popped them into Hugo's mouth.

"*You are such a tease.*" Hugo mumbled with his mouth full.

The Maitre d' interrupted their fun banter, '*Excuse me gentlemen are you ready to go to your table?*"

"Yes thank you."

The Maitre d' picked up their drinks in the chunky cut glasses, with the ice clinking against the glasses as he put them onto his silver tray.

"I'll take these for you, please follow me."

Hugo slid off his stool again, which was a bit too high for him to make a gainly decent, as he relied on clutching the edge of the bar again for support.

The Maitre d' walked ahead with Rogan and Hugo following. As they passed the table of Rod Stewart and his wife, Rogan looked directly at Penny. "Hi Penny, good to see you."

Penny Lancaster smiled sweetly, and Rod raised a glass as a greeting toast.

Walking on, Hugo looked back at Rod and Penny.

Penny was shaking her head, bemused of Rogan's personal greeting and Rod was laughing.

The Maitre d' led them to a table, which had a double seat sofa, for them to sit alongside each other looking out to the other diners.

"Do you know Penny Lancaster?"

"No." Replied Rogan.

"But you said, good to see you, as if you do know her?"

"I was just making her feel good, there is nothing wrong in that, Is there?" Rogan said in defense.

"No, I suppose not." Reflected Hugo.

A waiter arrived at their table and handed some menus to each of them.

"Good evening, tonight I can recommend Thermidor Lobster, Dover Sole meuniere, Fillet of John Dory with roasted artichokes."

Hugo interrupted, "We will have some Jersey Pearl oysters to start, six each, and two Bellini's, and if we can have a little more time to study the menu, thank you."

"Certainly Sir." The waiter said as he turned to leave the pair.

Two hours later, Hugo had paid the £350 bill, and was eager to get back to his flat to have sex with Rogan.

"More champagne M'lord?" Rogan said being attentive as he filled Hugo's glass, not waiting for his answer.

"Wonderful!" Hugo took a sip and opened a white envelope that had been sitting on the coffe table. Inside was a small plastic bag containing cocaine. Hugo spread it out on the glass top table, into two lines.

Rogan was amused at the envelopes stamp marks, and picked it up to take a closer look.

A crown sitting on top of large typeface red initials 'E.R', and stamp mark, 'Buckingham Palace SW1A 1AA'. Addressed to.

Mr H. Walford.

Ranley

Luxury Goods Store.

South Audley Street, Mayfair.

London.

Laughing, Rogan waved the empty envelope at Hugo, *"I've not seen this before, don't tell me you get your supply from the Palace!"*

Hugo snorted through his straw and looked up and laughed.

"Are you suggesting the Queen is my dealer? My coke is fit for a Queen dear, but she didn't send it! I brought the envelope from work to put on show for fun, and peoples reactions."

Rogan took a metal straw handed from Hugo and snorted the line.

"Well it works! Pity I would love to have a toot with the Queen and some 'Charlie' with Charlie boy! Do you know the Queen?"

Hugo sat up and looked grand, *"No, but I often go to Buckingham Palace when one of the secretaries telephones Ranley, to have a Selection of gifts brought to them for the Queen to choose as a present for some dignitary visiting, or one of the Royal family's Birthdays that the rest of the family want to choose. Sometimes for security reasons, they come into the store after hours, to look around when we've closed.*

Rogan looked surprised. *"The Queen!"*

"Yes, after all my boss is a member of their firm." Hugo said smugly.

"Firm? Firm?" Rogan reiterated.

"Yes, King George the fourth said; we're not a family, we're a firm! Now the Duke of Edinburgh also refers to the Royal establishment as 'The Firm'." Hugo explained.

Eddy was right Hugo was familiar with Royalty, although in the past he had referred to them as 'Royal Tarts'.

As another few hours passed, and after a few more drinks and several more cocaine lines, Hugo made an advance on Rogan who had set the scene whist dancing provocatively to the song tracks playing on Hugo's Spotify collection.

Hugo got up from the sofa and joined with Rogan to dance closely, whilst at the same time undoing the buttons on Rogan's shirt, revealing his tanned rippling muscular torso. As he ran his hands across Rogan's chest he slid it down to his six-pack, and bent to sensually lick and kiss his flesh. Undoing his belt and the top of his trousers, Rogan unzipped his fly and lowered his trousers to reveal his tight white 'Budgie Smugglers', with the uplifting pouch, which pushed his package forward, that he had bought on the Internet.

Hugo lowered and knelt to kiss his bulge through the underpants, as he clung to Rogan's bum cheeks.

Before he could go any further, Rogan pulled up his trousers and fastened them with his belt.

"Now-now Hugo you've been a very 'Snorty Boy', you will have to wait until next time, the shop is closed, I have to go as I have a meeting first thing tomorrow morning."

Hugo was disappointed that Rogan was cutting short their anniversary night.

As he lifted one bent leg to stand, he held out his hand for Rogan's support. Rogan offered his hand and then sharply took it away again as a tease, causing Hugo to fall backwards onto his back, flat onto the floor.

Rogan laughed at Hugo, who was humiliated and struggling to get up, which satisfied Rogan's sadistic personality disorder.

"You look like a Cockroach on your back, kicking out your little legs."

Helping Hugo to his feet, Rogan insincerely showed some care, and then cruelly added a final put down about Hugo's weight.

"We really must get you fit, I'll give you some exercises we can do together next time. You'll soon loose that paunch!"

Treat them mean keep them keen!

Guys and Dolls

"Where are we going?" Rogan asked Eddy.

"A walk on the wild side." Eddy said laughing.

Eddy and Candy walked each side of Rogan, holding on to his arms to steady him, as he was slightly drunk after another boozy night at Mauies club.

They entered a dimly lit alleyway in Earls Court, a section patronized by some dubious characters.

Candy held on to Rogan's arm even tighter, as she balanced and totted in her seven-inch high stilettos across the cobblestones, that were reminiscent of Dickens early Victorian England, the settings for his fictional repulsive underclass characters, that he constructed for some of his dark novels.

In the dimly lit shadows, boys and girls lingered, this was where they looked for *'Business'* from punters looking to pay for their sexual services and quick relief, most nights right there in dark doorways! Amongst the groans of ecstasy, skirts were lifted, trousers and pants down, glimpses of bare bums heaving forward as intercourse was taking place. Old men with balding heads were on their knees between the strong thighs of young studs.

Nothing much had changed since Victorian England, even the stench of urine on the walls from drunken heterosexual men, who whilst taking a pee, believed they were taken advantage of from either a male or female prostitute, who had masturbated them.

They would convince themselves of any guilt, with an excuse that all hands seemed the same in the dark?

Payment in Victorian England would be a shiny gold sovereign worth one pound, compared to present day, a red crispy £50 note for a doorway quickie!

Eddy and Candy guided Rogan up to a door with a sign above, *'DOLLIES GATEWAY TO PARADISE '.* A clandestine venue underground that welcomed Transvestites, Transsexual, Transgender and the curious?

Candy pushed the door and entered, walking down a narrow wooden rickety staircase, balancing herself on her heels, by outstretching her arms on the side walls, followed by Rogan and Eddy behind.

At the bottom of the stairs they came to a caged window next to the main club door. A very camp looking male receptionist wearing eye shadow, false eyelashes and lipstick peered through the window, *"Are you aware this is a 'T' Club darlink?"*

"T club?" Rogan mused slightly slurring.

"Are you drunk?" The receptionist asked.

Eddy pushed forward past Rogan and put his face close to the caged window, *"it's okay sweetheart I'm with them, tell Dolly Eddy is here".*

Eddy had been a regular customer at the club, but had not been there for some time, and was unknown to the new receptionist.

The receptionist disappeared for a couple of minutes before returning to the caged reception window.

"Okay come through, but make sure he doesn't cause any trouble." referring to Rogan.

"Ees alright don't worry, 'ees a pussycat!"

"Strikes me as bit of a Tiger!" The receptionist quickly responded admiring Rogan.

A buzzer sounded as the door was released and Candy pushed it open, for them to enter.

The receptionist was standing by the door.

Rogan clawed his hand like a Tiger's paw, and motioned a striking action at the receptionist and growled.

"ROARRR!"

"Ooo, you can have me for dinner any time!" The receptionist said pouting his lips.

As they walked through the crowded underground club, Rogan suddenly stood still, his mouth half open with an amazed expression, as he looked around at the crowd.

"There are so many birds in here!"

"Look again, they're T girls." Eddy said laughing

"That's what the receptionist said." Rogan said, still confused due to being slightly drunk.

"They're, Transvestites Transsexual and Transgender." Eddy explained.

"What's the difference?" Rogan asked.

"Transvestites are men who enjoy cross-dressing as a woman, Transsexual is a pre-operative person undergoing male-to-female operations. Transgender are people who do not identify with the sex they were born with. It's a lot to explain and that's why they are called 'T-Girls' to simplify, they're all looking to be who they want to be!

Rogan looked blankly at Eddy, as it seemed to go over his head. *"I've got to go for a piss, get me a whisky coke."*

In the toilets an old man in his 70s was struggling in his dress, as his arms could not reach around his back to pull up the long zip.

"Just a minute mate, I'll help you after I've had a slash." Rogan said turning half around at the urinal.

"Slash! Oh you're so butch." The old man said as he glanced at Rogan putting his penis back into his trousers.

Zipping the elderly man's dress up, Rogan commented as he straightened the man's bob style wig.

"You're wig is a bit skewiff."

The old man was pleased to get attention from the good-looking hunk.

"Oh thank-you you're so kind, have you been here before?"

Rogan laughed, *"No, this is a new experience."*

The old man enthused, *"You are going to love it! Dollies **IS** the best club in London!"*

Rogan laughed, *"What have I been missing, I've been going to a club called Mauies, which I thought was the best club in town, and all this time I've been wrong!"*

Walking towards the toilet exit door, he looked back at the old man who was gazing and squinting to see his reflection into a cracked mirror on the white tiled wall. Being shortsighted he smudged and overlapped his lips with the pink lipstick he was applying, which gave him the appearance of a clown!

"You look great!" Rogan called out with an affectionate wink as he added the sound of a kiss.

"Thank you we'll have a dance when I'm ready." Said the old man flattered at Rogan's remark, and was now smudging eye shadow on to his crinkly eyelids.

Rogan laughed and gave a 'thumbs up' as he left and went to the bar, where Eddy and Candy were waiting.

"Here Rogan, you're looking sober again, get this down yer! Whisky, splash of coke and." Candy joined in unison with Eddy. *"One cube of ice as usual."*

"At last I've found home." Candy said looking around at the other T – Girls.

"You sound like Dorothy in the Wizard of OZ." – Eddy teased, mimicking Judy Garland with a soft voice. *"There's No Place Like Home, There's No Place Like Home."*

"And you sound like The Wicked Witch, or should I say BITCH of the West!" Candy quickly hit back.

Eddy laughed, *"Come on there's a table in the corner, the show is about to begin."*

The three sat down in an alcove that was set beneath the road, and next to the stage.

"Well done Eddy, that was lucky to find a table right next to the stage." Rogan said, as he took his jacket off and put it onto the back of his chair, and then took a drink of his whisky as he sat back.

The coloured lights around the edge of the stage started to flash in a chase sequence, and the song track 'Hello Dolly' began to play as an introduction for the owner and compare Dolly to appear for her cabaret spot.

Suddenly the lights went out, and the stage was plunged into darkness.

"Michael the lights! Michael the lights! Where's my fucking lights?" Dolly's voice boomed over the speakers from

backstage, where she was waiting to make her grand entrance.

"Please give her a big hand on her entrance, as her boyfriend won't after he lost his torch! The one and only, as there won't be any more room on stage for anyone else! – Dolly."

The lights came back on, and Dolly walked on stage holding a microphone, to a thunderous cheer from the audience gathered around.

The overweight drag compare bulging out of a gold sequin dress and a Dolly Parton style blonde wig, gave a disdainful look at Michael the DJ operating the sound tracks and lights in a booth off stage, who had introduced her.

"You did that on purpose, just because the spotlights are for me, whilst you are in the shadows, and must find what lights you can? Any more remarks like that and you'll end up in a box, and I don't mean a DJ box! I'll get you later!"

The audience cheered and laughed at her put down.

"Good evening ladies and germs! Do you like my new glitzy dress? You should do, YOU BOUGHT IT!"

Dolly burst into song, as she swaggered provocatively around the stage.

"Don't you wish your girlfriend was hot like me? Don't you wish your girlfriend had a Cock like me? Don't cha? Don't cha?

The audience laughed and cheered.

"I've invested in a new weather cock. If I want to know what the weather is going to be like in the morning. I pull back the bed covers and look between my man's legs. If it's lying on the left, It's gonna be sunny, if it's lying on the right, it's gonna be rain."

A voice from the crowd called out. *"What if it's standing straight up?"*

Dolly laughed. *"Who cares about the weather?"*

Her attention suddenly redirected from the front, to the side of the stage where Rogan was seated. *"Oh! What do we have here?"*

The spotlight followed her as she stepped off the stage and sat on Rogan's lap and licked the microphone as a phallic symbol.

"The Dream Factory has sent the hunk I ordered on Amazon."
I love ordering on Amazon you can try things out for fourteen days, and if not suitable YOU CAN SEND THEM BACK!"

The audience gathered around the front of the stage screamed with laughter at Dolly's sexy and funny innuendos, as she kept them coming fast and all directed to Rogan.

"If I flip a coin, what do you reckon my chances of getting some head tonight?"

Rogan laughed as Dolly begun to undo the buttons of his shirt and holding it open to reveal his abs.

"Your body is Wonderland and I want to be Alice."

"Do you know what'd look good on you? Me!" Rogan was roaring with laughter as Dolly stood up and took his hand leading him onto the stage.

"Your Jeans are very tight, lets see the back." Dolly said as she guided him to turn and then stroked his bum. *"That reminds me, I must get some Buttocks for my face."*

Rogan looked back over his shoulder, *"Don't you mean Botox?"*

"HONEY, I KNOW WHAT I MEAN!" Dolly laughed as she squeezed his bum.

"You can sit on my face, it seats SIX!"

The audience cheered, as she turned him back again.

"Trust me, It will only seem kinky the first time!"

Dolly walked behind him and lifted his arms, as she guided them to be placed on the back of his head in a vulnerable pose, leaving his body at her disposal.

"Oh boy, his got his guns out." She said panting and feeling his bulging biceps. *"Will you be bringing out any more pistols to shoot from? Is that a gun in your pocket, or are you just pleased to see me?"* She added whilst wrapping her arms around his waist, and hovering over his jeans fly. The crowd hollered, *"LET'S SEE IT!"*

"What has 142 teeth and holds back the incredible hulk?" She asked the audience. *"HIS FLY ZIPPER!"* She shouted as she pulled his zip down.

Rogan laughed and walked off stage zipping his fly back up, as he went back to his chair with cheers from the audience. Eddy and Candy were hysterical with laughter.

"You bastards, you set me up whilst I went for a piss! I wondered why this table so close to the stage was still available, I'll get both of you for that." Rogan said laughing as he affectionately grabbed the back of their heads and pulled them towards him, as if he was going to bang them together.

"Yea, well you can get us a drink first, it's your round!" Eddy said with a cheeky grin.

Rogan reluctantly went to the bar and looked back at the pair still laughing at their successful planned cabaret spot for him.

Rogan shouted at them. *"I'm getting a bottle of champagne and you two are going to pay for it!"*

As he stood waiting in the crowd to be served amongst the T- Girls and their male admirers, who were looking lovingly at the imagery created by the young men who had become T-Girls, a voice alongside Rogan asked, *"What are you drinking?"*

The club receptionist was next to him, sipping a drink through a straw.

"Hi." Rogan was surprised to see the receptionist amongst the crowd.

"Time off for good behavior?"

"I'm never good, I'm like the poem, 'When he was good, he was very, very good, but when he was bad, he was even better!" Rogan smiled, *"You're spunky."*

"And your sexy, I watched you on stage."

"What's your name?" Rogan asked as he placed his hand around the receptionists' waist.

"Martine when I'm here, and Martin when I'm at my day job."

"What's your day job?"

"I work in Selfridges on the Tom Ford perfume counter, squirting men with Black Orchid as they walk by, hoping one will stop and buy an eighty pound bottle of cologne, so that I get bonus commission on top of my wages for selling more than six bottles in one day!" Martine enthused.

"That sounds like fun squirting men all day long. Are you also into water sports?" Rogan joked as he lowered his arm around Martine's waist to give him a gentle squeeze on his bum cheek.

"You're quick for a straight guy!"

"Yea I'm straight, straight to the point, I want to fuck you!"

"We'll have to see about that?" Martine said coyly as he sipped more of his drink through the straw, and then closed his eyes briefly as he gave Rogan a submissive look.

"Where's our drinks?" Eddy shouted at Rogan, as he fought through the crowd.

"Sorry mate, I got caught up with this hot little number!" Referring to Martine.

"I'll get them! I can go behind the bar, what are you drinking?" Martine took charge.

"Thank's there was mention of champagne?" Eddy replied.

"No I was supposed to get their drinks, you mustn't pay." Rogan said as he pulled out a fifty-pound note from his pocket, and offered it to Martine.

"No! It's okay as management I get drinks for nothing.

"Champagne?" Rogan queried.

"Well Dolly is back stage, and she won't miss one bottle." Eddy smiled *"I like you already."*

"Hands off, I saw him first!" Rogan said giving Eddy a gentle push on his shoulder.

"Champagne it is!" Martine disappeared through the crowd and reappeared behind the bar. Taking a bottle of champagne from the fridge he placed it into a bucket of ice and balanced four glasses on top, so that it looked majestic for a celebration.

Rogan met him at the end of the bar and took *the champagne bucket from his hands, "Let me take that for you."*

Eddy led the way pushing through the crowd to the table, where Candy was sitting talking to two T-girls who had joined her.

"Make way Royalty coming frough." Eddy announced to the T-Girls, who reluctantly stood up as Rogan and Martine arrived, to take up their seats at the table.

"I'm Roxy and I'm Amber." The two T-girls introduced themselves to Rogan and Eddy.

"Amber that's a nice name." Eddy said.

"Thanks it's short for Ambidextrous, I can wank two people off at once!" What are you two doing later?"

Eddy and Rogan laughed.

"You were so sexy on stage, what's your name?" Roxy said as she put her arm around Rogan's waist.

"Rogan. - Get some glasses, and you can have some Champagne with us."

"Rogan and Roxy, it has a ring about it, doesn't it Amber?" Roxy said trying to out do Amber's advances, as she threw her head backwards and laughed.

"The only ring you'll get, is around your neck when I throttle you, don't make moves on MY man!" Martine said firmly.

"Ooo! The Princess of Dollies has spoken, come on Amber, we're off we don't need their champagne let's have a dance."

"Your man?" Rogan said laughing as he leaned in and gave Martine a kiss on the lips.

"They're two of the biggest bitches." Martine said as he held Rogan's hand.

Candy and Eddy laughed. *"That's it girl, tell it as it is!"* Eddy said refilling Candy's glass with champagne.

"Do you wanna line?" Rogan asked Martine referring to cocaine.

"Yea!" Martine replied with a smile, as he stood up and led Rogan by his hand through the crowd to the toilets, where they went into a small cubicle and immediately kissed.

On one of the walls someone had written with a felt tip pen,

'TRANNIE LORRY DRIVER WANT'S A FUCK IN HIS TRUCK'.
Underneath someone added ' CALL THE AA YOU MAY HAVE SOME LUCK?

Rogan chopped two huge cocaine lines on top of the lavatory lid, and offered Martine a rolled up fifty-pound note to go first and snort.

Whilst Rogan was bent over snorting his line off the lavatory lid, Martine wrapped his arms around Rogan's waist, and as he stood up moved his hands lower to unzip his trouser fly. Rogan turned around and passionately kissed him again, as Martine slipped his hand inside the fly to grope and perform oral sex.

After they had finished, and realizing they had made loud sounds of ecstasy groans and banging noises against the wooden panel walls in the cramped cubicle, Martine gingerly opened the door.

Standing at the urinals with their backs to the cubicles, and skirts lifted to pee, Roxy and Amber both turned their heads to see who had been making so much noise and that was coming out of the cubicle.

"Told you he was my man, and he is a BIG-BIG man!" Martine smugly emphasized, laughing as he crossed three of his fingers; licked them and placed them into his mouth, and as he pulled them out, wiped his lips.

"The princess has fallen from grace, and is now a slut! Wonder if she swallowed or spat?" Roxy said to Amber in a bitter tone, as she screwed up her face with a sour expression, and tucked her penis back into her lace knickers.

"Come on girl lets go back to the spotlights, remember head back, teeth, tits and arse."

As the two eavesdroppers left, Martine and Rogan both laughed out loud at the sight of Ambers skirt, caught up in the back of her knickers!

Boys in lace knickers shouldn't throw insults!

Mandarin Hotel – Nelson Bar

Rogan sipped the cocktail of the moment, 'Blue Door'. - Gin, Sherry, Crème de Cacao, Orange and bitters.

Spreading his legs apart, he sank back into the comfort and intimacy of the soft burnished gold colour cushions on the sofa, set in the coves of the Mandarin Hotel's 'Nelson Bar' in Mayfair.

Hugo had called him earlier to meet, but he wasn't in the mood to see him, and made an excuse that he had a headache.

This was another hotel where the rich and famous stayed, a long way off from the seedy depths of Dollies underground nightclub.

He caught site of his reflection in the mirrored bar opposite his table wearing a 'Dior' royal blue suit, and smiled as he thought back to last night and the conversations, when he escorted 63-year-old Dorothy ('Dixie' to her friends) Burnstein, to a dinner party at the flat of socialite Gertrude (Girty' to her friends) Abrahams.

The flat in Lowndes Square Belgravia Knightsbridge spanned laterally across two buildings, and had a private gold lift that opened directly into the flat.

They were a little bit late on arriving due to heavy traffic at Hyde Park corner.

"I would have asked what kept you? But I can see why." Girty said to Dixie, as she also greeted Rogan.

"So handsome." She moved in, stroking his shoulder.

"It's better to arrive late looking fabulous, than early looking a mess!" Dixie said laughing as she took possession, and clutched Rogan's arm, who responded on cue by kissing her on the cheek.

Girty laughed and stroked Dixie's glamorous emerald green coat, trimmed with an emerald green fur collar and cuffs, and kissed the air next to Dixie's cheek, without making contact with her.

"*Mwah-Mwah! New clothes same old faces!*"

"*I might not be good-looking, but I sure got style!*" Dixie said, wanting the last word.

As they hugged, Dixie looked over Girty's shoulder, through the open double doors leading off the hallway, to friends of a similar age who also had nicknames Baba and Nana, seated in the palatial living room drinking champagne with their husbands.

"*Baba and Nana are here on loan from Madame Tussauds Waxworks.*" Girty bitched out of ear-shot to the propped up women, sitting on the edge of the gold ormolu Empire style chairs like wax dummies!

As they saw Dixie, both waved and barely mouthed a silent hello, due to their facelifts and Botox injections restricting their facial muscles.

"*I see what you mean!*" Dixie said trying not to laugh out aloud, as they both giggled at their bitchy remarks.

"*Come through and help me wind up the keys in their backs, or they wont be able to get up!*" Girty said from the corner of her mouth.

Rogan was unexpectedly taken aback, not from the remarks, but because he recognized Nana's husband Harvey, a rich punter, whom he had sex with several months ago in a sleazy hotel in Vauxhall, within the shadows of the MI5 Building.

Harvey had made advances to Rogan in the 'Hard Rock' Gay sauna steam room (Affectionately known as the 'Hard Cock' Sauna) by sitting close to him, with his knee touching Rogan's.

Rogan was aware of Harvey's interest and let the towel wrapped around his waist full open, revealing his legs wide apart and semi erect penis, to seduce Harvey in parting with his fat wallet.

The hotel 'LAS VEGAS' in Vauxhall used by rent boys for a quick fuck for cash, couldn't be further from the opulent luxurious hotels that dominate the Las Vegas strip in the USA, and not the usual 5 star rating and standard Rogan would circulate, looking for wealthy trade, but was close to the sauna and convenient for Rogan to entertain Harvey, after stopping off at a Cash Point hole in the wall machine, for Harvey to draw out £750 for Rogan's fee, using several bank card limits.

The Greek male receptionist charged Harvey £30 for the room, and said it was for two hours only, which suited Rogan as he had another client before 9pm.

The 65 year old man looked nervous when he saw Rogan, and had more beads of sweat on his bald head, than he did in the sauna, but Rogan was professional and acted as if their meeting was a new introduction, remaining charming and discreet. Although he enjoyed the power of being the dominant party as they shook hands.

Dixie owned a ranch and avocado orchard plantation in Southern California and was a multi-millionairess due to inheriting all of her late husbands fortune. When she was in London she was a regular client of Rogan, and his services were just to escort her to various dinner functions or the theatre without any sex involvement.

Although aged 63 she had great personality and was a lot of fun to be with.

Her generosity had spread to her buying Rogan's Dior suit for him to wear at Girty's dinner party and other engagements, beside his regular £500 escorting fee.

His designer clothes image was important for him to blend in with the elite, who travelled the world following the sun to millionaire playgrounds. Cannes, Monaco, Florida and the Bahamas, and were all places on his hit list to visit and be paid for.

Five star hotels were perfect hunting grounds for Rogan, when he was looking for *'Business'*, and for tonight the Nelson bar was his shop window, as it was him who was for the *'MALE FOR SALE'*.

The waiter brought him another cocktail he had ordered, *'The Composer'*, a mixture of vodka and Louis Roederer Champagne, with a touch of Italicus Rosolio di Bergamotto that added citrus hints of rose with lavender, and a Rhubarb cordial to give its rose colour.

In a corner the pianist played laid-back American Jazz, as a young woman that accompanied him sang songs made famous by Ella Fitzgerald, Billy Holiday and Peggy Lee.

The waiter who was passing, carrying a silver tray with a few empty glasses he had collected from tables, stopped at Rogan's table.

"Will you be dining tonight Sir? I can make a reservation for you in the Savoldo Grill the food is wonderful. It has Michelin three stars and headed by Chef Ru Jacques."

Rogan checked his watch, an Oyster pink gold Rolex," *I'm not sure yet, thank you, and I'm not keen on this cocktail, but I will have another drink".*

"Would you prefer another Blue Door cocktail?" The waiter said as he picked up Rogan's empty glass and placed it on his silver tray.

"No, just a straight scotch whisky please."

"Which whisky would you like?"

"A Johnnie Walker Blue label will do fine, thank you."

"On the rocks?" The waiter said with a friendly smile.

"One piece of ice only" Rogan gave his usual reply to the question every barman asked, as he adjusted his glasses by pushing them with his forefinger further up his nose.

He didn't need glasses and although they were a 'Valentino' design, the lenses were clear glass with a tint. Sometimes he would wear them as a fashion statement just to look affluent and sophisticated.

The waiter returned with his drink and a fresh dish of large Spanish Queen olives and nuts.

"Excuse me, is anyone serving?" An attractive young woman asked the waiter as he turned to go back to the bar.

"Yes madam, what would you like?"

Rogan jumped up and intercepted, *"I'll get that."*

He had spotted the beautiful sophisticated young woman and was mesmerized not only by her beauty, but also by the enormous diamond ring she was wearing, sparkling under the overhead spotlights, and not on her marriage finger! (Not that it would have mattered to Rogan) It was nearly as big as the melting ice-cube, still bouncing about in his whisky.

The aroma of her perfume was the smell of money, and had wafted to his table.

"Do I know you?" She asked.

"I seem to know you? Were you skiing in Courchevel? " Rogan said smiling and turning on his charm.

The young woman smiled and looked puzzled, *"No, I was in Aspen this year."*

"I've got it!" Rogan said enthusiastically, as he gestured with a sharp flick movement of his hand. *"St Tropez!"*

The young woman laughed and also looked puzzled as she tried to place Rogan's face.

"I was there for a few days, when my father moored his yacht."

Rogan had taken a long shot that paid off, he knew the hot spots of the rich and if he mentioned several different playgrounds, he would certainly get one right.

"Yes that's it! You were sitting opposite me at an open-air restaurant on the promenade de la Croisette in front of the yachts."

"Oh you mean 'Pieros restaurant', I love it there!"

Rogan snapped his fingers. *"Yes that was it!"*

Second strike! Rogan had made her say a restaurant name, although he had never been to St Tropez!

He often studied the pages of Hello and OK magazine, taking in and learning the names of hotspots where celebrities hung out.

"How nice to see you again." She stretched out her hand to shake, as she was now convinced she knew him.

Rogan shook her hand and could not help himself to glance again at the diamond on her finger, as he sat on a stool next to her.

"My name is Rogan."

"Hi, I'm Francesca von Bryssen, but please call me Frankie, all my friends do".

"Okay Frankie what would you like to drink?"

"A white Lady cocktail, please."

Rogan ordered the drink.

"What's a beautiful young lady doing in a bar alone?"

"I'm staying here with my parents for a few days, but they have gone out for dinner to some friends, and I think at twenty four I'm just a little bit too old to go everywhere Mummy and Daddy go." She said sarcastically and laughing.

"I got fed up sitting in the suite watching the TV and thought I would see if the hotel offered any action?"

She was used to a lot of action, having recently graced the pages of many showbiz and society gossip magazines, with photos of her in an embrace, captioned *'Heiress Wild Child hangs out with Rock Star Emilio in a Mauritius nightclub 'Les Enfants Terrible'.*

The waiter placed her cocktail on the bar.

"Thank you." She said as she raised her glass, to toast and make contact with the top of Rogan's raised glass.

Although well spoken, Rogan picked up on her slight accent.

"I'm trying to work out what accent you have?"

Frankie laughed, *"No matter how hard I try, people always pickup I have an accent, even though I went to finishing school in Switzerland, where we were taught to say; The rain in Spain stays mainly in the Plain, and in Hertford, Hereford, and Hampshire, Hurricanes Hardly ever Happen."*

Rogan laughed and leaned closer to Frankie showing his interest. *"I've seen that film too! You are my Fair Lady who is drinking a White Lady, but seriously where are you from?"*

"Austria." Came a quick reply after a sip of her drink.

*"**Headache gone**?"* A voice boomed beside Rogan, which made him swivel around on his stool to see whom it was. Hugo was standing next to him!

"Hugo! What are you doing here?" Rogan said in surprise as he jumped off the stool and hugged him.

"I am on a secret assignment, to catch Pinnochio!"

Rogan laughed at Hugo's inference that he had lied about having a headache.

"I took a couple of Paracetamol and bingo, my headache went. I didn't call you as I thought you were settled in, and I didn't want to mess you about."

Hugo laughed and said sarcastically, *"Wonderful! Miracles still happen, you'll be walking on water next dear boy, and who is this beautiful lady?"* Hugo took Francesca's hand and kissed it.

Francesca smiled. *"My name is Francesca Von Bryssen."*

Hugo was familiar with her surname; recognising members of her family had shopped at Ranley and were a wealthy dynasty.

Turning on his heel he felt smug, as he could introduce a more impressive title. *"Let me introduce you to Viscount Alexander Ranley."*

Alexander who was standing next to Hugo smiled and put out his hand to shake.

Rogan realized by his surname, the Viscount was the owner of 'Ranley' and a member of the Royal Family that Hugo had told him about.

"And this is Rogan, a friend of mine." Hugo explained as he introduced him to the Viscount who put out his hand to shake Rogan's.

"Pleased to meet you, Hugo has told me you are a wonderful boss."

"He's still not getting a rise." Viscount Ranley said laughing and giving Hugo a friendly pat on his back.

"Alex and I have been working late in the office, and he invited me to dine with him here."

Rogan was beaming and impressed that he finally had met Viscount Alexander Ranley and 'Pressed the flesh' of the young royal who had told many Royal inside stories to Hugo, and who in turn repeated them to him.

As Hugo worked closely with the Viscount, he did not address him by his title and shortened his name to Alex, only introducing him by his full title on meeting new people.

Hugo put his hand gently on Frankie's shoulder.

"Alex and I are going for dinner in the Savoldo Grill, would you both like to join us Francesca?"

"Oh please call me Frankie, yes I would love to join you."

He did not need to ask Rogan twice, as he knew Rogan would never say no to a free dinner.

"The food is wonderful, Michelin three star Chef Ru Jacques runs it." Rogan said remembering the waiters' words, and giving the impression he had eaten there before.

Hugo knew Rogan probably had never eaten there, and was trying to impress the rest of the guests.

As the four walked through to the dining room, heads in the crowded bar turned as they nudged each other to look, as some recognized Viscount Alexander Ranley, who as a junior member of the royal family, was always on the balcony of Buckingham Palace on royal state occasions with the rest of the family, and although his position on the balcony was far to one side, he was still with the rest of the royals, to be alongside the Queen.

As the Viscount and Frankie walked in front of Rogan and Hugo chatting, the on-lookers tongues were wagging, of the identity of the stunningly attractive brunette young woman that he was accompanying?

"Is she oh? You know, whatshername? She was in the film Girl With The Pearl Earring."

"Scarlett Johansson?"

"Yes! Yes! That's her!"

"No, I don't think so? She looks more like Britney Spears. Yes! That's who she is!"

Frankie's body was well toned, and her chic little black dress gripped every contour, revealing her stunning figure. Scalloped Black lace covered her upper chest to the neck, and sleeves to her wrists, only the low cut V-back plunging down to just above her bum revealed any flesh. Her diamond ring was the only accessory.

As Rogan and Hugo walked behind the pair, Rogan knowing Hugo's weakness for sex games, whispered sexy promises to makeup for his excuse of being unwell.

He wasn't going to let his introduction to the Viscount go to waste, as social climbing meant more introductions to society who had lots of money and treats.

Hugo warned Rogan not to bring up any conversation about the Royal Family, as it would be in bad taste and the Viscount would be offended.

Over dinner Frankie, said that being in the UK was a stop off for her parents to catch up with friends, before going onto the fashion shows in Milan, where she and her mother would buy some of the collections shown for a fashion store she was opening off Bond Street Mayfair.

Many of their favourite designers Fendi, Prada, Salvatore Ferragamo, Roberto Cavalli, Versace and Victoria's Secrets, would all be showing.

Her father was a successful industrialist and had companies in Italy, so would be in business talks, leaving them to enjoy themselves, buying for the store and adding to their own wardrobes.

After dinner when the bill arrived, Hugo insisted he would pay, and that he and the Viscount must leave as they both had an early start at Ranley.

As they got up to leave, Hugo turned back and spoke softly into Rogan's ear. *"Come for dinner on Thursday, I've got the day off, we can have some fun?"*

Rogan and Frankie carried on having a nightcap liqueur and coffee.

"I've never been to a fashion show." Rogan said as he sipped a Drambuie liqueur.

"Then you must come with us." Frankie insisted.

"Really!" Rogan looked surprised at Frankie's quick response.

"Yes, you will be my excuse to go to the Men's fashion shows as well, and look at all those gorgeous models!"

"Will your parents mind?"

"No, I will tell them you are a friend who is going to be opening a Designer Menswear shop, and I am going to help you choose clothes from a woman's prospective."

"When are you going?"

"In two days."

"But I won't be able to book a plane ticket in time, and the planes are probably full with so many buyers going?"

Frankie laughed. *"Don't worry about that, you can come with us, my father always books a private Learjet, there's plenty of room."*

"But you hardly know me."

"That's why it's so much fun! And by the way, I haven't been to St Tropez!" Frankie said laughing as she had caught him out.

"You're crazy!" Rogan said affectionately.

Touché!

8.0 pm Machiavelli Oriental Hotel - Milan

Rogan was in his room at the Machiavelli Oriental hotel in Milan, sipping a whisky (with one piece of ice!) and relaxing before going down to the restaurant in the hotel, to have dinner alone with Frankie, as her parents were going out to dine with business associates.

They had gone to the last of the men's fashions shows, and over the last several days it had been a whirlwind of rushing from one show to another, as Frankie had arranged entry tickets for her mother and Rogan to all of the top designers couture fashion shows, whilst her father attended business meetings.

Her mother in her mid 50s, was very chic and sophisticated, and liked Rogan as he was full of compliments, which he had mastered over time, by flattering older women, making them feel special, who were paying for his special services. - He fancied her!

Her father was a little bit more distant, and had questioned Rogan, enquiring of his profession in business.

"Property Developer, I'm putting together a portfolio of properties."

His answer was loose and enough for him to lie, conjuring up the vision of a prestigious business, acquiring and renovating properties.

The reality of being a Gigolo as a profession would not have gone down too well.

His mobile played its ringtone of an incoming call. Rogan answered. *"Hello".* The voice on the other end was Hugo.

"Where are you?"

"Oh hello Hugo, I'm in Milan."

"Milan!" Hugo said in surprise. *"What are you doing there, you were supposed to be coming here for dinner tonight!"*

"I'm at the fashion shows with Frankie, It was last minute. I've been here for two days. Frankie asked me to help her decide which designer clothes she should order for her designer wear women's shop she is going to open, and wanted a mans prospective of choice." He said reversing the same excuse Frankie had given to her parents.

"Well a call would have been decent! We planned this last week! You knew this was my day off; I've been cooking dinner thinking you were about to arrive and you're in Italy! Now I've got to throw half away in the bin, I am so angry! Fuck you! Fuck off!" Outraged, Hugo said furiously and hung up.

Rogan sat on the side of the bed and had a gulp of his whisky, wondering if he should call Hugo back and what to say?

Hesitantly he dialed Hugo's number.

Recognising the number that came up on his mobiles display screen, Hugo answered in a clipped and angry speaking manner, *"Yes!"*

Knowing how to get on the better side of Hugo, he spoke with a loving caring voice. *"Baby, I'm sorry, you are always on to me saying I should get a job, and Frankie offered to pay me to accompany her, I thought you would be pleased?"*

"I would have, if you would of told me before you jetted off, and not let me down, I was so looking forward to our night together, and I made you your favorite Salmon and Truffle."

Rogan laughed, *"You liar, I know you, you've had it delivered in from Prunier the French restaurant."*

"Well, I had to make the telephone call!" Hugo said with his quick wit.

Rogan laughed as he turned the tables on Hugo's anger, and into him being as the guilty party. *"We've been seeing each other for three months, and you are still trying to make me believe you've been slaving over a hot cooker! You don't even know where your kitchen is!*

Don't throw it away put it in the fridge if you can find it! I shall be back tomorrow evening and will come straight over to eat it right off your body, and after you can give me a spanking for being a naughty boy!"

"Okay, but don't you dare let me down again."

"Can't wait! I'll be there, love you." Rogan hung up and muttered, "Old git."

No sooner had he hung up on his mobile, the room telephone on the bedside table rung. It was on the opposite side of the bed to where he had sprawled himself whilst talking to Hugo.

Edging his body across to reach the receiver he lifted it to his ear.

"Rogan." It was Frankie.

"Rather than eating in the hotels boring restaurant, I'm ordering dinner from room service, which we can eat here", have a look at the menu in your room and ring me back."

"Okay" Rogan walked over to a desk and picked up the menu and perused the main dishes.

Picking up the room phone, he dialed Frankie's room and gave his order of food dishes as soon as she answered.

"Steak Béarnaise, medium cooked, dauphinoise potatoes and asparagus. That will be fab! Be there in twenty minutes, I'm taking a shower first."

"Okay" Frankie hung up.

As they were not going out, after his shower Rogan dressed casual, and put on a white T-shirt and his tight skinny jeans.

Just as he entered the lift to go to Frankie's room on the ninth floor, a young handsome guy dashed to get in before the door automatically closed.

Rogan had spotted him coming towards the lift and held onto the door restricting it from closing.

"Thanks." The young man's face lit up with a broad smile at Rogan's good deed.

"What floor?" Rogan enquired as his finger hovered over the floor buttons.

"Ninth, thank you."

As the lift journeyed up, Rogan could not take his eyes off the beauty of the young man standing opposite, with long black curly hair pushed back behind his ears.

A long silver chain with big links hung around his strong neck and dangled over a black vest he was wearing loosely over his jeans. Part of the vest was tucked into the side of his jeans in a casual way, so that his crotch was not hidden. Uncannily a picture of 'Che Guevara' the Argentine Marxist Revolutionary leader that was printed on it, looked like an older version of him.

A famous quote of Guevara was also printed on the vest under the picture, but some of the wording was hidden as it was tucked into the boy's jeans.

Rogan read it out aloud.
"The revolution is not an apple that falls when it is ripe."

Not being able to see the rest of it, which was tucked into the jeans, he asked the boy. *"What do you do if it is not ripe?"*
The boy smiled as he pulled his vest from the side of his jeans, and stretched it pulling it out wide, revealing his navel button on his hairless body, and the last line of the quote to show as he recited.

"You have to make it fall!"

"Mmm." Rogan broke into a broad smile and was salivating, transfixed on the boys sexy naval, and averted his eyes to the lifts flashing indicator lights on the wall to the left of the boy's body.

The floors passing were getting closer to their destination. Rogan was hoping '9' would never light up, and that their lift may break down for several hours, trapping them to get to know each other better, and maybe the chance to shake his tree?

'Ping!' The lift came to a stop as the 9th floor light flashed, and the door slid open.

The young man was slightly ahead of Rogan as they walked along the hallway, and stopped at room 911 to knock on the door.

Rogan stood next to him and grinned. *"Hi."* Frankie opened the door, and laughed. *"You came together."*

"Not yet!" Rogan used her words as an innuendo. *"I gave him a lift."* Rogan said laughing as he placed his hand on the young man's back, ushering him to walk in before.

"Santiago, meet Rogan, Rogan, meet Santiago." Frankie said as she handed them both a glass of champagne.

There was an obvious attraction between the two as they gave each other long lingering looks.

"Santiago is one of the models, we saw today at the Dolce and Gabbana beachwear show we went to earlier."

Rogan gave a broad smile. *"Yes of course, you were wearing the trunks with gold crowns printed on them."*

"You're very observant." Santiago said as he took a sip of champagne.

"I couldn't forget seeing your crowning glory!"

"Was I sticking out that much? The cod piece padding must have slipped?" Santiago said laughing as he gave his crotch a tug.

"I met Santiago after the show, and after my mother had left, and when you went off to the toilet. I thought him so delicious he would be great to have for dinner." Frankie said wrapping an arm around Santiago's shoulders and bumping her hip on his, to the beat sound of the song track she had playing.

Rogan jokingly licked his lips and still playing on Frankies words for innuendos. *"Yes, I'd love him for dinner! Mmm I could gobble him up, In-fact cancel my steak, he's much more juicy!"*

Their sexual innuendos were interrupted by a knock on the door.

Frankie opened it. A hotel waiter wearing a white jacket, with the name of the hotel *'Machiavelli Oriental'* embroidered in gold on his breast pocket, pushed a trolley through.

"Would you like me to put the food out onto your table madam?"

He asked Frankie in an Italian accent.

"No thank you, that's okay." Frankie handed him a twenty-euro note tip.

As the waiter left the room, Frankie lifted the silver terrine lids off the three meals.

"Chicken! That's yours Santiago, Sea Bass! That's mine and Steak for you sexy!" Frankie said as she placed the meals on the table.

The three sat down.

"Do you live in Milan?" asked Rogan.

"No I am from Argentine", replied Santiago.

"How old are you?"

"Twenty six."

"More champagne?" Frankie interrupted. Rogan and Santiago were in conversation and had heavy eye contact, but broke as they held their glasses up to meet the champagne bottleneck that Frankie was putting between their faces, as she stretched across the table.

Her Apple Tablet was booming out a song track that she did not like any more, which was playing from the selection she had on a download.

Moving on to another track, she picked up the beat and started to dance swinging her hips as she went back to the dining table. Standing behind and in-between the two boys seated, she placed an arm around each of them, and kissed both in turn on the cheek.

"I've got desert, when you two have stopped gazing into each others eyes, and have finished your dinner."

Rogan's attention to Santiago immediately changed to Frankie's announcement, as he was familiar with the term desert in these circles did not mean coffee Tiramisu or any other sweet. This was desert for the Big Boys and Girls, who would rush through their dinner for a line of cocaine!

As the evening went on, the lines kept coming along with the alcohol.

2am Room 911

The volume of the Apple tablet pumping out the song tracks
was very loud, as Frankie had turned the dial setting to its
maximum sound level.

Rogan and Santiago kissed and hugged in-between dancing
and fell onto the sofa in an embrace.

Stoned on cocaine and very drunk, Frankie could hardly
stand as she stumbled around the room clutching the nearly
empty champagne bottle.

Taking a swig straight from the bottle, she finished it off.

"Look at my two sexy boys." She said as she fell on top of
them and dropped the empty bottle onto the floor.

Gently she pushed Rogan's head to one side. *"It's my turn."*

And put her tongue into Santiago's mouth and reached
down, to rub his penis bulge that had become semi erect
from kissing Rogan.

Rogan responded by reaching out to join her hand, and also
caress Santiago's erection, as he kissed Frankie.

The trio, were in a sexual liaison *'Manage de trois',* and were
on the same page for the rest of the night.

Santiago lowered his head onto Frankie's breasts and licked
in-between them, as he crossed over her and Rogan's hands,
reaching to unzip Rogan's jeans and feeling inside.

As dawn broke, a beam of light shone through a break in the
heavy draped closed curtains.

Santiago got up from the king sized bed, and walked naked
over to the curtains. Opening them slightly to take in the
early morning sunlight, he looked back to the bed at the two
naked bodies he had spent the night feeling, performing oral
sex and entering.

The sunlight on Rogan's muscular body highlighted his six-
pack abs, and stirred him as it hit his eyes causing him to
semi wake, and his penis stand to it's regular morning
erection.

Unable to ignore the spectacular sight of Rogan's naked sexy body, Santiago walked back to the bed, and knelt down beside, leaning over.

Rogan's groans of ecstasy as he ejaculated, stirred Frankie, who muttered in her sleep and turned over onto her front, on the far side of the bed.

Late afternoon, a knock on the door stopped Rogan from packing his suitcase, and he went to open it.

Frankie fully recovered and wearing a camel colour coat, swished in as if she was in a hurry.

Tearfully she dabbed her eye with a handkerchief. *"Darling the plans have changed, my parents aren't going back to London, we have to go home back to Austria now! As my fathers mother has been taken seriously ill, and he has been advised she may not live until tomorrow!"*

"I'm sorry to hear that." Rogan said sympathetically *"But how will I get back to London?"* Putting his dilemma first.

Frankie reached into her chocolate brown calf leather designer *'Fendi'* handbag (Known to be in the top ten most expensive handbags at £1,890).

Rogan did not know how much the bag cost, but was aware Frankie would not be carrying a handbag from Marks and Spencer, and judging from its style and quality, if the bag could speak, would say *"I am rich!"*

Frankie pulled out a wad of fifty-pound notes and handed them to Rogan.

"There's five hundred there, it should get you a first class ticket back to the UK?"

Rogan eyes lit up at seeing the wad, and took the opportunity to push for more.

"I've also got a bar bill, and got to get to the airport in Milan, and from Heathrow to home. I did tell you coming here; in the hurry I left my wallet and credit cards at home."

"Okay, yes I forgot." Frankie reached into her handbag again, *here's another five hundred that should settle everything? We'll meet up in London soon, bye darling."*

They both kissed as Frankie turned on her heel and left. Within one minute there was another knock on the door. Rogan threw the wads of money onto his un-maid bed and covered them with the duvet before he opened the door. Frankie was back?

"I had a great time last night, but can't remember which one of you fucked me?"

(Rogan took a cab to Milan Malpensa International airport for 80 Euros, (£70) and bought an economy airline ticket back to London for £72, and then a ticket on the Heathrow Express, back to Paddington station for £25, and a taxi for £33 straight to Hugo's flat. A total of £200, leaving him to pocket £800 of Frankie's gift of £1,000 for first class travel that he never intended to follow through? He did not feel bad about it after all he had fucked her, and in his business that always comes with a price!)

Murder on my mind

"Hi Peter." Rogan was often visiting Hugo's at his flat, and acknowledged the concierge at reception as he marched by. Although not lovers, his relationship with Hugo that had started out casual had developed into a close relationship over the past year.

Hugo had given him his own key to his mansion flat as a token of trust. Hugo regarded him as his companion with perks of sex.

Hurriedly Peter picked up the house phone to inform Hugo, that Rogan was on his way up to the flat.

As he entered the hallway in the flat, he could hear the reception house telephone that was still ringing. The bedroom door opened at the other end of the hall, and Hugo in his black kaftan robe, walked hurriedly up the hallway, intending to answer the phone sitting on the marble console table that was half way up the hall.

He was surprised at seeing Rogan walking towards him, at the other end and speeded up his steps as he tried to reach for the telephone inbetween them before Rogan did, but Rogan got to it first and lifted the receiver to his ear, as he stared coldly into Hugo's eyes and listened to the revealing message. *"Mr Walford, Rogan is on his way up, he walked quickly past me before I could let you know! Sorry."* Peter uttered.

"Thankyou Peter", Rogan said as he hung up and stared at Hugo with a cold expression, sensing that there was something not quite right at Hugo's shifty behaviour and Peter's attempt of a tipoff to his arrival.

"Too busy to answer the phone?"

"I thought you were coming back later this evening?" Hugo said, uneasy at the sight of Rogan's serious face, which was unusual and frightening.

"I got an earlier flight, as I knew you were counting the hours that we would be together again baby. Thought we could have lunch?" Rogan said in a sarcastic manner, and then embraced Hugo with a kiss, that of Judas identifying him to his executioners?

"You must be dying for a drink? Go into the living room and pour one for me as well, I was just getting dressed, won't be a moment." Hugo said nervously and on edge, as he had never seen this side of Rogan.

Rogan walked into the living room and poured three drinks of whisky, and then took them to Hugo's bedroom.

Holding the three glasses tightly against his chest for balance, he pushed the door open with his foot. *"Thought your friend would like one too?"*

A naked young man was hurriedly stepping into a pair of jeans, and looked nervous at being caught with his pants down, in Hugo's bedroom.

"Alright mate! Thanks for giving me the night off." Rogan said stretching out his hand, as he offered the drink.

Noticing a pair of underpants lying on the floor next to the bed, Rogan stooped, picked them up, and sniffed them at the crotch.

Playfully he threw them at Hugo. *"Here smell these, anyone you know?"*

Hugo looked guilty, and tried to switch the uneasy atmosphere to being relaxed as he giggled and motioned his hand, waving in a stroke of flamboyancy. *"Honey I thought you would like a coming home present, and I was just going to test Alex before you arrived."*

Realising Hugo had paid for a 'Rent Boy' Rogan jumped to the occasion at the sight of the boy's semi erection, and grabbed hold of it. *"You can't leave Commando, and let that go to waste big boy, don't bother putting those trousers back on, it's' time to get the party started! Thanks Hugo, nice of you to invite me to lunch!"*

The three engaged in sex stopping occasionally to have more alcohol and lines of cocaine. Rogan still felt angry Hugo had wanted sex with a younger boy, although it was okay for him as it was his business. He wanted to have Alex all to himself and get back at Hugo.

Unbeknown to Hugo or Alex, he secretly mixed a small amount of MDMA ecstasy powder with the line of cocaine Hugo was to snort, knowing it would knock him out.

The MDMA was dangerously too strong for Hugo, and after a couple of hours he was drunk, hallucinating, and having hot flushes.

As he tried to speak, he was involuntary jaw clenching, causing him to mumble, and fall about the room, finally collapsing onto a small sofa in the corner of his bedroom, Rogan and Alex were also high on cocaine and oblivious of Hugo's state as they continued their fantasy sex acts.

Half opening his blurred eyes, Hugo could make out a hazy scene of Rogan naked on all fours with a full erection, being led around the room by Alex tugging on a belt strapped around his neck.

Alex in a dominant role, wearing a leather jock strap, occasionally pulled on the belt jerking Rogan's head backwards to choke and excite him, giving him masochistic sexual pleasure to maintain his erection.

Rogan had experimented alone with paraphilia asphyxia, depriving himself of oxygen to heighten his state of sexual arousal, and wanted to explore S and M further.

(**WARNING!** Paraphilia Asphyxia is an extremely dangerous life-threatening act, (Not to be tried) which has often led to the act going wrong and resulting in death).

Hugo had slipped from the sofa onto the floor and tried to speak, but his speech was slurred. *"What the fook are youse doin?"* And passed out again.

After Alex left, Rogan knelt by Hugo, who was slumped on the floor by the bed, and gently slapped his face to waken him.
"Come on, wakey-wakey."
Still stoned on drugs and paralytic, Hugo stirred and half waking came round.
Rogan put his arm under Hugo's, and struggled with Hugo's weight as he lifted him. *"You need some fresh air."*
Hugo with the help of Rogan pulled himself up, gripping the side of the sofa, and was stumbling to remain on his feet, as they walked to the French doors leading to the small balcony overlooking the private gardens.
On the balcony unable to keep his balance, Hugo clenched the railings swaying forward and back, as the air accelerated his stoned condition of dizziness.
For a moment Rogan thought, a gentle push and Hugo would topple over the top.
The coroner would declare his stomach was full of booze and drugs, and that it was an accident.
Being over weight, his body would hit the ground in 30 seconds, his head smashed, his brains spewed on the pavement, he would never survive.
Hugo had talked of his will and told Rogan he would be a beneficiary, but never said how much he would receive or who else may benefit? Rogan couldn't be sure if Hugo had left him a large some of money, or just a Silver frame with his own photo to haunt?
In the past, Hugo had joked he was going to leave Rogan a naked photo and a video he had filmed of him on his Iphone, one drunken, drug fueled night, dressed in a woman's bra and frilly pink panties dancing the French Can-Can. Whilst dancing he had pulled down the panties, and bent over for

Hugo to stick a fifty pound note into the crack of his bum, as a tip!

"Be careful you could fall? Lets go back in". Rogan couldn't let anything tragic happen to Hugo, he needed to be financially secure, he had not seen the written will, and it was still early days to weave a web?

Where there's a will – There will be a way?

Monkeys Tea Party

Fortnum and Mason an up-market department store in Piccadilly that holds a Royal warrant as suppliers to the Queen, were holding an afternoon Tea Party invite to high society aristocrats and A-lister celebrity, for an exclusive first view of the works by world renowned Greek Surrealist artist *'Ilias Constantinos',* which were to go on display within the store.

Viscount Alexander Ranley had been invited, and in turn asked Hugo to accompany him.

As they walked into the famous 'Tea Salon' a waiter greeted them at the door with a glass of champagne.

The room was packed with guests admiring the works of art, mounted in the arms of giant fiberglass molded monkeys, standing around the edges of the room.

"Didn't know you were bringing me to a Monkey's tea party Alex."

"What did you think I brought these bananas for?" Alex joked, as he grabbed one from the fun centerpiece displays on the tables set for tea.

The two laughed and ventured around the room, looking at the surrealist art.

"Allo Hugo." a cockney voice boomed out from the crowd.

"And you must be Alex?" Eddy stepped forward pushing through the crowd of the well heeled, well spoken, socialite crowd, and nouveau riche wannabes.

Grabbing Hugo he placed a kiss on his cheek.

Hugo was embarrassed, at Eddy referring to the Viscount by his first name, which would be evident that he had spoken about him in close circles using his shortened name.

Rogan was just behind and was angry at Eddy's bold greeting to the Viscount whom he had never met, but had been told about by both Hugo and himself.

From Hugo and Rogan's description, he had guessed the young man with Hugo was the Viscount, and as Hugo always referred to Viscount Alexander as 'Alex', it was typical of

Eddy's cheekiness and disregard of the Royal Family, that he was not going to address him with his formal title.

Hugo pretended he and the Viscount had not heard the cockney bellow, and officially introduced him to the Viscount. *"Eddy this is Viscount Alexander Ranley."*

"Nice to meet ya." Eddy said putting out his hand to shake, but to his surprise the Viscount clenched his fist to give a 'street knuckle bump'.

"Boom! And nice to meet you." The Viscount said with a smile. Eddy laughed *"Nice one."* And responded by engaging the Viscount's knuckles with a fist dap greeting.

Rogan standing alongside Eddy put out his hand, and undermining Eddy's familiarity addressed Alex by his full name. *"Hello Alexander."*

"Please I told you when we had dinner at the Mandarin to call me Alex, I'm not really into titles!" And repeated a street knuckle bump greeting to him.

"That's a surprise seeing you two here." Hugo said as he downed the last of his champagne in his glass.

"There are actually three of us."

A very attractive slim woman, wearing a pale blue Chanel boucle suit, navy silk blouse and diamond earrings, stood next to Rogan and smiled as she removed her large tinted glasses.

"This is my mother Lisa."

Hugo smiled back, and commented at her youthful look.

"Surely you mean sister!"

Lisa laughed, and grabbed Hugo's arm in friendship. *"I like you, Rogan has told me so much about you, and we're going to get on famously."*

"Let me introduce you to Viscount Alexander Ranley - my boss!"

"Yes I know, Rogan has explained."

The Viscount put out his hand to shake.

"What no knuckles?" Lisa said laughing.

"I wouldn't want to harm such beautiful hands." The Viscount said in his charming manner, as he bent his head and kissed

the back of her hand. *"And please call me Alex, Eddy already does!"* Everybody laughed as they turned towards Eddy, who was also laughing and could not resist a comeback remark as he put out his fist again to knock.

"Good on ya mate!"

"My mother is a friend of the head PR at Fortnum, and he kindly invited us", Rogan said explaining of their status to have an invite.

"Lovely! Shall we all sit and take tea?" Hugo took charge and was dismissive of Rogan's explanation, putting the importance squarely on the Teacakes, scones and Battenberg slices he noticed the waiters placing on the tables.

"E luvs ees grub!" Eddy said grabbing and hugging Hugo around the waist from behind, and giving his paunch a friendly wiggle, as they took their seats at a table.

"Eddy!" Hugo was flustered at Eddy's familiarity in front of Alex who was already seated, and did not seem to show any reaction to Eddy's antics, as he reached for a pastry.

Lisa sat next to Alex, and during conversation kept touching his knee, to mark a point in an over friendly way.

Alex was uneasy of her tactile friendliness. She was old enough to be his mother and he was younger than her son. He felt the touching un-appropriate.

"Where's Eddy gone?" Rogan suddenly noticed his absence.

"Think he went to the loo?" Hugo said shrugging his shoulders.

A man stood on a stage and made an announcement.

"Ladies and Gentlemen Illias Constantinos, has kindly donated three of his paintings to be auctioned in aid of the WWF World Life Animal Fund. This is such a worthy cause, I hope you will give generously, you won't be able to get these for peanuts!"
He said laughing as two men wearing monkey suits, crawled onto the stage swinging their arms and dragging their knuckles on the floor.

"Pay peanuts and all you'll get, are these monkeys!"

Everyone in the room laughed, as the Monkeys lifted one of the paintings to be auctioned, showing it to the people.

"The title of this wonderful painting of animals hanging out in a nightclub, is titled 'Serengeti Safari meets Zanzibar.

Who'll start me at say, three thousand pounds?" The auctioneer called out.

A man sitting at a table near to Rogan's party raised his hand.

"Three thousand, thank-you Sir."

"Do I see three thousand five hundred?"

A woman on the far side raised her hand.

"Thank you Madam, three thousand five hundred, do I see four thousand?"

The first man raised his hand again.

"Thank you Sir. Four thousand pounds, do I see four thousand five hundred?"

The room was quiet, as everyone was looking around to see if there were any more offers.

The auctioneer continued. *"No more? Come on Ladies and Gentlemen this is for a wonderful cause; think about those endangered animals that need your help. No? Okay, four thousand pounds once, four thousand pounds twice, make no mistake about it I will sell Illias Constantinos magnificent painting for four thousand pounds.*

Suddenly a voice from the back called out. *"Four thousand Five hundred."*

Everybody in the room turned their heads to see the person who had swooped in before the hammer went down.

Rogan was standing with his arm raised above his head.

Lisa and Hugo looked shocked at Rogan's sudden bid, knowing he was not in the same financial bracket as some of the wealthy people in the room, and could not afford to spend so much money on a painting.

"Thank-you Sir, that is very generous of you. I have an offer of four thousand five hundred pounds. Going once, Going twice."

"Five thousand pounds!" Everyone gasped at the new last minute bid.

The auctioneer looked towards Rogan who was still standing.

"Sir Five thousand Five hundred. It could be yours?"

Rogan shook his head and sat down.

The auctioneer banged his gavel down with a thud on the stand he was behind conducting the auction.

"Sold! Five thousand pounds to the gentleman on the right, thank-you Sir."

Everyone in the room clapped.

The excitement of the auction had stimulated Rogan. He never intended to buy the painting, and not knowing if he would be out bid, gave him a thrill.

"What were you doing?" Lisa said clutching her chest that was turning red with her anxiety.

"Bumping up the price, I do it all the time."

Lisa knew he was referring to his tantalizing techniques in the bedroom with clients.

"You were showing off." Hugo chipped in.

The Viscount laughed, if ever you consider being a sales man, come and see me?"

Hugo raised an eyebrow.

Rogan suddenly realized Eddy was still not back from the toilet.

"Eddy still not back? He's missed my act!"

After the Auctioneer finished auctioning off the lots for sale, the men in the Monkey suits roamed around the tables; sitting on the guests laps and running off with their bottles of champagne, they had grabbed from the tables.

One of the Monkeys sat on the Viscounts lap put his arm around the Viscounts neck and bounced up and down, as he picked up a bottle of champagne from the table and swigged from it through the hole in the costumes mouth.

The Monkey took off the head of the costume.

"Eddy!"

Everybody looked surprised to see Eddy dressed in the furry costume, still sitting on the Viscounts lap..

"Was that you on stage holding the paintings?" Hugo said laughing.

"Yea, when I went to the toilet, a guy wearing a Monkey suit was kneeling over the lavatory being sick. Some PR girl was standing next to him saying you won't be able to go on stage in your state. The paintings are really heavy; I'll find someone else to help. That's when Batman came to the rescue!"

Everyone on the table laughed at Eddy's heroic stand in story.

"Well done! Eddy." Alex said admiring Eddy's spontaneity.

"You had better get out of that Monkey suit before they put you in a cage!" Hugo joked.

"Wouldn't be the first time?" Eddy said laughing.

Alex turned towards Hugo who was sitting alongside, scoffing another cream scone with strawberry preserve, and raised half up from his chair, which was a gesture and a cue to Hugo of his time to leave.

"Got to get back, I'm off to New York in the morning."

Eddy put out his hand still in a Monkey costume glove, and knuckle bumped Alex outstretched knuckle.

"Let's be 'aving ya Alex!"

Alex was not sure what the cockney term meant, but laughed as he left with Hugo.

Eddy went off to the toilets to get out of the costume, and get payment from the PR girl for his quick action of stepping in, for his role as a Monkey.

When he returned Rogan tore into him, as he was jealous of Eddy getting on so well with the Viscount.

"What the fuck are you playing at!"

"Wot do you mean?" Eddy retaliated.

"Getting all familiar with the Viscount sitting on his lap and calling him Alex! You don't even know him!"

Lisa was sitting between them.

"Boys! Stop it! To be fair Rogan, Alex did laugh, I think he enjoyed somebody not pandering up to him".

"Okay but next time we all meet, hold back his mine!"

"Mine?" Eddy repeated the remark, but took it no further, realizing Rogan must have ulterior motives for the friendship with Alex he was cultivating.

Lisa changed the atmosphere. *"A friend of mine owns a club 'Oh Jo!' In Curzon Street Mayfair, I think we could all have dinner there on the house!"*

"Sounds good to me, you up for it Rogan?" Eddy said putting his arm around Rogan's shoulders in a gesture of their friendship.

"Last at the bar buys the drinks!" Rogan said laughing and back on track with their friendship.

"No need, Jo will give us drinks on the house! Referring to the clubs owner. *"I'll make sure of that!"* Lisa said with a wink as she laughed and put her tinted glasses back on.

Like Mother – Like Son!

Oh - Jo!

Lisa pressed a buzzer on the door intercom.

"Oh Jo says hello, can I help you?" A receptionist replied with a greeted script.

"Hello, tell Jo Lisa is here."

A buzzer on the door sounded as the catch was released, allowing the three to enter the darkened interior of the nightclub, which was virtually empty except for a couple at the bar, a foursome of two boys and girls lounging on the sofas, and a few couples dancing on the under-lit colourful dance floor.

A cheerful portly character with a gravel sounding voice, greeted Lisa with a kiss on her cheek.

"Hello darling, 'aven't seen you in a while, where 'ave you been? Monaco? Los Angeles? Or up Romford market?"

Romford was dear to Jo's heart as he had started his career running a fruit and vegetable stall there, and later moved on to running a greasy spoon café in Holland where he sold under the counter cheap alcohol and cigarettes. He then moved to Calais where he made his fortune selling cut-price booze to British holidaymakers.

Although he became a multimillionaire, he could only speak one word in French (Bonjour).

Returning to London, his flamboyancy dress style of wearing only outrageous suits and cockney accent, did not fit the snobby profile for London's glitterati nightclub membership, so as a 54 year old multimillionaire and not a person to be reckoned with, he opened his own nightclub opposite the Celebrity haunt 'Toffs' (One of the nightclubs that had rejected his membership application).

"Yes I've been travelling" Lisa said leaving an open answer to Jo's enquiry.

"And who are these two young men? Your bodyguards to fight off all of the blokes trying to get into your knickers?" Jo said laughing at his own gross remark.

"Well you can get us a drink, and we shall find out cheeky!" Lisa said as she poked Jo in his fat belly.

Rogan was offended of Jo's familiarity remark to his mother, but at the same time knew of his mother's strength of character at being able to deal with anyone who made any verbal attack, both in anger or humour, and that they would pay for it.

"This is my son Rogan, and his friend Eddy." Lisa said turning to the boys.

Rogan put out his hand to shake, and after the handshake wondered if Jo was a member of the Freemasons or fancied him? As Jo's middle finger was bent into his palm as he pressed his hand into Rogan's, and could be regarded as a secret sign given by the Freemasons fraternity signaling another member? It also used to be a secret sign for Gay men before 1967, when it was illegal to be Homosexual. (It was due to crippling arthritis!)

Eddy just nodded acknowledgement with a flippant *"Alright mate!"*

Sitting at the bar on a stool, a boy with long hair down to his shoulders was stretching and leaning across to a pretty girl facing, who was sitting on a stool next to him. For balance he was resting his hands on her knees, as he repeated pecking kisses on her lips, and as she gazed lovingly into his eyes.

Looking around at his guests, Jo leaned on the bar. *"Right what you 'aving?"*

"Dom Perignon will be fine before dinner." Lisa said in an instant!

Jo pulled the lining of his pockets out of his trousers to show they were empty. *"Dinner as well! I'm not made of money!"* He said jokingly as he put on an innocent expression by raising his eyebrows and turning down the corners of his mouth, and then laughed. *"Send a waiter with the bottle and glasses to my table."* He instructed the barman listening to take the guests drinks order, as he ushered the party through to the restaurant area.

A custom made round table with sofa seating wrapped around, was mounted on a one step up plinth.

All of them shuffled around the seating, allowing each other to find a seated space, as there were only two entrances to sit at the enclosed table.

The Dom Perignon arrived, and the last glass to be filled by the waiter was for Dave seated at the head of the table.

"Fasten your seat belts 5,4,3,2,1, it's time for take off!" Jo said as he pressed a button mounted on a box that was fitted on the table next to his seated head position.

Suddenly the whole table and seating began to slowly revolve.

Eddy motioned swaying his head spinning, *"Cor blimey everyfinks spinning, I've only 'ad one sip of this champagne and it's gone straight to me 'ead! Although, I did do a line of coke in the loo just now!"*

Everybody laughed.

During dinner, Rogan dropped his napkin and bent down under the table to pick it up, catching sight of Jo's hand under Lisa's skirt!

Sitting up again he looked directly at his mother, who winked and smiled shamelessly of her seductive move, in allowing Jo to fondle her.

Rogan smiled back, knowing his mother had now secured dinner to be definitely on the house!

She had taught him, with his handsome looks of high cheekbones, he had inherited from his Irish father Patrick Ford who had abandoned them, her thick Italian hair and the toned athletic physique he had built with regular visits to the gym, there is always someone else who will pay for your good times and buy you presents, when you use your God given assets.

He had discussed his bisexuality with her in his teens, and to his amazement she confessed at being bisexual as well, and that it was a lucky gift that he should use to better himself in life.

When he was five, Rogan's father had walked out of the marital home to live with another woman in County Galway Ireland where he originated from, and left his mother penniless after an acrimonious divorce, forcing her to live in a small flat with one bedroom and Rogan having to sleep on a sofa in the living room until his age of twenty-one, when as part of his gift and as a surprise, she told him they were moving into a luxury flat in Shepherd Market a small quarter in Mayfair, which had been made possible and paid for by a boyfriend named Henry, a tycoon from California, who would come to stay for the weekend and would pay for Rogan to move out, to stay at one of London's central hotels, so that he could be alone with his mother.

Rogan accepted this was his mother's way of looking after them both and to live in luxury.

He didn't mind, as he loved spending time in the luxurious hotels, where he took the opportunity of taking a leaf out of his mother's book, by sitting around in the hotel's bar, waiting to be picked up by men who were either tourists or staying there on business.

He would take them to his hotel room, and at first he would charge them £50 for a blowjob and £100 a fuck, but soon realized if he teased and excited them with other sex games and roles, he could get £500 to £1,000 out of them, to satisfy his desired irrepressible lifestyle he embarked on.

This was easy money and he became so good at his seduction tease, the money was pouring in. His bank balance was soaring, affording him to buy designer clothes, jewellery and to pay rent on a luxurious flat, as the men came back again and again to pour over his young firm flesh, telling their wives they had to travel again on another business trip.

What's good for the Goose is good for the Gander he thought, and increased the opportunity of selling his body for sex, by escorting and servicing women as well. - He had stepped up from being a Rent boy to becoming a Gigolo.

The only assets Lisa had besides her glamorous looks and sharp calculating brain were her voluptuous breasts and tenacious personality to succeed, which she used playing on the scene of mixing and sleeping with affluent people.

Although Lisa had several other regular boyfriends, she also had two girlfriends. One was a well-known Member of Parliament for the Conservative party, the other a woman television newsreader; they both showered her with gifts and money, making sure she was kept happy enough not to sell them out!

Henry still came to stay at least once a month, and after his visit, Lisa would hit the designer clothes shops, spending some of the money he had treated her to.

Determined to squeeze every penny she could out of him, she also took back some of his gifts to the stores where he had bought them, saying they were not suitable, and exchanging them for cash refunds.

On one ocassion she showed Henry a fake diamond necklace that she already owned, and lied telling him she had it on approval from the jewelers, but decided at £3,000 it was too expensive for her. Henry blinded by her enticing ways gave her the money to buy it.

As Jo ordered liqueurs for everyone, two petite identical twin girls walked up to the table.

"Allo, Vodka and Tonic 'ave turned up." Jo said as the 19-year-old girls both leaned across the table to kiss him on each side of his fat cheeks. *"I call my Russian dolls those names, 'cause one pours Vodka down my froat, as the other gives me a relief massage, which is a tonic! I met them at Stringfellows lap-dancing club and was so impressed with their sexy dancing, I thought they could dance around my bedroom every night, so they moved in."*

"*Go back to the flat, I'll be up later.*" Jo said referring to his flat above the club. As the girls turned to leave, he stood up and stretched out his arms, to give both of them a pat on their bums at the same time.

Lisa grabbed the opportunity of Jo focusing his attention on the young girls, and got a breather from Jo's wandering hands.

Standing up she slid past Eddy who was sitting next to her. "*I'm just going to the ladies.*"

"*How would you like to earn two thousand quid?*" Jo asked Rogan.

"*I would!*" Eddy interrupted eagerly.

"*I'm not talking to you!*" Jo said in a stern manner.

"*What's involved?*" Rogan said curiously, and interested.

"*It's alright nothing illegal, I want you to fuck the twins whilst I watch.*"

"*When?*"

"*After Lisa and pretty boy (referring to Eddy) here leave.*"

"*Payment first.*" Rogan insisted.

"*No problem.*" Said Jo as he pushed his salivating tongue into his brandy glass, and licked out the last remaining drops clinging to the inside.

It was an ugly sight, to see his tongue wriggling in the glass, like a worm looking for a way out, but Rogan could only think of the unexpected windfall, and raised his glass in a toast accepting the deal.

He had never experienced having sex with twins before, the closest situation being brothers he met in a gay sauna he had gone to whilst in Berlin.

An elderly businessman had taken him there on a three-day business trip, as a paid escort, and only wanted his company at dinner and not for sex.

Rogan was eager for some action to satisfy his high libido sex drive, and as he had his own room in the hotel, snuck out late one night to the sauna where he met the handsome young brothers who took him to one of the private guest rooms, and shared him at the same time.

Lisa came back to the table.
"Ready to go?" She asked Rogan.
"Jo and I are going to discuss some business, Eddy will make sure you get home safe."
Lisa knew better than to ask any questions and kissed Rogan on the cheek, as Eddy would fill her in later. *"Alright honey."*
Jo stood up and put his arms around Lisa giving her bum a squeeze, as he kissed her full on the lips.
"Lovely seeing you darlin, give us a ring, we can go shopping up Romford! Ha-Ha."
After their goodbyes, Jo went to his office set behind the bar, and re-emerged with an envelope that contained Rogan's payment.
"You've got half an hour of play, and then I'm coming up to see you deliver. Come on, I'll let you into the flat. I've already rung up to tell them to expect you."
Rogan did not move.
"What's wrong?"
"You Pay, I Play! I told you, money first."
"Alright, alright I'm not leaving the Country!" Jo handed Rogan the envelope.
Rogan peered inside at the wad of crisp fifty-pound notes.
"Alright, it's all there, I just printed them, Ha! Ha! Come on."
Jo motioned Rogan to walk with him to a door that led to his flat above. At the door Jo pressed code number keys to release the entrance lock.
Waiting at the top of the stairs, the twins wearing matching black bras and panties stood provocatively, and both grabbed Rogan's arms to lead him into a bedroom.
Stripping him of his clothes except for his underpants, the twins edged him onto the bed.
Lying on each side, they caressed his body as he fondled them.

After a while Jo entered the room and sat in an armchair beside the bed, watching as the three bodies entwined in various positions.

As Rogan was having intercourse with one of the girls, he caught sight of Jo who had removed his clothes, and was about to move onto the bed, and take part in an orgy.

Rogan withdrew from intercourse and sat up.

"You didn't say you were taking part, that will be five hundred extra."

This was his business, and his time and sex-motion were all valuable.

"Yea-Yea, don't worry, I'm not into boys, we won't come into contact."

"Doesn't matter, the deal was for you to watch, jumping in is extra."

"Okay you'll get it before you leave."

"No! The deal is pay before play."

"You're a tough negotiator, you should work on the stock exchange. You can carry on, I'll be back in a minute."

Jo returned with the money, and the orgy continued with Jo only fondling and licking the twin's breasts, whilst Rogan fulfilled his deal of fucking them.

"How much did you get out of him?" Lisa went straight in, before Rogan could say hello, as he answered his mobile later in his flat.

"It's two thirty am!"

"I think I deserve half."

"Half! I had to work hard for the money, and be with that fat pig all night!"

"Alright I don't want to know the details, if it wasn't for me you wouldn't of had any, I introduced you and I did get you free champagne and dinner!"

"Alright I'll drop two fifty off tomorrow."

"Two fifty! Is that all? I know you! You don't work for less than a thousand. Anyway Eddy said you were offered two thousand."

"Well he's wrong! Okay three fifty and you can do my washing this week."

"You know I don't do washing, I'll give it to Maria when she comes in this week to clean. I'll have to pay her extra, so you can throw in another twenty. Make sure you come by one o'clock, I'm meeting my girlfriend Ruth for lunch at Harvey Nichols roof top at two, and want to buy a Marc Jacobs design bag I've seen there."

As he hung up, his mobile rang again, Eddy's name appeared on screen.

"Allo 'ow did you get on? Any chance of loaning a Monkey?"

"Bloody hell! Yes! I've not even had time for a piss yet, with you vultures on my case!"

"Vultures?"

"Yes! You and my dear robbing mother! And why did you tell her I was getting two grand? You know she's Fagin in drag!"

"Sorry mate, but you know how much she digs. I was drunk and didn't fink."

"Okay, okay, I'll whack five hundred in your bank tomorrow, now can I go and have a piss?"

"No! I need it in readies, I owe my dealer and 'es getting a bit narked, as I've owed it for a month."

"Okay, pop by tomorrow."

"Fanks. And Rogan..?"

"What!"

"Piss off! Ha, ha, ha." Brrrrr.

One week later.
Mother came too!

Hugo owned a luxurious open plan apartment in the hills of the Millionaire playground of Marbella, and invited Rogan to spend a week for a break there with him.

When the taxi Hugo was travelling in that he had booked to take them to Heathrow airport, pulled up outside Rogan's flat to collect him at their arranged meeting time, to Hugo's surprise Lisa was with him, and wheeling her suitcase towards the taxi.

"Hi Lisa, are we dropping you off somewhere?" Hugo asked as Rogan followed her into the cab.

"Mother is coming with us. She has been feeling depressed recently, and you both get on so well, I thought you would really cheer her up. She is always saying you are one of her favourite people. Can we get her an airline ticket at the airport?" Rogan said, expecting Hugo not to refuse him.

The euphemism of *'We'* he used in his conversation of *"can we"* really meant *'You'* pay for the ticket.

Hugo forced a smile and gritted his teeth, thinking she would be in the way of what he thought would be a romantic trip, and even worse not wanting to upset Rogan, he was being forced to pay for her. *"How nice the three of us together, we'll have so much fun."*

At the 3-bedroom apartment in Marbella, Lisa was given a small single bedroom at the end of the hall, which was a reasonable distance from Hugo's master bedroom, where he and Rogan would sleep and use as their playground.

As Hugo and Rogan began to unpack their suitcases, Lisa walked into their room. Redness was forming on her neck and chest from anxiety.

"I can't stay in that tiny room, it's too claustrophobic!"

"But you've got wonderful views from your terrace, overlooking the hills towards the beach, the other bedroom

doesn't have a balcony, and the views are not as good." Hugo said attempting to pacify her.

"I don't care about the views, we shall be out anyway." Lisa said, as she took over and made a decision over their itinerary.

"Okay Rogan, grab your mothers case and put it in the room next door." Hugo said reluctantly at having his adopted mother-in-law within ear shot of their erotic sex moans and groans he was longing for.

Waikiki Beach Club

It was Sunday, and Hugo had arranged for them to go to a late lunch at the fashionable Waikiki Beach Club, where the young rich and famous hung out.

As they walked in, photographers were taking photos of them. Rogan loved the attention and stopped to occasionally pose, holding the side arm of his Gucci designer Aviator sunglasses, and his other hand tugging on his trouser belt in a cool manner.

The photographers worked at the beach club, and photographed most of the clientele as they entered, making them feel important as if he had just been *'Papped'* by the international paparazzi.

Holding out the flat palm of his hand at the false paparazzi, he said, *"That's all boys!"* And walked on, as the young waiter showed the three to their booked table.

"They thought I was Matt Damon from the Jason Bourne film franchise! I get it in so many places." Rogan joked as he lapped up the attention.

"Get you franchise! Really! I mostly get mistaken for the lavatory attendant at the cottage toilets franchise in Piccadilly circus!" Hugo said, and was the only one laughing at his own send-up joke.

"That's because, you're always in there!" Rogan was quick to add.

The three sat down at a table overlooking the big swimming pool, filled with good-looking boys and girls, gyrating with dance movements in the shallow end that sent ripples, across the water towards a trio playing on musical instruments of bongo drums, guitar and saxophone on the side of the pool terrace.

Several Cuban girls who were professional dancers, wearing Indian feather headdresses, shell bras and grass skirts, shook their booty in time to Latin beats booming out across the pool, to the rest of the boys and girls dancing around the edges.

"Dom Perignon!" Hugo answered the young waiter, who had asked for their drinks order.

Being very attractive, sexy and stylish in her clothes had its uses, when Rogan would flaunt his mother in front of wealthy men, willing to pay for their nights on the town. Sometimes he would encourage her to go back with a 'Trick', [as they called the men with money] in order to get them on a hook for further benefits.

They were a duo working the scene together, both being charismatic as they took others for a ride.

A handsome man in his mid fifties with thick silver grey hair brushed back, giving him a sophisticated look, sat alone at the next table sipping a cocktail as he watched the crowds of dancing boys and girls.

Lisa looked across to him and smiled, she had noticed his 'Patek Philippe Chronograph' gold watch with a brown crocodile leather strap, peaking out from his navy shirt cuff, and knew it to be worth in the region of £200,000, as she had seen it in a advert featured in one of the glossy magazines.

Each month she like Rogan would buy Harpers Bazaar, Hello, OK, Car and other magazines, studying and memorizing the names of society and wealthy people attending glamorous events, photos of their luxurious homes and the finer fashionable trappings of life, that were advertised and reaching out from the glossy pages, as trophy flags of the rich, and magnets for them both to be attracted to.

As he lifted his gold-rimmed sunglasses, he locked eyes with her and smiled back, motioning with his glass held up and a backward nod, to join him at his table for a drink.

Lisa did not need a second nod, and stood up pushing her chair aside.

"Where are you going, to the toilet or bar?" Rogan asked. *"I could do with a whisky if you're going to the bar?"*

"No, I'm going to get married!"

"Married!" Rogan said laughing, as he watched his mother put out her hand to shake with the sophisticated George Clooney lookalike on the next table, who gentlemanly stood behind the chair he set for her, and at the same time push it gently towards the table as she safely sat down.

Hugo was pleased to get rid of Lisa for a while, so that he could enjoy and be alone with his handsome companion Rogan.

"Toot time, you go first." Hugo handed a wrap of cocaine to Rogan under the table.

Making his way to the toilets snorting cabins, located in a small building on the other side of the open-air dance floor, he walked past the bar.

In front of him seated on stools beside a tall cocktail table, was a good-looking young guy, with a cute looking girl wearing gold lamé shorts, a black Basque top and thigh length black patent, laced up boots.

They were sipping exotic looking drinks with pineapple and strawberries on sticks popping out of the top of their glasses.

The guy in an American accent asked an out of the blue question to Rogan, as he was about to pass. *"Do you know where we can get some coke?"*

"Putting his hand on the guys shoulder in a friendly gesture, Rogan asked. *"Why would you think I know where you can get drugs?"*

"Because you look cool." The guy said in admiration, as the girl opened her eyes wide in a hopeful expression, smiled and put down her glass.

Stopped in his tracks Rogan was flattered at the guy's compliment that had a double-edged sword meaning. *'Do I look that obvious?'* He thought.

The guy was wearing a Cowboy Stetson hat, an open multi-coloured shirt, which was slipping back revealing his tanned shoulder, and young firm body.

A large dark blue tattoo with red and green pictures and words entwined ran down his arm and one side of his sexy body.

They would have personal meaning to him and maybe to others, if they could decipher them?

Rogan pulled the guy's shirt open even wider, to reveal more of the tattoo on his shoulder.

"Beautiful!" He said suggestively, first looking at the tattoo and then into the guy's eyes as he lingered his hand on the tattoo.

Rogan felt the guy push his body forward enjoying the pressure of Rogan's hand on his body.

"What's your name? He said turning to the girl, not wanting to leave her out or causing any friction between her, him and the guy?

"Kara."

"That's a beautiful name and unusual."

"I'm American Italian."

"And where do you live?"

*"We're both from Philadelphia Pennsylvania, **Good ol' USA!"***
Rogan laughed as Kara's personality came to life, emphasizing her American accent as she said, *"Good ol' USA!"*

"And what's your name Mr Tattoo."

"Tyler."

"Tyler Tattoo." Rogan said laughing as he introduced himself. *"I'm Rogan good to meet you,"* and quickly turned his head to Kara so that she did not feel excluded from his greeting, although he had the 'Hots' for Tyler!

"Tyler," give me a couple of minutes and follow me to the Mens, you wait here, for the next serving."* He instructed Kara

with a wink, who smiled as she took another sip of her cocktail.

Tyler waited outside the toilet cubicle doors, not knowing which cubicle Rogan was inside.

Rogan opened the door slightly peering out and called softly *"Tyler, Tyler."* Alerting him of the cubicle he was in, and then closed it again, as he saw some other men entering and going to the urinals.

When the coast was clear, Tyler knocked twice on the cubicle door, Rogan opened it and Tyler slipped in quickly, pressing his back against the door as Rogan slid the lock on. Without saying a word, so not to alert any attention to their cubicle, Rogan pointed to a line of cocaine on the lid of the toilet seat, he had chopped up, and handed Tyler a rolled up euro note to snort through.

Many people like Rogan of all classes and sex, used the lavatories as their private office to get their hits of cocaine, and although occasionally the club staff would make an obvious presence in the immediate area, they often turned a blind-eye as two people would emerge from a cubicle, and then look inside to see if there were any pickings left for them to scoop up?

After his snort, Tyler straightened up from bending over the toilet seat, and kissed Rogan on the lips, pushing his tongue deep into his mouth.

Rogan immediately got an erection as Tyler's erection pressed against him in the tiny space.

Suddenly there was a bang on the cubicle door. *"Date prisa, otros estan esperando."*

Rogan responded. *"What?"*

"Hurry up, others are waiting." Came the translated reply.

Tyler reached down feeling Rogan's bulge.

"Not now." Rogan said panting with excitement, as he took a deep breath to control his desire to continue, and peered out of the doorway.

Outside was the lavatory attendant, who smiled but did not say a word as they passed and he slipped in to clean up?

"Here Kara." Rogan discreetly handed her the wrap of cocaine, as she jumped off her stool.

"I thought you two ran away!" She said laughing, and went off to the ladies toilets.

"There you are!" Hugo said pushing his way through some dancing revelers.

"I thought either you fell down the toilet or you were in trouble?" He chuckled. *"I was right, you were in trouble!"* He continued as he looked at Tyler seated close to Rogan.

"Well howdy Cowboy, who could resist a face and body like this? Are you a rustler or a hustler? Introduce me quickly Rogan, before he takes out his six shooter!"

Tyler jumped off the stool and put out his hand to shake, realizing from the concerned questions Hugo was asking Rogan, that he was a close friend.

"Hi I'm Tyler."

"And I'm Hugo, come and join us at our table for some Champagne."

"Thank you, but I'm just waiting for my girlfriend to come back."

After a short while whilst they were chatting, Kara returned.

"This is my girlfriend Kara."

Hugo reached out and wiped some white powder from her nostril.

"Hello darling, been powdering your nose?" An action and comment he often said to both sexes, to people who had obviously been secretly snorting the drug.

"Agatha Christie strikes again!" Rogan said, referring to the famous 'Who Dunnit' author, to send up Hugo fancying himself as an amateur drug sleuth.

Kara looked slightly embarrassed, as she took a tissue from her clutch bag and handed it to Tyler, whom she trusted, to wipe her nose and make sure there were no more traces of cocaine.

Hugo held up his closed hand in a fist to his face, and opened up his clenched fingers with his other hand, imitating holding a powder compact as he mimicked applying powder to his nose, whilst looking into the compact mirror. *"Max Factor darling, non smudge, I use it all the time!"*

"You are so funny." Kara and Tyler both laughed.

After their introductions, they took up Hugo's Champagne invitation, and made their way through the crowd to the table.

Lisa was still infatuated with her Clooney look-alike, and was acting like a young girl, as she giggled at his remarks, and suddenly noticed Rogan's return.

"Excuse me for a moment." She said as she gave the man's hand a squeeze, and went over to Rogan.

Being secretive, so others seated at the table could not hear her, she spoke in a soft whisper close to Rogan's ear.

"His name is Carter Bass from Texas, Goggle him and let me know if he's worth my time?"

Looking across the table at the two unknown guests, and putting on a false smile, to look as if she was genuinely interested, Lisa asked. *"Who is this handsome young man and his friend?"*

"Do you mean me?" Hugo jumped in.

"This is Kara and Tyler." Rogan said, as he stopped and looked up from his mobile, which he had on his lap out of sight, as he typed the name in of Carter Bass on Google to read his Wikipedia page.

Hugo stopped a passing waiter, to ask for some more champagne glasses for his guests.

Turning half in his chair so not to be heard, Rogan informed Lisa, *"He's fifty four, a Texan billionaire worth three billion dollars, made his fortune from Henna hair products, that he discovered whilst travelling through the Middle East, and introduced the product to the world, and then investing in real estate in the USA. Hang on to him!"*

"Strange he's all alone, I've got no competition so he's all mine!" A broad grin spread across Lisa's face as she turned

and went back to Carter, ignoring being introduced to the young couple.

Before she could sit down again Carter jumped up. *"Aren't you gonna introduce me to your friends?"*

"Of course, I came to get you." She lied, and held on to his arm as they walked over to join everyone at their table.

"Everybody this is my new friend Carter."

The group responded as Lisa went around the table introducing them.

"This is my son Rogan, his friend Hugo and Tyler, and Tyler's girlfriend Kookie."

"Kookie!" Kara said laughing.

"My name is Kara."

"Oh! I'm sorry darling, I got mixed up, I meant to say Kara, who looks so Kookie in those hot pants Kylie Minogue made famous back in the nineties. It's good to see there has been a revival!"

Lisa never felt comfortable when any other woman were around, no matter how old. The stage was always for her as the star and main attraction.

Kara forced a laugh, knowing Lisa was really being bitchy and probably jealous of her youth and petit figure.

"I'm not old enough to remember that long ago, I was still at junior high school! Were people still smoking in UK clubs then? So gross!" She hit back with a distasteful look on her face

Lisa knew Kara wasn't referring to the cigarettes?

"Rogan help Carter bring their chairs to join us for some Perignon, and stop a waiter to bring more Champagne glasses. Oh! And another bottle." Hugo said lightening the awkward moment, as he topped up everyone's glasses with the last of the Champagne left in the bottle.

After a few more glasses of Champagne and more comfortable in Lisa's company, Carter explained to her that he had been married, which ended in an acrimonious divorce, and that he enjoyed going out alone, to see what was going on with the present social scene.

"I would like to invite you all to dinner." Carter said.

"How nice thank you." Hugo politely thanked him, as everybody joined the same gratitude.

"Do you have a car here?"

"No, we came by taxi."

"Us too." Tyler added.

"Not to worry, good, I shall ask the parking valet to bring my car around to the door, it may be a squeeze but we shall all get in."

"I can sit on Tyler's lap." Kara said as she kissed him on the lips, to show they were a couple.

Carter went to the reception to ask for his car to be brought to the front of the club.

As they walked to the exit, Rogan put his arm around Kara, to win some of her affection and redirect her thinking that he was making a play for her boyfriend, after her suspicious comment earlier of,

"I thought you two ran away!"

Parked immediately outside the Waikiki beach club with its cream roof down, a royal blue Bentley convertible with Cream and Navy piped leather seats, gleamed in the sunshine, it's engine gently purring ready to roar off.

Carter opened the front door for Lisa, as the rest squeezed up in the back.

"Where are we going?" Rogan said leaning forward from sitting behind Carter's driving seat.

"It's a surprise." Carter said as he took the road to Puerto Banus, where the Luxurious Super Yachts were moored.

'La Dolcé Vita'

Arriving at the quayside harbour, Carter pulled up his Bentley alongside a 67.15m long white Super-yacht.

The name *'La Dolcé Vita'* was painted on its bow, and a helicopter sat perched ready for take off, on top at the helipad deck, a popular feature amongst the yachting elite.

"Welcome aboard." Carter announced to the group as he stepped out of the Bentley.

All of the guests stood on the quayside admiring the fabulous yacht.

"Is this yours?" Lisa said, resisting licking her lips.

"La Dolcé Vita that's Italian for The Sweet Life, I thought you were American?" Hugo quizzed as he read aloud the name painted on the side of the yacht.

"It was a film by Fedorico Fellini back in the sixties, about a gossip columnist who wrote of fading aristocrats, second rate movie stars, aging playboys and women of the night."

"Bit like us!" Hugo laughed.

"My ex-wife was Italian and named it, but now we are divorced I shall get rid of the yacht."

"Wouldn't it be easier to rename the yacht?" Hugo suggested.

"No, this yacht has too many bad memories of her.

She was 'That Women of the Night'! Every time we docked somewhere, she ran off to spend my money in all of the designer and jewellery shops, arriving back loaded with carrier bags of clothes, Fendi, Vera Wang, McCartney, Victoria's Secret, Bvlgari.

The final straw was in London, and although I wasn't there, I had a private detective follow her, as she kept making excuses to keep going there. She said her best friend who was going through depression and not well, needed her, or she needed her hair tinted".

"Tinted!" Hugo said shocked at the feeble excuse. *"Couldn't she have her hair tinted in America?"*

"Her hairdresser moved from California, and had opened a salon in London's Mayfair. At first I thought it a little crazy, but thought this is what women do, visit their friends and gossip to their hairdressers.

One time she flew him back to the States, to do her hair for a big party we were attending, so I was sort of used to her devotion of his skills, she would say, "No one does my hair like Duke," Duke! He should have been called Duchess! If he hadn't been Gay I would have thought she was having an affair with him!"

When the Private Detective I hired showed me photos of a well-built guy with blonde hair, kissing her in the restaurant of the Lanesborough hotel, I could see the guy was definitely not her hairdresser who had long brown hair. I don't know who he was, I couldn't see his full face as the angle of the photo was a side view, probably some gigolo she paid for?"

Rogan breathed a sigh of relief to hear Carter explain the gigolo had blonde hair and was not he, as at first he had wondered if Carter's wife had been one of his clients, remembering he had serviced an oversexed American woman staying at the Lanesborough Hotel.

Although he was not, for a moment he enjoyed fantasizing the possibility and thought of being able to please Carters wife more than he could with all of his millions! What were the chances of Carter being her husband, and he one of the reasons for their divorce, and now by chance, being invited to dinner with him!

Waiting at the top of the yachts quayside boarding steps, a young man wearing a loose white cotton shirt over white cotton Chinos, with the yachts name *'La Dolcé Vita'* monogrammed in navy blue on his breast pocket, greeted Carter and his guests, as one by one they climbed the steps to board.

"This is Mario, my right-hand man and Confidant, who looks after the running of the yacht, he knows every inch of it."

Hugo mumbled under his breath. *"I would like to know every inch of him!"* And as usual when meeting any good-looking young men, was infatuated by the young man's Mediterranean looks and sex appeal.

Touching Mario's breast pocket with the monogram, he laughed, *"Looks like you will have to get a new shirt soon."* Referring of his suggestion to Carter, to change the yachts name.

Mario looked bewildered not knowing what Hugo was talking about, and asked Carter.

"Is there something wrong with my shirt?"

"No, no Mario don't worry, it's just a joke, tell the chef, we have five guests joining me for dinner, could he come to let me know what he can prepare, and bring a bottle of Champagne. Thank-you Mario."

Carter led his guests to an on deck built in semi round sofa, with a rosewood base and soft leather orange cushions, piped in gold. Opposite eight matching armchairs all set around an oval rosewood wooden dining table, with Marquetry inlay of Pewter, Lapis Lazuli and Agate, that was scintillating as the last of the days sunshine spread its rays across the table and picked out the magnificent colours.

Mario came back, and having changed, was now wearing a different coloured shirt, which was navy and also had 'La Dolcé Vita', monogrammed on the breast pocket.

Hugo smiled with affection that Mario was not party to the conversation about changing the yachts name, and thought there was something wrong with his shirt, and had changed. He placed the tray with a bottle of Cristal champagne and glass flutes on the table.

"Shall I pour Sir?"

"No thank you, that will be all."

"I spoke to chef, he will come up shortly to discuss tonight's menu is there anything else I can get you?"

"Yes a crudité of dips, olives etcetera, and a charcuterie platter of Cerrano and Parma ham. You know what I like!"

"Yes sir, right away."

Carter poured the champagne and served Lisa first, who sat back into the engulfing soft leather sofa, making herself at home.

'I could get used to this'. She thought as she reached out to squeeze Carters hand.

All of the guests were eager to see the rest of the Super-yacht.

"How many floors are there on the yacht?" Rogan asked.

"There are two main saloons, one on the main deck, and the second on the upper deck with a cinema screen. Two dining areas, this one for al fresco and a formal dining area that seats sixteen on the main deck. On the bridge I have a gymnasium, as I like to keep fit, and on the sundeck a fresh water swimming pool, next to a Tiki bar, which sort of cancels out all the good work I've done in the gym!" Carter said laughing.

"There is also a sauna, to sweat out the alcohol, before a massage from my masseur and if you want to get away fast, I have a helipad on top deck. Come let me show you."

Everyone got up still holding onto their champagne glasses excited to see the luxuries that were on board, as they followed Carter to a lift that took them to the lower deck.

"Oh this is fabulous!" Kara said as she looked at the freshwater swimming pool.

"Can I have a swim?"

"Sure be my guest, there may be a spare bikini in the changing rooms?" Carter offered.

"No need for that!" Kara said as she took off her boots and unfastened her sexy basque before jumping into the pool still wearing her gold lamé shorts.

Lisa turned away, as the view of the semi naked nymph like, young girls beautiful body offended her, making her become conscious of her own body stretch marks of age.

"I can't wait to see your cinema, do you serve popcorn?" She said falsely laughing wanting to move on from Kara getting

all of the attention from Carter's transfixed eyes on her firm little body.

Suddenly there was another splash, as Tyler also dived in only wearing his pale blue underpants.

Rogan had watched Tyler and Kara strip off, and was not going to miss out of another opportunity to get up close, as he too stripped and joined the two beautiful semi-naked bodies gleaming as they bobbed up in the water.

"A Mermaid and two Mermen, is something fishy going on?" Hugo joked.

"When you beautiful bodies have had your swim, come back up to top deck for dinner." Carter called out as he Lisa and Hugo walked off.

Lisa was not pleased at being upstaged by Kara revealing her perky breasts to Carter.

Hovering at the dining table now laid with the crudité, the chef greeted Carter.

"Sir, I have been told by Mario there will be six of you dining. I have lobster, Oysters, crab and king prawns, so I could make a big platter of seafood with an exotic salad?"

"Yes that sounds good, but I think we could have some Beluga Caviar and crisp breads as well, whilst we're waiting."

After a half hour Rogan, Tyler and Kara arrived at the table, with all smiles and their hair still wet.

"What have you three been up to? Teaching each other the back stroke, the front stroke, or just having a stroke?" Hugo giggled.

"Ooo caviar, I've never tasted it before." Kara said innocently as it was served.

"Darling I usually buy it with my weekly shop at the Supermarket, but it goes so quickly." Lisa said smugly.

"Yes I've seen it in there, but I'm confused because although it says caviar, it also says on the tin Lumpfish, which I thought was the poor man's version?"

Lisa turned her back on Kara ignoring her cutting comments.

"Carter, this Cristal Champagne is my favourite."

"Let me top you up. When they serve the seafood I'll tell them to bring another bottle."

During dinner, Lisa asked Carter if she could use the toilet.

"Certainly, but the staff are currently cleaning them on this floor. Come with me, I'll take you to mine in my suite next to the pool."

Lisa was pleased to go to Carter's private suite accompanied by him, and took his invite as a sign to be alone with her?

They took a lift next to the one they had all taken earlier, but this was Carter's private lift, that went directly down into his cabin suite.

As the lift door opened, Lisa took a breath at the lavish opulent décor before her, and gazed up at the hexagonal shaped blue opaque glass ceiling, surrounded by an inlay dropped strip of soft gold lighting above a Queen sized bed, which took centre stage of the luxurious bedroom.

The bed faced floor to ceiling glass doors, that were open leading to a huge terrace and balcony overlooking the sea, with reclining pale blue sun loungers and ivory coloured table and chairs.

Lisa could not hold back of how impressed she was. "This is fabulous." She said as she sat on the edge of the bed.

"Thank-you, I wish I could take the credit, but it was designed by 'Fendi', following my ex wife's wishes. She certainly knew how to spend money!"

Lisa took the opportunity of delivering a corny line as she laughed and joyfully bounced her bum suggestively on the mattress. "You need a new Queen to fill this King sized bed."

Her comment either went over Carter's head or he dodged it, as he pointed to a half open door, which hinted a view of the ivory coloured marble floor with a black onyx inlay design.

"The toilets through there."

Carter turned to leave, disappointing Lisa of her moment.

"When you are ready, take the lift and press the button marked Royal bluebird deck."

After dinner and another tour of the yacht, Carter said he would order two cars to take everyone back to the places where they were staying.

Slightly uneasy on her feet from being drunk, Lisa hung on to Carter as she thanked and kissed him on the lips, which took him by surprise, but laughed it off as Rogan supported her to walk down the gangway stairs to the quayside, where two Limousines were waiting.

Carter retired to his suite.

Lifting the receiver of the telephone on his desk, he pressed the connection button marked 'MARIO'.

"Hello Mario, please come down to my suite, my gold Montblanc Boheme Papillion pen is not on my desk?"

Mario used Carter's private lift to arrive directly into the suite.

Carter was on his knees looking under his desk.

"I'm sure it was on my desk this morning before I went to the Waikiki Beach Club."

"Was it the Diamante Van Cleef and Arpels?"

"No my ex-wife took that! She knew it was worth seven hundred and thirty thousand dollars.

At my Solicitors office, she enjoyed taking it out of her handbag to use signing our divorce papers to wind me up, Bitch! It's the Gold limited edition Boehme Papillion Montblanc, only worth two hundred and thirty thousand dollars, too cheap for my wife!

"Oh my god! I remember when you bought it in Monaco, and asked me which pen did I prefer from the choice the Bvlgari sales man brought on board."

Mario got on his knees and joined in with the search, looking under tables and chairs and areas around the suite and bathroom.

The penny dropped as Carter realised. *"Lisa! She used my suite during dinner."*

"Yes, but the three young guests were swimming around alone in the pool next to your suite for some time? Just saying?" Mario suggested as alternative suspects?

"Rogan, Rogan come here." Lisa called out from her room the next morning.
"What does she want now?" Hugo mumbled rolling over in bed, as Rogan got out naked.
Slipping on his underpants he walked up the hallway to her bedroom, but did not enter, only popping his head around the half opened door, as his morning erection had not gone down.
"Look!" Lisa was sitting on her bed, waving the gold fountain pen at Rogan.
"I opened my eyes and the first thing I saw was this pen on my bedside table!"
Rogan's erection went down from the shock at seeing his mother holding the priceless decorative gold pen, and walked into the bedroom taking the pen from her.
"Wow this looks expensive, how did you get it, did Carter give it to you?"
"I don't remember! I was drunk! We must take it back immediately before he calls the police. I will tell him how drunk I was, and sorry as I must have picked it up in my stupor."
Rogan agreed and explained to Hugo, who was still half asleep, of the urgency of rectifying his mother's moment of Kleptomania, and they were taking a taxi to Puerto Banus quayside where 'La Dolce Vita' was moored.

On arrival at the quay, there was a huge empty space between the other moored Super-Yachts.
"Gone!" Lisa said, thinking she had just awoken from a bad dream about a vanishing yacht.

Back at Hugo's apartment, Lisa explained to him her embarrassment of taking the expensive fountain pen and that she wanted to return it.

Hugo took on his professional managerial role, and traced the next docking of 'La Dolce Vita' yacht by satellite on his computer, which was Tangier Morocco, and then organized 'Courier Service to Super Yachts Company', to deliver the gold pen back to Carter with Lisa's apology letter.

"Rogan and I are going to the Waikiki beach. I've arranged for the courier to come here and collect the pen from you."
Hugo handed Lisa a note-let with two phone numbers written on it. *"This is the telephone number of the courier if you need to check on his arrival, and the cab service number for you to come and join us at the beach."*
"Okay see you later."

In the afternoon Lisa arrived at the beach club, and joined with Rogan and Hugo seated at the restaurant by the pool.
"Ah! just in time for lunch. Did the courier arrive?" Hugo said as he passed the lunch menu for Lisa to order.
"Yes, all's well. I think I shall have the Tiger prawns and smoked salmon mouse with tropical salad." Lisa said being dismissive of the theft and putting her appetite first.

Rogan had not swapped contact details with Tyler or Kara, and although he visited the Waikiki beach club several more times over his two-week stay, Tyler and Kara never showed.

'Ships that pass in the night!'
Henry Wadsworth Longfellow.

The Monarchist League Banquet – Cameron Hall London

"You look very smart, I fancy you." Rogan said complimenting Hugo as he gave his white bow tie a tug, making sure it was straight, and adding a provocative remark, as he stepped out of the chauffeur driven Bentley car, Hugo hired to take them to the 'Monarchist League White Tie Banquet', at the exclusive 'Cameron Hall' overlooking the Thames on London's Embankment.

"Why thank you kind Sir, you look hot yourself!" Hugo said in a grateful jokingly manner.

Rogan was also wearing the formal traditional evening dress code required, consisting of a black dress tailcoat, white starched shirt, Marcella waistcoat and the eponymous white bow tie around a standing wingtip collar.

The Marchioness of Beckingham, a regular client at Ranley Luxury goods store, had invited Hugo and a guest to attend the dinner that her husband The Marquess Chancellor of the Monarchist league headed.

At the reception hall entrance, a toastmaster announced the names of all guests attending.

"Mr Hugo Peregrine Walford and Mr Rogan Ford."

"Peregrine! You kept that quiet. I thought he said Penguin! Mind you, we both look like couple of penguins in these tails." Rogan said laughing as they walked up to the line of dignitaries headed by the Marquess and Marchioness waiting to greet guests.

"It means Wanderer." Hugo explained.

"Now I know why your hands are always wandering over me!" Rogan said out of the corner of his mouth, still laughing.

After they made their way along the line into the reception room, they took a glass of champagne from the silver trays, waiters were holding to serve all of the guests.

"She was on fire!" Rogan said, as he took a drink of the champagne.

"Who?"

"The Marchioness."

"Really, did you fancy her?"

"No, it's her diamond tiara that's hot! I'd love you to wear one of those in bed."

Hugo roared with laughter. *"I'd look like an old queen, if I wore one of those!"*

"I've got news for you, you don't need a tiara!"

Both of them laughed and walked on into the throng of guests, gathered at the reception.

The invitation notes had stated their table for dinner was named 'Tudor King Henry V111', and would be on a display card in the centre of the table.

Their seating was L7 and L9, leaving L8 in the middle for another guest to be seated between them.

All of the invitation table places had spilt couples up, to sit alternately next to a stranger, to make sure conversation was spread around each table.

Rogan and Hugo took their places standing behind their chairs, like the rest of the room, waiting for their hosts' procession to enter and take their places at the top table. A trumpet fanfare filled the room by two Military Royal Household guards, dressed in red tunics, as the imposing giant floor to ceiling double mirrored doors, that reflected the drop crystal Chandeliers in the dining room, were opened simultaneously by two young men, wearing short waisted purple velvet jackets with gold braided epaulets, and mustard corduroy breeches, over black tights and wearing traditional black patent shoes with gold buckles. Just as the procession entered the room headed by the Marquess and Marchioness, a young man in his early 40s accompanying a glamorous looking women in her mid 50s, who were late arrivals, took their opportunity and entered through a side door, whilst everyone in the room were standing and probably would not notice them, but they were wrong, as heads turned to see the couple, anxiously searching for their table number.

The woman was wearing an off the shoulder flame red Shantung silk dress, ruched with glittering beading, which made her entrance stand out like hellfire!

They walked fast to be respectively etiquette at their table, before the procession of hosts reached the top table.

"Is this my seat?" The woman said with a French accent to Hugo, finishing with an electric smile that would light any room.

"I think your seat is L10." Hugo replied pointing to the seat on the other side next to Rogan, as he had spotted the handsome aristocratic looking young man with her and wanted to save L8 to keep him close.

Around his neck he was wearing, a striped ribbon of the French tricolour colours, blue, white and red, with a medal dangling from it, which sat 3 inches above the top of his white Marcella waistcoat.

Looking bewildered of where he should sit, he asked Hugo.

"Then is this my seat?"

"Yes! You're here, L8." Hugo tapped the top of the chair next to him, making sure he would be in easy reach and able to get to know him.

Rogan did not object to the seating arrangements Hugo had orchestrated, as he was happy to be sandwiched between the dream team couple.

"Hello, my name is Rogan."

"Hello I am Gisiline, our car got held up in the traffic." She said in a French accent explaining their late hurried arrival.

"We're two glasses of Champagne ahead of you, but you've time to catch up." Rogan said as he leaned across the table to grab the bottle of Roederer Champagne (Always at arms

length) and filled Gisilines's glass, before turning to her escort and filling his glass.

He took a sip of the champagne. *"Thank you, I need this after our rush to get here, my names Stirling."* Putting out his hand as he changed his champagne glass to his left hand, so that he could offer his right hand to shake.

Smiling at him and putting down the bottle, Rogan introduced himself. *"Hi my names Rogan."*

When the Marquess and Marchioness and the rest of the entourage were standing behind the top table, the toastmaster called the toast.

"Your Royal highnesses ladies and gentlemen, the toast is to the Queen and Monarchy, God save the Queen."

"God save the Queen, God save the Queen, God save the Queen." The crowd of guests in the room bellowed back three times, and took a sip of their Champagne.

Still standing Gisiline and Strirling both turned inwards to Rogan.

"Nice to meet you." Gisiline toasted him as they clinked their glasses.

"Yes nice to meet you." Stirling repeated as he too clinked his glass with Rogan's upheld glass, and then turned back to Hugo to toast him.

"We haven't formerly introduced ourselves yet, but it's nice to meet you as well, my names Stirling."

"Just call me Hugo, after all it is my name!" Hugo joked as they clinked their glasses together.

Gisiline leaned across acknowledging Hugo, and held her glass high as a toast and said her name. *"Gisiline."*

Hugo reciprocated. *"Hugo."* adding mouthed words. *"Speak later after the speeches."*

The top table took their seats, signalling the room of guests to do the same, as light background music was being serenaded to them, by a string quartet, comprising of violins and cello that were accompanying a young woman playing a harp.

Rogan was infatuated, by Gisiline's star quality glamour and eye dazzling jewellery.

Her long black hair dressed behind both ears, to show off her long drop earrings, with exquisite emerald and diamond stones, were part of a set she was wearing, that complimented the emerald 12 stone necklace with a 13th huge emerald stone surrounded by diamonds as the centre drop resting on her cleavage.

"Are you a member of the Monarchist League?" Rogan asked Gisiline.

"Ha! No! They are a bunch of people believing they are Royal when in actual fact they are aristocrats of a deposed Monarchy. In 1939 Italy invaded Albania and removed the reigning self-proclaimed King Zog, ha! Don't you just love that name?"

Rogan laughed. *"Sounds like he came from another planet!"*

Gisiline carried on explaining. *"They instated their own King Victor Emmanuel the Third, as it's new monarch. This happened in many countries, China, Portugal, Yugoslavia, Bulgaria, Brazil, Egypt, I could go on."*

"How do you know all of this?"

"I have been studying and writing a dissertation on deposed monarchies around the world for an academic bachelors degree, and was invited here tonight, as I have just interviewed the Chancellor of the Monarchist League The Marquess of Beckingham."

"So will you become a Professor or Proferess?" Rogan joked.

"Ha! That's a long way off."

"Well when you are, can you give me detention and keep me in after school?"

Gisiline laughed at Rogan's suggestive remarks and picked up the menu to read.

"I can't make up my mind, whether to have the Venison or Dover Sole with Oysters? One, I have to get my teeth into, the other slips down my throat. What do you think I should go for?" Gisiline said being suggestive back to Rogan.

"I think you should let it slip down your throat, you can leave it up to me to do the biting!" Rogan said also being provocative.

Gisiline threw her head back as she laughed.

Cameron Hall

MENU

Turbot and Lobster Mouse

Roast loin of Venison in a Madeira Truffle sauce
Braised cabbage, cocotte potatoes, timbale of celeriac and butternut squash.

Or

Fillets of Dover Sole filled with Salmon and Oyster mouse on a bed of leeks with a white cream sauce, cocotte potatoes.

Pudding form of delice dark chocolate, mango and lime.

Fruits de Desert
*****

Liqueurs/Coffee

Wines
Nyetimber Classic Cuvée 2007
Puligny-Montrachet ler Cru 2006
Chateau Pichon-Lonueville Contesse de Lalande 1990

Taylor Vintage Port 1977

Stirling leaned shoulder to shoulder with Rogan, so that his voice would not carry.

"I was going to have the Fillet of Dover sole, but it's filled with salmon and oyster mouse."

"Sounds delicious!"

"I'm sure it is, but Oysters are an aphrodisiac, and I'm already oversexed!"

"Thought I recognised you, I've seen your photo, we belong to the same agency." Rogan winked.

"What a coincidence! Is Hugo your client?"

"You could say that, more long term. What's with the French medal dangling around your neck?"

"Gisiline gave it to me, to wear for tonight, belonged to her late father who was an Ambassador. She said I would look

important. I want more than a medal for sitting with these old cronies!"

"I know what you mean!" Rogan said as he looked across to Hugo, who smiled back, not knowing he had just been insulted.

Both of them laughed.

Rogan knew Gisiline was in the market for virile sex, as soon as he saw a young man on her arm. She had already shopped in 'Bargain Basement,' and as he had no scruples of allegiance to Stirling, he intended to take her shopping for a more exclusive experience to satisfy her?

Hugo told Stirling of his position as Executive Sales Manager at Ranley, and discreetly so that Rogan did not see, passed him his business card.

"Give me a call, and we will do dinner."

"Thank you, I'm busy this week, Gisiline and I are going to Paris, shopping for a few days, but I'll give you a call when I get back."

After dinner and during being served with liqueurs, Rogan felt Gisiline's hand on his thigh, moving slowly towards his crotch. At the same time, he felt Stirling's hand on his other thigh. For a moment he froze at the situation, as each of his admirers did not realise they were making a play for him at the same time.

Reaching under the table he grabbed Gisiline's hand to move it further down his thigh again, and unbeknown to her, let Stirling to have his turn for a fumble.

Looking straight ahead, and enjoying being groped, he took a drink of his Drambuie liqueur and spread his legs wide, so that the two hands did not meet under the table!

Both took their hand away, still unaware of their near miss.

"Are you wearing panties?" He whispered in Gisiline's ear.

"No." She replied breathlessly, being aroused at the question.

"Touch yourself, and put your fingers in my mouth."

Hugo's flat

Later that night at Hugo's flat Rogan had changed into a pair of jeans to relax in, and after a few lines of cocaine and several glasses of whisky, he challenged Hugo.

"Did I see you passing your card to Stirling?"

"He wanted to come to Ranley to have a look around."

"Liar! Liar! What's wrong, am I getting too fucking old for you?"

"Don't be so silly, calm down you've had too much whisky and cocaine, anyway you've never complained at me having a few rent boys in the past! I think you fancied him and you're jealous!" Hugo tried to pacify him with reason.

"Silly, that's it! I AM NOT SILLY, but you're a silly old fool, thinking he would fancy you with your fat gut! He's on the game and only after you for your money!"

"And like you're not! I've always known as long as I line your pockets with money, buy you gifts, and pay your rent, you'll drop your pants!"

"My cock is the powerhouse that lays old fools like you! I'm worth every penny! Rogan get me a drink! Rogan hang up my coat! Rogan give me a wank! Well I'm fed up with it! Toss yourself off, I'm going!"

Rogan was furious and threw his glass of whisky at Hugo's face, and then threw the empty glass against the red Japanese lacquered double doors that were open inwards, chipping off some of the gold leaf, painted on the giant crane birds that adorned the doors.

Hugo was afraid of Rogan, and had never seen him get this angry. He was much younger, stronger and taller, and had turned into a monster that was capable of all kinds of retaliation?

"Get out! Get out! Hugo screamed.

"I will, you old fart! Fuck! Fuck!" Rogan screamed back and left.

The impact of using the expletive word more than once had lost being shocking as an insult, and sounded petulant although it was still insulting.

Hugo bent down to pick up the empty glass Rogan had thrown.

The internal phone rang, and Hugo shaking with distress trudged up the hall to answer it.

"Mr Walford, is everything alright, Rogan just rushed past me and Mrs Osband next door to you, has reported screams."

"Yes Peter, just a lovers tiff." Hugo forced a laugh and hung up.

Sitting back into an armchair, feeling alone and heartbroken, he began to sob.

Broken hearts don't come cheap!
                    Bari Bacco Author.

The Blue Berlin Club

Rogan was still angry, and at first did not notice the rain that beat down on him, and later did not care, as he walked along Bayswater Road, busy with traffic that had slowed down, as their windscreen wipers were outrun by the heavy downpour.

In his mind he was going over the argument he had with Hugo, but wasn't going to let it get to him.

His anger had released endorphins in his brain, and stimulated his sexual prowess.

The mannequins in Selfridges Store windows, placed in summer beach scenes complimenting furnishings and displaying clothes, looked attractive and friendly.

Rogan peered in at one of the wet windows displaying a group of good-looking Mannequin Girls and Boys wearing designer beach wear, standing at a props beach bar under a straw sun umbrella. Two girls were seated at the bar and two boys were standing alongside, holding cocktail drinks. The scene looked so inviting and cool, transporting Rogan's mind to the life he loved.

In a surreal moment he wished he were inside the window, enjoying being with the fun crowd on display.

Turning away from the summer scene, and back into the reality of the rain still beating down, he realised that he had walked along the whole length of Oxford Street, and that subconsciously he was looking to fulfil his wild side.

Walking on he wondered of what direction to take, to satisfy his rebellious and deviant mood he was now in, and although drenched from the rain, sat on the bench in a bus shelter to collect his thoughts.

To the Right; Soho bars, to the Left; the Sadomasochistic *'Blue Berlin Club'*... He turned left!

Cutting through Newman Street and Cleveland Street into Goodge Place, he looked for *'Blue Berlin Club'*, an underground fetish and bondage club.

He had remembered the name, from several weeks ago, when he serviced a young rich housewife, a client whom he had visited at her suburb home in Essex and had told him about the BBC sex club, after he had spanked her with a leather strap, and had anal intercourse whilst she was bizarrely sucking on a chocolate Mars Bar, as she bent over a vibrating washing machine set on 'Fast Spin'.

At first when she had told him of the Blue Berlin Club, she had referred to it only by it's initials BBC, which made Rogan laugh, thinking there was some deviant den at the BBC Television Centre, that Newscasters popped into before reading the 10 o'clock news.

She said her husband had often gone there with her live in boyfriend, and without her. They had been in a Polyamory relationship, but she felt her husband had become more involved with her boyfriend, and that she was being eased out of the relationship. It was time for her to seek sex with Mars Bars somewhere else!

Eventually he spotted a small sign 'BBC' that hung on black painted railings, with a small waist height swing wrought iron gate, which led to the basement entrance.

It was illicit and exciting.

Rogan pressed an entrance button on the video security camera, mounted on the door, and a buzzer sounded as the door was released for him to enter the inner sanctuary.

Inside the dimly lit venue, a six-foot muscular giant of a man approached him.

His baldhead and face were completely tattooed with pictures of Zombies, crosses and daggers. On his chest he had giant wing tattoos each side of a skeleton skull, surrounded by a bleeding rose flower, and was wearing a leather strapped body harness attached to rubber shorts with metal studs.

Towering and intimidating in his bikers studded boots, he spoke with a soft camp and cockney lisp and could not pronounce 'Rs', which brought him down to size!

"You 'avent been 'ere before 'ave yer mate." He said as his bottom false teeth rose up on its plate.

"No, first time, is that a problem?"

"Na, just thaying. I know all the wegulars. That's fifteen quid." He said putting out his hand.

Rogan took out a slightly wet twenty-pound note that was crumpled in his jeans pocket, and handed it to him.

As the man took the note, Rogan noticed the tattoo that ran from the back of his hand, up his arm and onto his bicep, was of a python snake, with a muscular naked man straddling it between his legs, that gave the impression of a phallic symbol.

On his bicep the tattoo snakes head disappeared into the crotch of a naked girl with enormous breasts, her long flowing blonde hair cascading onto her shoulders, facing the young muscular guy at the other end.

The man saw Rogan studying his tattoos.

"Me fithting arm." He said with a grunt and laugh, as he bent his arm to show off his bulging muscular bicep.

Taking Rogan's twenty-pound note, he stuffed it into a small leather bag strapped across his chest that dispelled the look of his hard butch persona, and gave away his camp feminine side.

Fumbling through the bag of money he pulled out a five pound note." *'ere fiver change. If you go into the changing woom, fough that door."* The man indicated. "You can get out of those wet clothes, unless you're into water sports? *You'll find all sorts of wear to hire, if you need any? You don't 'ave to wear anyfink; it's up to you mate. All the wooms are further down the 'all. Each woom is a different theme; 'ave a good time."*

As he walked along the hallway past deep-set recesses that went under the pavement, the few red lights and flashing strobes allowed glimpses of erect penises poking through 'Glory holes' in wooden walls, waiting to be orally stimulated.

Suddenly a hand came out of the darkness and grabbed his crotch.

"Do you want me to piss on you?" A mysterious voice begged. His soaking wet jeans from the rain were giving the wrong impression, and he had to change into something more fitting to satisfy his own kink. He pulled away without answering, and went into the costume room.

A cute effeminate boy was standing in a corner, with his arms stretched above his head to slim his waistline, as a girl in a black Latex head to foot suit, was fastening hooks, and pulling on laces to fit a sugar pink corset the boy was forcing his body into.

"You look great." Rogan complimented.

"Thanks."

"Thanks."

Each said in turn, thinking the compliment was for them. Another girl dressed as the DC Comic fictional character 'Cat Woman' in a rubber suit and mask, was seated on a bench pulling up thigh length black patent boots over her spandex tights.

"Have you got a spanking paddle?" She called out to a well-built muscular boy, standing behind a counter in front of an adjoining room, filled with kinky and bizarre looking costumes dangling from hangers on clothes rails, and stuffed into boxes on the floor.

Although muscular with bulging biceps, the boy was surprisingly dressed, wearing his idea of kinky perversion; black rubber maids outfit with a white lace pinafore attached.

He rustled around in a box, and came back to the counter with a leather single rod whip that had a small square of leather attached at the end, that looked more like a fly swatter, and a short stubby black leather oblong paddle. The girl went over to the counter and picked each one up in turn.

"Take that you bitch!" She said as she cracked the paddle down hard onto the counter.

Picking up the rod, she teased the boy behind the counter. Leaning across, she poked it under the front of his short skirt, and lifted it. He did not move and seemed mesmerized enjoying being humiliated, as she ran the tip along the bulge in his tight white Lycra G-string, and then put the tip of it into his mouth, which he responded to, by licking the end.

"I'll take the rod, I like to tease before I punish – Ha!"

"You'll have to leave another fiver deposit, and get three quid back when you return it along with the rest of your hire." He said, taking back control.

The girl unzipped the front of her tight figure hugging shiny black latex suit, reached inside and pulled out a ten-pound note.

Slamming it down on the counter, she followed through with her rod, which made a swishing noise as she banged it on the note.

"Take that again! You bitch!" She said laughing and turned towards Rogan who had stood back from the counter sharply.

"Just practicing." She said laughing again, as she snatched up her five-pound note change, and pushed it down the front of her costume as she left the room.

The costume maid turned to Rogan, who was laughing at the girl's antics.

"What's your bag?"

"Have you got Black tails, winged collar shirt and a Bow tie?"

"Get you mate! Where do you think you are Buckingham Palace?"

Rogan laughed at the Maids butch response that did not match up with his submissive costume.

"Just joking. A white shirt, mine's soaking wet."

"Is that it?"

"Yes."

Okay, here's a key for a locker to put your clothes in. The minimum deposit fee is a fiver, and you get three quid back on return."

"Cool."

Rogan got the shirt and went to his locker, where he stripped off and hung up his wet jacket, shirt and jeans.

The boy now tied securely in the corset and frilly panties was staring and admiring Rogan wearing only white pants; his eyes focused on Rogan's assets.

"Sexxxy!"

Rogan laughed and enjoyed at being admired, no matter how many times he had heard it before.

Leaving the shirt open to show off his six pack abdomen, and rolling up the sleeves half way, Rogan walked further along the hallway.

The overhead ultra-violet lights enhanced the whiteness of his shirt and brought attention to his glowing pants.

Venturing into a dimly lit and smoke filled room of bodies, Rogan cruised around the edges watching both men and women semi-naked wearing leather submissive harnesses' and in embraces, whilst having oral sex, and engaging in both front and anal intercourse.

Pornographic films of all kinds were projected onto screens mounted on the surrounding walls, and every few minutes a blast of smoke bellowed out from machines attached onto the walls in each corner of the room.

As he stood by a wall watching through the fog of smoke the orgies of bodies, a projected film of a girl on her knees giving oral sex to three naked men surrounding her, beamed across his white shirt, and by chance projected onto his crotch, giving him a fantasy blowjob.

Several hands appeared from the darkness, caressing his six-pack and rubbing the bulge in his pants.

Whack, Whack, Whack.' A cracking noise was coming from an adjoining room.

Rogan pulled away from the cluster of hands, feeling and touching his body and followed the sound to the other room A naked girl and a naked boy were side by side, spread-eagled across a leather padded bench, their hands and feet secured by manacles on chains, and padlocked to bars attached to the bench.

The 'Cat Woman' he had met in the changing room, was using her whip to lash the backsides of both the naked girl and boy strapped down and secured, unable to move.

Around the edges of the crowded room, men and women of all sizes and ages wearing rubber or leather masks were fondling each other in orgies, and like the previous room rolling about on mattresses, as they enjoyed the sadomasochistic scene and sounds of punishment.

Rogan had both sadistic and masochistic tendencies, which although being paid, had satisfied him throughout his life as a Gigolo selling his body for sex.

Some clients had required he took a dominant role, inflicting pain or control during sex; others had wanted to dominate him in fantasy games.

He had been able to turn on either tap, whatever the client wanted.

After watching the scene for a while, he also wanted to be humiliated and punished, to satisfy his masochistic guilt of being so aggressive and sadistic towards Hugo, although at the time, had enjoyed it.

The bright red bums of both the girl and boy, with welts from the rod, looked appealing; he wanted the same.

The pain of flagellation would stimulate and heighten the release of serotonin and melatonin production in his brain, which would transform his painful experience into pleasure, and reward him for pleading guilty of being an opportunist and sociopath.

"Dinosaur!" The boy called out. Which was his release escape word, to be taken seriously and stop the beatings, which he had preset with the Sadist inflicting the pain.

"Margaret Thatcher!" The girl also called out as her escape words.

The Cat Woman gave her another swipe with the rod. *"That's from Maggie!"* And laughed.

The bald tattooed giant Rogan had met when he arrived released the two.

Without a word, Rogan took off his shirt and threw it to one side as he bent over the leather bench, his arms outstretched, his body arched as the bench pushed into his stomach.

"I am Spartacus, your Master."

An intimidating fearful looking muscular man spoke with an authoritive voice.

He was covered in tattoos and dressed as a Roman Gladiator, wearing a silver metal helmet designed with a central strip hanging down to protect his nose, if he had been going into battle.

Grabbing Rogan's wrists he fastened them with manacles and chains, and attached them to the bench.

The rest of the costume gave him a dominant and powerful appearance. A half chain mail vest, dangled down from his broad shoulders to just above his ripped six-pack abdomen, which was glistening from the oil.

Around his waist he wore an apron skirt made of leather panel strips, revealing his strong thighs, a powerhouse in supporting his thrusts when fucking.

Leather bindings strapped tightly around his arms to enhance his bulging biceps, metal spiked gauntlets and spike studded boots, added to his overall erotic appearance.

Holding the sides of Rogan's bum cheeks, the Master ripped off his pants with his teeth, stripping him naked, and at the same time kicked the calves of his legs open wide apart, to spread eagle him, and then attached the manacles and chains around his ankles.

"Lovely arse." The Master said as he stroked and caressed it. Rogan turned his head to speak to the man.

"I'm fucked up."

"That's why we're all 'ere! What's yer release word or words? I'm going to whip yer arse in more ways than one?"

"Don't Stop."

"That's gonna be confusing?"

"It is always by way of pain one arrives at pleasure."
                                     Marquis de Sade.

Ranley

Several weeks went by, one afternoon Stirling walked into
Ranley.

As usual the store was empty during lunch hour.

The Clientele, who patronised the store, would still be eating
lunch in Michelin star restaurants, and at the smart hotels
Ritz Piccadilly or Connaught by Berkeley Square.

Hugo saw him immediately, and got up from his desk, where
he had been munching on a chicken and mayonnaise salad
sandwich, whilst going through some of the orders.

Swallowing his last bite he went to greet Stirling. *"Hello how
nice to see you."* Greeting him with an affectionate hug.

*"I was in the area and thought I would take you to lunch, if
you are free?"*

*"How kind, but I can't leave the store, all of my staff are at
lunch at the moment, so I was just having a chicken sandwich
for my lunch."*

Stirling took the silk handkerchief Hugo had flamboyantly
arranged in the top pocket of his jacket, and wiped some
mayonnaise from the corner of Hugo's mouth. *"You've got
creamy lips."*

"Creamed up and ready to go, how convenient." Hugo fired
back with his usual quick and suggestive wit.

"How was it in Paris, and the lovely Gisiline?"

"Smelling of garlic!" Stirling said laughing.

"How's Rogan?"

"We've split."

Stirling falsely showed some concern. *"I'm sorry."*

"I'm not!"

Some of the staff wandered onto the shop floor, from the
staff room.

Hugo looked at his watch. *"It's two, lunch is over, and I have
to get back to work. Come back at six thirty and we can go for
dinner and talk more."*

"Great see you then." Stirling said and put out his hand to shake, so as not to look too familiar in front of the staff.

In the evening at six o'clock, Hugo saw the last of the staff leave and locked the front door. As he turned to go back for his coat, there was a tap on the door.

Rogan was standing outside, holding a bunch of long stem blood red roses.

The blood drained from Hugo's face, as if it were the roses that had sucked him dry, but it was the possibility of another angry confrontation again that frightened him, knowing Rogan's temperamental outbursts, if he were to come face to face with Stirling in the next half hour?

He had no choice and opened the door to let Rogan in.

"Hello Baby, It's no good, I can't stop thinking about you, I'm sorry." Rogan wanted his regular meal ticket back and hugged Hugo, kissed him, and rested his cheek next to his.

"I thought it was over?" Hugo said affectionately.

"It's not over." Rogan's expression was cold as he stared ahead at the luxury goods he desired, and thought *'Til I'm done?'*

As Hugo looked over Rogan's shoulder, he was horrified to see Stirling approaching the front door!

Holding up the palm of his hand behind Rogan's back, he indicated a warning, not to approach.

Stirling realised the back he could see, was that of Rogan, so turned and left.

Bishops Avenue

4.15 pm. Rogan was updating and loading his new photos, taken by a photographer who specialised in the male form, onto the *'Pleasure par Excellence Escort Agency'* website that he belonged to, and to his own website, for clients who had got his calling card from the Concierge's on his payroll of London's 5 Star hotels.

Alongside the updated photos he typed in his details.

Rogan.

Rogan is a professional model, and ambitious with lots of interests and passions. He loves to travel have fun, play sports, go to the theatre, meet people and socialise, but just as happy on a one to one evening.

He enjoys fine dining, and is a great respectful companion.

Nationality. British.
Height. 6. 1"
Hair. Dark Brown.
Eyes. Blue.
Chest. 44".
Waist. 32".
Inside leg. 32".
Weight. 13 stone
Spoken language. English/ Italian/ French. (He lied)
Hobbies and Sport. Art, Swimming/Football.

Sexual preference. M/F In or Out.

He added COCK 8 inches just to make him laugh, but then deleted it.

Three different individual styles of photos were taken, portraying his sex appeal, to suit different fantasies clients might desire, who would book him to carry them out at a price?

His 'Quintessential Man about Town' business image, wearing black horn rimmed glasses, and dressed in a black suit, white shirt and tie, sitting on the front of an office desk, with his legs wide apart, projecting Power and sex, was often desired by women or men with little confidence.

As he uploaded his Swimwear beefcake shot, taken at Camber Sands beach, chosen to look like a beach in Acapulco Mexico, with waves crashing onto the rocks behind him, he smiled as he recalled, It had been bright and sunny that day on the beach, but the temperature was low, and he was conscious that his penis had shrunk from the cold in his 'Aussiebum' trunks, so he stuffed a sock down the front to enhance his attraction? Which made the photographer laugh and comment, *"With a packet like that, there will be a queue at your door!"*

He also belonged to another sex service website 'Only Fans', a site for customers to belong to, and pay for nude frontal photos and video clips.

The *'Pleasure Par Excellence'* escort agency did not allow full frontal photos on their website, but Rogan still had a way around the rule and uploaded a provocative photo that would still create a picture in the mind of clients desiring his body.

"This is worth at least a thousand and a tip!" He said out loud, and not resisting his vanity, kissed the last photo.

The photo was his 'Prick Teaser – Money Shot' to be uploaded on both websites.

A back shot of him naked in a shower, with shower-gel foam running down his back onto his rounded glistening bum cheeks, with his head turning looking seductively over his shoulder towards the camera, and a sexy expression on his face, would tease and leave the voyeur client, wondering and eager to pay for their pleasure, to see what the image on the front of his body was like?

Rogan was a master in seduction, even by posing on a photo, he knew how to get women or men lusting after him, and ready to pay for his sexy body.

Just as he pressed the Enter button on his keyboard to upload all of the photos, a fanfare tune played. The timing made him laugh, as the fanfare seemed to be announcing and heralding his arrival to his public admirers scanning the agencies website, but it was his video entry intercom in his flat that was announcing a caller.

"Allo, Allo." The voice on the intercom was repeating.

Rogan wondered who it was, as all he could see on the intercom screen, was a close up of an ear pressed up to the intercom, trying to hear if there was an answer.

As the caller backed away from the camera, Rogan could see it was Eddy who again squashed his ear against the camera of the intercom at the outside main door, waiting to hear a response.

"Weyhey Eddy boy." Rogan was pleased to see his close friend.

"Come down Bro, I've got a new car."

Rogan did not wait for the lift, and raced down the stairs eager to see Eddy and his new car.

"Roll up! Roll up! Eddy said laughing, standing alongside the open drivers door of a red 1980s Silver Shadow Rolls Royce convertible.

"Red! I thought the block was on fire; all you need is a hose and bell! Rogan said as he climbed into the white leather driver's seat.

Eddy laughed at Rogan's send up comment.

"You animal! Where did you get it?" Rogan said as he stroked the steering wheel, and the wooden inlay dashboard. *"Bit smeary, the steering wheel is sticky."*

"Fuck! I fought I cleaned it all up."

"Cleaned it up?"

"Yea I banged one out when I picked it up.'

"You what!"

"I 'ad a wank and shot me load over the driving wheel and dashboard."

"Yuk!" Rogan wiped the palm of his hands on his jeans. *"You're fucking sick! A nutter!"*

"Chief nutter if you don't mind! Well it's not every day you get a Roller, and I got an'ard on, when I got behind the wheel. I couldn't 'elp it, I got excited."

"You're a sicko."

Knowing Eddy who was always short of money, and often dodged paying his fare on a bus, by getting on at the back and running up the stairs to top deck, before the driver caught sight of him on the drivers monitor in his cab, he asked. *"Whose motor is it?"*

"I'm looking after it for a while, belonged to a mate of mine, who got banged up for four years, for an attempted bank job. 'E 'ad an accomplice bird working behind the counter, who was going to pass him ten grand, when he was holding her up with a dummy gun. Soppy cow, was late back from lunch, so the teller sitting in her place, pressed the alarm system button, that sent the steel protective barrier crashing down onto the counter." Eddy started to laugh uncontrollably. *" 'E 'ad a pair of tights over his head, but laddered them with his beard when he pulled them on, revealing the centre strip of his moush! I fink the police were looking for a bearded lady 'Oose lost 'er tights!"*

Rogan laughed at Eddy's funny story and the way he told it. *"Get in the passenger seat buddy, I'll take you for a spin, we're gonna Kick-Arse and burn some rubber!"*

Eddy took great pleasure swanning through town in the flashy Rolls.

As he drove in front of Buckingham Palace, he half turned his head to Rogan. *"Wave to the Poor!"*

Rogan laughed. *"That lot are eating baked beans on toast, off gold plates."*

"Then show me the Money! I am your Queen!" Eddy screamed out as he drove twice around the memorial monument of Queen Victoria's statue, in front of the Palace.

As they continued around Hyde Park corner, up Park Lane and the Edgware Road, Rogan asked.

"Where are we going?"

"Gonna show you the 'ouse I'm going to buy." Eddy bragged.

"Shame the Queen took her For Sale sign down." Rogan said laughing.

Cruising down The Bishops Avenue, Hampstead's Millionaire Mansions, mainly owned by billionaire Russians, Arabs and Greek shipping magnets.

Eddy pulled up outside one of the palatial homes, and gazed at the entrance behind the giant gates. Four tall stone Doric columns supported a Palladian architectural triangular top, based on Venetian architecture of 1500, stood impressively surrounding the oak front door.

"I'm gonna live in an 'ouse like that one day."

Rogan took a pound coin from his pocket and handed it to Eddy.

"Here take this, just twenty nine million, nine hundred and ninety nine thousand, nine hundred and ninety nine pounds, to go!"

Both of them laughed and drove on cruising slowly along the avenue, admiring the rest of the fabulous mansions.

"Stop!" Rogan shouted as he slapped the palm of his hand onto the top of the leather dashboard, enforcing his command.

Eddy pulled to a sudden halt, as Rogan opened his door and jumped out without explaining, and ran towards closed wrought iron gates surrounding a mansion.

Holding on to the bars he called through them.*"Gisiline, Gisiline!"* He had spotted Gisiline whom he had met at the Monarchist League Banquet several weeks ago, getting out of a pale blue Alfa Romeo sports car with it's white hood down, in the forecourt entrance of a Mansion.

Pulling out some smart carrier bags, with designer names printed on them, from her car, she turned to see who was calling her name.

At first she did not recognise Rogan, and walked a little closer to the gates, and removed her big black-framed 'Celine' sunglasses for a clearer view.

"Rogan!" What are you doing around here, what a surprise?" She said with a big smile as she gazed from the other side of the gates that were separating them.

"We were just driving through, when I spotted a stunning lady!"

Gisiline laughed at the complimentary and forward remark. Looking across at the red Rolls Royce, she wondered whom he was with.

"You are with a friend?"

"Yes his an Aristocrat, Edwin the first." Rogan laughed at the bogus title he had given Eddy, as he remembered of Gisilines studies on deposed monarchies she had told him about at the banquet.

"Edwin the first of where?"

"First at the Bar!" Rogan said laughing.

"Ask him in for a drink, if you both have the time?"

"We'd love too, I'll go and tell him." Rogan had made up Eddy's mind without him being asked.

"Who's the star?"

"She is that beautiful woman I told you about, that I met at the Monarchist League banquet. She lives here! Look at the size of that mansion, I didn't know she was that rich! She's invited us in for a drink."

"Bit of a gaff! I'll 'ave some of that!" Eddy said beaming with delight of being invited into the mansion.

The ten-foot tall gates slowly opened, as Gisiline pressed her remote control, allowing Eddy to drive onto the forecourt in front of the house.

"Slowly, don't fucking knock the gates down." Rogan said fearfully, peering out of his side window, as Eddy who was not yet used to the long body of the Rolls, came close.

Gisiline dressed in a white 'Givenchy' double-breasted fitted jacket suit, stood by the porch as they got out of the car.

"Alright, nice to meet you." Eddy said putting out his hand to shake.

The door opened without Gisiline using a key.

A man in his late 40s dressed in a smart black suit, shirt and tie, greeted her, as she passed to him, several shopping bags to carry for her.

"Thank you Orlando."

"That was good timing, were you just nipping out?" Eddy joked as he walked past Orlando holding the door and bags.

Gisiline laughed. *"You are so funny, anyone approaching the front door sets off my security cameras, alerting Orlando who can see them on a screen. He keeps me safe as a JiuJitsu martial arts black belt."*

"Whoops better mind my Ps and Qs, or me JiuJitsu's."

Rogan raised his eyebrows and shook his head at Eddy's corny remarks. *"Eddy never stops."*

"I like him, he makes me laugh. Come through to the living room." Gisiline said walking across the white marble floor with peach veins running through.

A sweeping double stairway each side, that met in the middle at the top, dominated the hall.

Half way up, floor to ceiling peach mirrors reflected the magnificent classic long drop crystal 'Swarovski Schonbek' light, which gloriously took it's place as guest of honour.

As they walked through the middle of the reception hall between the staircases, Gisiline threw her 'Birkin' shoulder bag on to a huge round table veneered with fret marquetry and elaborate gilt bronze mounts. A sister double to a table in the French Palace of Versailles, and once owned by Queen Marie-Antoinette, was positioned in the center of the walk through.

A vase full of exotic Birds of Paradise, had been placed on the table with their bright orange heads above banana leaves, complimenting the arrangement, toned with the orange veins in the marble floor.

Both Rogan and Eddy were looking side to side at the ornate lavish décor, and stopped to admire two life size Stallion horses, one black marble the other brown marble, rearing up on their hind legs, sculptured in a jumping motion, that flanked the glass doors leading to the living room.

"These are fabulous!" Rogan said patting the black marble horse, which gave him the feeling of being connected through its tactile feeling.

"You are patting 'Mr Pepperoni', and Eddy has 'Mr Chips." Gisiline said laughing.

"Lovely, mine's an English horse, beats your pizza." Eddy said laughing.

"Chips! Perfect! You talk a lot of Cod! Mine is like me, an Italian Stallion!" Rogan quickly responded the banter.

"You're not Italian?" Eddy quizzed.

"My mothers half Italian." Rogan said proudly.

"My late husband was Italian," Gisiline interrupted. *"And although he was in shipping, he loved racing his horses at Ascot and other tracks. We lived partly in Newmarket and had stables, where his team bred and trained them. One day he took a new horse out to ride on our land, and fell at a jump, and as he wasn't wearing a riding hat, he had concussion and a bleeding haemorrhage on the brain, that was that!"*

"I'm sorry." Rogan said sympathetically.

"I'm not! He was seventy one and an old bastard, I much prefer my sexy young Italian Stallion!" Gisiline said laughing and stroking Rogan's cheek, as she threw her head backwards, causing her long black hair to fall behind her shoulders and reveal her 'Christian Lacroix' diamond stud earrings, as she led them on through the double glass living room doors, that were etched with the gold Versace logo of Medusa in the centre of each door.

"What would you both like to drink? Whisky? Vodka?" Before Rogan and Eddy could answer, Gisiline decided. *"Lets have some Champagne and celebrate to new friends, Ha!"*

Slowly and seductively undoing the buttons on her jacket, she took it off and placed it by her side, over the arm of the sofa that she sat down on, posed sitting on the edge with her long legs poised coquettish to one side.

Rogan sat alongside her on the elegant silver grey linen sofa, with a deep studded-button back, and Eddy sat facing on a sapphire blue armchair, trimmed with silver studs around the edges.

Gisiline's butler Orlando, walked into the room. *"Can I get you anything?"*

"Thank you Orlando, A bottle of Champagne.

"Certainly." Orlando turned on his heel and went to fetch a bottle.

"Do you live in this big 'ouse by yourself?" Eddy said.

"No Orlando and his wife Marguerite live here in the North Wing, and look after all my needs."

"All your needs?" Rogan said giving a sexy broad smile, as he stretched out his arm and placed it in the space between them, as a gesture of closeness by filling the gap, and then edged a little closer to Gisiline.

Gisiline crossed her legs, and wiggled her foot in a circular movement.

Inside her 'Christian Louboutin' shoe, she bent her toes down in pleasure. *"Why, do you know anyone who could fulfil me?"*

Before Rogan could add any more flirtatious remarks, Orlando walked into the room carrying a silver tray with a bottle of champagne in an ice bucket with Cristal champagne flutes, and placed it on the coffee table in front of them.

"Shall I pour?"

"Yes, thank you Orlando, and that will be all this evening."

Orlando passed the flutes of champagne around, took his cue from Gisiline and left.

"I'm feeling left out over 'ere." Eddy said as he leaned forward to chink his glass in a toast with Gisiline.

"Ah, come sit here, Gisiline beckoned and patted the sofa seat next to her.

As he took his seat, Eddy leaned across her, and brushed her breasts with his hand as if by accident, as he made contact with Rogan's glass in a joint toast.

"Christmas has come all at once, I've got two handsome sexy young men to entertain me."

"I fought, you were going to entertain us?" Eddy said, being his cheeky self.

Gisiline fluttered her eyelids. *"Mmmm? You're very fast."*

Rogan's mobile started to vibrate in his jeans pocket, indicating a phone call. He had forgot he turned the sound tone off the night before, leaving it on Vibrate only, when he had gone to the cinema to see the latest Bond Film. An on screen warning notice had appeared before the film commenced reminding patrons to turn off mobiles.

Gisiline looked at Rogan curiously as he fumbled in his jeans pocket.

"My Vibrator is going off."

"I wondered what that was in your jeans wriggling about?" Gisiline said laughing.

Eddy and Rogan both laughed at her quick reaction.

Rogan pulled his mobile from his pocket, and looked at it to see the name of the caller.

"Sorry, I need to answer this." He said, as he got up and walked to the window out of earshot of his conversation, and gazed out at the landscaped garden and swimming pool, as he listened to the call.

He cut the call short and returned to his seat on the sofa.

"Sorry about that, work! My agency called to give me a job for this evening, it's an offer I can't refuse."

"Your agency? That's as in Escort Agency?"

"Yea, how do you know?"

"My escort Stirling, you met at the Monarchist League banquet told me, that you were on the same agencies books."

"Oh yes I forgot about him."

"Yes so have I now." Gisiline replied looking side to side.

"How about we do a private booking?"

"Private booking?" Eddy chipped in.

"I think Gisiline was talking to me Eddy."

"Well actually, I thought you both could be booked?"

Rogan looked across to Eddy. "You game?"

"Yea, gorgeous lady like this, what do you fink!"

"Ok, but it's not two for the price of one."

" Or BOGOF." Eddy quickly added.

"Bogof? "Gisiline was bewildered at the word.

Eddy laughed. "It means Buy One, Get One Free!"

'That's a funny word, is it English, I've never heard that before."

"Don't you shop in Aldi or Morrisons?"

Gisiline was naïve. "No why? Everything is sent in by Harrods."

Rogan laughed at Eddy hopelessly trying to explain the abbreviated word for bargains in the Supermarkets.

Gisiline stood up. "Excuse me for a moment, I have to see Orlando before he signs off." And walked out of the room.

Eddy rubbed the palms of his hands together, which was his gleeful expression, before receiving money. "Ow much you gonna ask 'er for."

"Fifteen hundred."

"Great!"

'You're getting five hundred, I met her first."

"Alright, alright keep your shirt on."

"Actually I shall be taking it off, and my pants!"

Eddy laughed. "Lucky you got that call from your agency, it edged 'er on!"

"I didn't get a call from my agency."

"But I saw you talking, although I couldn't 'ear you right over there?" Eddy said looking bewildered, as he pointed to the window, at the far end of the room.

"There was nobody on the other end. I have an App download 'Secret Caller' that rings my number every two hours, in case I *need an excuse to get away from a situation. Good job, I had the vibrating mode on, came at the right moment."*

"Yea, I come at the right moment!"

"So you fucking lied when you said your agency called?"

"What do you think?"

The two of them burst out laughing as they gave each other a high five.

After a short while Gisiline came back into the room. Rogan stood up with respect for her.

The attention to playing 'A Gentleman' was part of the detail he had acquired for his role as an escort to both women and men.

Eddy followed suit on seeing Rogan jumping up.

She had changed her clothes, and was now wearing a red silk low cut neck dress revealing a lot more of her breasts.

Rogan handed Gisiline the glass of Champagne she had left on the table, which he had topped up for her.

In her other hand she was holding a wad of pink fifty-pound notes and placed them on the coffee table in front of Rogan.

"Two thousand, is that alright, lets get it out of the way, I'm sure you both will be worth every penny!"

Rogan was pleased he had not asked for fifteen hundred, and had gained five hundred extra, although he would only give Eddy an extra two hundred.

Rogan picked up the cash and put it in his jeans pocket.

"Buisness before pleasure, coming right up!"

Rogan grabbed Gisiline pulling her towards him, and gave her a long kiss, pushing his tongue into her mouth, whilst Eddy put his hands around her from behind, rubbing her breasts.

She could feel Eddy's erection pressing into her from the back and Rogan's from the front.

"Lets go to my bedroom."

Stepping into the lift, Gisiline turned the overhead light off, to make their ride erotic groping each other in the dark, as the lift ascended to the first floor.

Rogan and Eddy ran their hands over her body, kissing and licking the side of her neck, and breasts.

As the lift came to a halt, Gisiline groaned in ecstasy and reached down to feel both of their erections, wanting to have them inside her there and then.

Rogan pushed the door open and stepped out with Gisiline and Eddy following.

Eddy was behind and wrapped his arms around Gisiline, feeling her breasts, as she at the same time reached behind rubbing his erection; the three stumbled into her bedroom and fell onto the bed.

Gisiline broke free from Rogan and Eddy's wandering hands, and stood up.

'Wait! Wait! I've got some cocaine."

She went to her dressing table opened a drawer and took out a wrap, along with a bundle of fifty pound notes. After she cut three lines and snorted hers, she threw the bundle of notes into the air, which landed and spread over the floor and bed.

"Pick a note to snort through, and then fuck me on top of the money.

The more you fuck, the more extra money you take!"

Eddy grabbed a handful of notes and shoved them into his pockets. "I like this game! This is just a deposit for your first fuck!" He said laughing.

At the dressing table, he snorted his line and opened a bottle of Champagne Gisiline had placed there earlier, and had set the scene when she changed her clothes.

There were no glasses, which didn't stop Eddy from drinking it straight from the bottle.

After snorting a line he stripped off down to his pants, and went over to the bed, where Rogan was already naked on top of Gisiline.

She was still dressed, and had her hands wrapped around Rogan's waist, squeezing and stroking his firm bum cheeks.

Eddy sat on the edge of the bed and kissed her cheek, at the same time stroking Rogan's lower back, and joining Gisiline's hand stroking Rogan's bum.

"I need another line." Gisiline manoeuvred her way from under Rogan's body, and went to the dressing table.

Rogan turned over lying on his back, his penis erect.

Eddy began to pull down his pants.

"No! Leave them on! That's my job." Gisiline called out, as she returned to the bed.

Royal Garden Party at the Palace

"Just a bit straighter." Hugo adjusted Rogan's Silk Top Hat.
"I've never been that straight!" Rogan joked.
"Yes dear, I've noticed!"
"Oh! I forgot my buttonhole flower, I left it on the kitchen island."
"You're such a panic dear, calm down I'll get it for you."
"Well I've not met the Queen before."
"And you probably won't today! There will be about Eight thousand people there, more interested in scoffing sticky buns, and having cold cups of tea!"
"Come on, Peter just rung up, our car is here." Rogan said excitedly.

Hugo walked a little faster up the hallway, and stuck the stem of the yellow rose bud, into Rogan's buttonhole on his black tailcoat lapel.

"Marvellous!" Hugo said admiring his finishing touches to Rogan's official quintessential sartorial dress, they both hired from 'Hackett Gentlemen's formal wear hire', required for the Palace Party.

As they got into the back of the chauffeur driven black Bentley Hugo had hired, and sat down, a button flew off Hugo's waistcoat and hit the back of the Chauffeurs head!

"Don't shoot the Chauffeur, they'll think we're Terrorists!" Rogan roared with laughter.

"I'll have to go back up and change, I have another waistcoat, I can't meet the Queen with a button missing!"

"Yes, she'll think you ate all the sticky buns!"

Hugo got out of the car and ran back to the block of flats. Rogan lowered his window and shouted, as he laughed at the comical sight of portly Hugo, with the tails of his coat flying and holding on to his topper, which was now on the wonk!

*"Oo ate all the pies? Oo ate all the pies? You fat bastard, you fat bastard, **You** ate all the pies!"*

As Hugo entered through the entrance door to the block, he turned and gave Rogan a 'V' sign with two fingers. Remembering Hugo had told him at the Monarchist League Banquet, his middle name *'Peregrine'* meant Penguin, Rogan called out again still laughing. *"You look like 'The Penguin' in Batman. Ha, ha, ha."*

Viscount Alexander Ranley had arranged and given Hugo the invitation to the Queen's Garden Party, which allowed a guest to accompany him.

For security, all cars dropping off guests were not allowed through the main Palace gates. Guests, who had been allocated invitations, were required to enter on foot through different door entrances around the Palace. Hugo and Rogan joined the queue for the North Wing entrance and joined the queue, slowly making their way through the Palace and to the garden.

"I'm dying for a piss." Rogan said as they shuffled along.

"Hold on we're almost at the entrance, can't have you doing your water sports in-front of the guards.'

"That wouldn't be unusual to them, I've heard if they're standing in those guard boxes, and they gotter go, then they go!"

"Where did you hear that?'

"Some of the guards told me in The Troubedor pub Knightsbridge, back of their quarters, where they hang out."

Hugo started to sing in a low voice as they moved nearer to the entrance. *"All the nice girls like a soldier."*

"I thought that was a Sailor?"

"Who cares? As long as they are in uniform, or better out!"

As they entered, the first thing they saw, mounted on a facing wall, was a picture of the Queen dressed in a soft pink two piece suit with a matching hat, smiling as a welcome to her party.

"Hi Liz!" Rogan blew her a kiss.

"Stop it! She'll send you to the Tower and have you hung drawn and circumcised!"

"Circumsised! Don't you mean quartered?"

"No, every inch lost to man would be a tragedy! Ha, ha."

Rogan and Hugo strolled through the Palace, taking in all of the ornate décor.

"Wow! Now I know where you get your decor inspiration for your home."

"Yes I took a leaf out of Her Majesty's book. It's not much, but we call it home!" Hugo chuckled, as they entered the gardens on the other side of the palace.

Rogan looked around anxiously, for a sign directing to the Men's Toilet "Wait for me, I've got to take that piss, where are they? I'm bursting!"

"It's over there." Hugo pointed to a sign marked 'Men's Washroom'.

Rogan followed behind other men clinging to their top hats, so they did not fall off, as the walked quickly towards 'Heaven's relief' waiting for them, in the mobile luxury designer toilet.

Inside the lavatory cubicle and feeling relaxed again, after emptying his bladder, Rogan took off his Top hat and pulled back the inside silk gossamer sweatband. A small clear plastic bag containing crack cocaine, fell into his hand.

He cut a bigger line than usual to last for an hour or so, as he did not want to take the chance of having to queue for entry again later, when guests had consumed and had to relieve themselves of a couple pints of tea!

After a half hour watching the Queens bodyguards Yeoman Warders, dressed in their red and gold braided tunics and black hats, parading up and down in choreographed marches, to the Military brass band playing hits from yesteryears, the Queen and all of the Royals made their entrance from the Palace.

The Royal family stood alongside the Queen, on the buildings upper terrace overlooking the crowds standing on the lawns, which had been infused with the calming scent of Chamomile, as the music changed to play the 'National Anthem'.

Rogan and Hugo pushed their way through to the front of the crowd, to get a better view of the Royals headed by the Queen, dressed in a matching hat and summer coat, in a striking cobalt blue colour so that she stood out from crowd, and to make it easier for people to spot her.

"Look, there's Viscount Alexander Ranley, standing to the right of the Queen, shall we go and say hello?"

"Don't point." Hugo pulled Rogan's arm down.

Two young Coldstream Guards wearing their Army Division Khaki colour uniforms who were standing in front of them, having been placed there along with other soldiers, who were spaced on the surrounding edges of the crowd, by the Lieutenant General to maintain a security presence, turned around on hearing Rogan's excited comment.

Rogan gave them a broad smile. *'He's a friend of mine."*

Hugo raised his eyebrows and looked to his side, ignoring Rogan trying to impress the young men.

"You've only met him twice, and he isn't even a friend of mine! I only work for him!"

"Well he did tell me to call him Alex, when I first met him at the Mandarin Hotel, and a knuckle bump greeting at the Fortnum Monkey's Tea Party event, so in my book that makes him a friend!"

"Such a Social climber." Hugo muttered under his breath.

The Soldiers standing in front were in their twenty's and both very good-looking. One of them blonde and angelic looking, with high cheekbones and full sexy lips that turned down at the corners, the other had a chiselled jaw, and blue eyes peering out from under the black shiny peak of his hat, which was worn forward and tipping down, at the required position of his regiment. His broad shoulders built like a brick-house, posed a barrier of protection and security to the Queen and Royal Family, which the general public would not cross, without consequences.

As the National Anthem ended, the Queen made her way down the wide stone stairs to the lawns, signalling 'Tea is served' and for the Military band to strike up again to play a selection of music from; My Fair Lady, South Pacific and Mama Mia, as a cue for guests to make a B-line for the Tea-line as they hurried to the marquees surrounding the lawns, that were serving a selection of finger sandwiches, with a choice of white or brown bread; Cucumber and mint, fresh Salmon and lemon, Benedictine cheese and cress, pastry fancies, Fondants and coffee éclairs, all to be gobbled up by people who are usually too smart to eat, and chase their peas around a plate at formal dinner parties, but this was the Queen's Palace Garden Party and it would be insulting to Her Majesty not to eat from her table?

Turning to each other the young soldiers spoke and looked back several times smiling, as they had heard Hugo's muttered remark.

Rogan tapped the blonde soldier on his shoulder. *'Would you mind taking your hats off, I can't see the Queen."* He joked.

"We can!" The other soldier said, turning his head and laughing, making a double-edged comment as he stared at Rogan.

Rogan laughed and put out his hand to shake. *"Touché! I'm Rogan and this is the fabulous Hugo."*

"Good to meet you, I'm Harry." Said the young blonde soldier as he put out his hand to shake, first with Hugo and then with Rogan,.

The other soldier also greeted. *"I'm James."*

"You look like models, not Soldiers?"

"We're from the New Model Army, but like Madonna, only strike a pose when we're on Parade!" James said laughing.

"What made two good-looking boys like you, both sign up for the Army?" Hugo asked.

"We met at Sandhurst College, Muscular Public School as we called it, and both didn't fancy signing up for guerrilla warfare or counter-insurgency blowing guys heads off! So instead we signed up to protect Queen and Country, Sir."

Hugo chuckled. "Call me Hugo, you don't have to call me Sir."

James explained. "As one of the colour sergeants said at Sandhurst, there's a famous quote by one of the predecessors in the 1950s who called every officer cadet "Sir", and he said to his cadets, "You'll call me 'Sir', I'll call you 'Sir', but the only difference is, you'll mean it!"

Rogan looked at Hugo. "I like it! From now on you can call me Sir, and I shall call you Madam and mean it!"

"Take him to the Guardhouse!" Hugo joked.

"Yes please do, both of you!" Rogan enthused.

Suddenly Harry and James stood to attention, as the Queen walked by.

"Why can't you be like them? Obedient servants to the Queen." Hugo said to Rogan, as they stood watching the Queen over James and Harry's shoulders.

"I thought I was? When I was in that Masochistic rubber outfit you made me wear last night." Rogan joked.

Both Harry and James with eyes front burst out laughing, just as the Queen stopped further along out of earshot, to meet a few pre-selected people from various charities.

Whilst on duty at the Queens Garden Party, all of the Soldiers were allowed to wander and mingle with the 8,000 guests, which would not pose an obvious sense of security, although they were alert and ready, to any unusual behaviour and circumstances.

After the Queen moved on, James and Harry relaxed again, ready to carry on conversation with their new fun friends.

"I was telling Hugo, that when Guards are on duty in their Sentry Boxes at the Palace, if they've got to piss they do. It's true isn't it?"

Harry laughed. "Yes, I've spent many a cold night standing in-front of the Palace hoping my Diaper won't leak with my piss to run down my leg."

"Diaper, you mean like a baby wears?" Hugo asked, curious of the revelation not usually brought to public knowledge.

*"Yes we are all given a monthly pack of them to wear on duty. Although Diaper is the American term for Nappy, the Army uses the abbreviation letters as, **D**isposable, **I**ndividual, **A**rmy, **P**ee, **E**xcretion **R**eceptacle.*

As they are padded, they also hide if you have an erection, but that's unlikely when you're standing on duty in the bloody cold for two hours!"

"Ugh soggy knickers!" Hugo said pulling a distasteful face.

"It can be worse than that, it's not wise to have a Vindaloo for dinner before Guard Duty!" James added.

What are you doing later? Come and have some Champagne at our flat, you'll need it after this waxworks tea party! We live near Marble Arch, neighbours with the Queen." Rogan said handing his card with his mobile number printed on it, and inheriting Hugo's address to impress.

The boys laughed. *"Well we are off duty after the party, although we were going to do a job for some extra money."* Harry said.

"Doing what?" Hugo said fascinated that they would hire themselves out.

"We are supposed to be serving drinks at some Woman's Birthday Party in Belgravia, pay is good, hundred and fifty each."

"I'll double that, if you want to come and serve us drinks later?" Hugo said with a wink.

"Each?" James quickly came back with.

"Yes! Is Harry up for it?" Hugo said turning towards him.

"He's up for anything that pays.

"Sounds like my line of business?" Rogan said laughing.

"I could do with a line, get it out." James said, referring to a line of cocaine, as he put his hand on Rogan's shoulder.

"What makes you think I've got any drugs?"

"I know you do! At Sandhurst one of the first things we learn as Officer Cadets is to recognise the smell of Crack Cocaine, in case it is smoked by the troops under our command."

Rogan was amazed at James detection and explanation.

"Are you seriously saying you can smell cocaine? Some people say Labradors and Bloodhounds can't really sniff out cocaine, only dope, and that it is the fear on people's faces that gives them away, thinking the dog is going to drop them in it. So how can a human smell it?"

"That's not true, crack cocaine often smells of burning rubber or plastic, although some coke has a floral smell. It depends on what it's cut with? You smell of rubber."

"Yea well, I was in a rubber bondage suit last night!" Rogan repeated his earlier joking comment to Hugo.

James laughed and turned to Harry.

"What do you think, serving drinks to some old bird, or a night on parade?"

Harry ignored answering James's question and directed his conversation to Hugo.

"I'll bring my riding boots as well."

Hugo laughed. *"It's not a fashion show dear. So I take it, that's a yes?"*

James added. *"Okay, we hadn't confirmed with her yet, as we said we didn't know what time we would get away from the Palace?"*

"If you bring your red tunic jackets and black trousers with the red stripes running down the sides, I'll add another hundred each!" Hugo said getting more excited at the thought of having uniformed guards in his flat at his command?

"How much if we bring our Busby hats?" Harry said, trying to bump up the fee.

Most of the guests were queuing at the marquees, peering at other Guest's plates, as they walked back past them.

Many dressed as a 'Dog's Dinner' with their dainty finger sandwiches piled high, as they were cut so small. Four of them could be eaten all together without anyone looking piggish!

Rogan saw it as an opportunity to have another line of cocaine and take James with him? As the toilets would not be that busy whilst the guests were eating.

"Come on, James let's do the 'Hokey Cokey in the Palace Pissoirs."
"You've just had some!" Hugo announced loudly.
"Shoosh! Why don't you put in your speech from the Throne Room! Anyway that was an hour ago, and if I have to look at these boring old farts gobbling like they do when they're incognito at Macdonalds, I think I need another! Have you noticed, all of these people have a certain look about them?"
"Yes, down their nose!" Harry interrupted.
Rogan laughed. *"I've got something to snort up your nose. Come on both of you."*
A few men were at the urinals, concentrating in a hypnotic state on the flow of their urine, as Rogan and James went into a lavatory cubicle in a separate area.
After their lines of cocaine, Rogan feeling stoned started to kiss James.
James backed off and reached to open the door lock. *"If I get caught in here, I'll end up in a Court Marshall."*
Harry had taken his hat off, and was hovering by the washbasins straightening his hair with his hands, so as not to look suspicious whilst waiting to be summoned for his line of cocaine.
As he slipped into the cubicle, Rogan sang softly.
"They're changing Guards in the Loos at Fucking-him Palace, I would love to suck both of their Phallus!"

"You're stoned we have to leave." Hugo said, catching hold of Rogan's arm; as he staggered out following James and Harry leave the portable lavatories.
"I'm okay the Queen said I can stay the night."
"How much coke have you had? Look at the state of you, your eyes are blank and your face is red. James, Harry, can you help get him out of here discreetly."

"Okay we'll take him out through the side gate of the garden on Grosvenor Place, next to the Queens Gallery, there's usually lots of taxi's driving along there." Harry said taking command of the situation.

"You were an embarrassment!" Hugo screamed at Rogan back at his flat.

"You're always an embarrassment, you old git!" Rogan shouted back as he snorted another line of cocaine.

Mimicking Hugo in a camp voice, Rogan added more fuel to their fire. *"I'll double your fee and add another hundred, if you bring your red jackets. You fucking creepy tart! What about me! You offered them four hundred each and lately you've been asking me for half the bill in restaurants, I'm fucking sick of you!"*

"And I'm sick of you, you sponger! Get out!"

Rogan jumped up from the side of the coffee table he had been crouched over to snort more cocaine, and knocked over an open bottle of whisky, that he had been drinking directly from the bottleneck.

As he lunged at Hugo he hit him on the side of his face, causing Hugo to fall backwards, and bang his head on a side console table, and fall to the floor amongst the spilt flowing whisky.

Rogan spat at him, turned and left.

The front door banged shut.

"Bastard!" Hugo called out as he slumped into an armchair. Bending over he reached for the whisky bottle at his feet, and swigged the last few mouthfuls left, straight from the bottle.

The argument and fight had heightened and aroused his emotions, turning him on, increasing his heart rate and blood flow, releasing endorphins that made him feel sexy. Suddenly he began to get an erection. The uncontrollable reaction made him ponder, would he feel better if he masturbated?

Just as the taxi pulled up outside Rogan's block of flats where he lived, his mobile rang.

"Hi Rogan, this is Harry how are you feeling, shall James and I come over now?"

"No mate, I've got a splitting headache and going to bed. You'd better go and serve that old bird. Call you some other time."

The call sidetracked Rogan's thoughts as he started to walk away from the taxi towards his block of flats.

"Aye! You 'aven't paid! The cab driver called out.

He turned and walked back to the driver's window and handed him a fifty-pound note.

"It's fourteen fifty on the clock, sorry mate I've only just clocked on and can't change that."

"It's alright, keep the change, there's plenty more where that came from!"

Several weeks later...Sunday morning - Hugo's flat

11.47am. Hugo answered his internal phone.

Peter the concierge was on the other end. *"Mr Walford, there's a messenger here with a Royal Mail special delivery for you, shall I send him up?*

"I'm not expecting anything, but yes, thank-you."

The door buzzer sounded almost immediately, as he put the receiver down.

Still wearing his dressing gown and slippers, he shuffled up to his front door.

Standing before him was the back of a Grenadier Guard wearing a full regal red tunic, with brass buttons, epulets and a red stripe running the side length of his black trousers, complete with a black bearskin hat.

As he turned around Hugo gasped with surprise, recognising the soldier was Rogan, holding twenty long stem red roses. Rogan bent his right leg up to his waist and stamped his foot back down onto the floor with a thud, and at the same time saluted Hugo as he handed the bunch of roses to him.

"Sir, I am your Royal Male reporting for duty, Sir."

Hugo shocked but delighted smiled, and was pleased to see Rogan and the effort he had gone to for reconciliation after their argument several weeks ago.

Rogan knew how to keep Hugo on his string, tempting and enticing him, feeding his insatiable appetite for sex.

The Soldiers uniform had worked, a symbol of authority power, protection, heroism, strength and manliness, a sexy erotic image for his bedroom?

"When did they let you out?"

"Let me out?" Rogan puzzled with the question.

"The Bloody Tower! I'll have their guts for garters! I told them to lock you up and throw away the key!" Hugo said laughing and clutching his roses. *"And at the same time, they can*

166

throw Peter in there as well, you just can't trust staff anymore!"

As Rogan bent forward to kiss Hugo on the lips, his tall black bearskin hat fell forward and hit Hugo on the head.

"Attacking me again dear!"

Rogan laughed as he pulled the hat off. *"Sorry babes, at least it's big and hairy."*

Hugo grabbed Rogan's arm.

"Come on we've got some unfinished business.

"Yes, you can show me those garters you mentioned."

Both of them laughed, as they marched playfully like children stomping their feet, and swinging their arms stiffly like toy soldiers, down the hall to the bedroom.

"I'm going to make you stand to attention, although you will be lying down!" Hugo said as he reached for Rogan's buckle on his belt.

After having sex, Hugo lay on his bed next to Rogan with his arm around his shoulder, enjoying their moment of closeness and having made up from their past argument. The red and gold tunic jacket was crumpled up on a chair, trousers and a jock strap on the floor, and the bearskin, had been placed on top of a bedside lamp for fun.

"Where did you get the uniform? No! Don't tell me! James, or was it Harry? I knew it wouldn't be long before you inspected the guards? "

Rogan laughed. *"Both. The trousers were from James, the Jacket and bearskin from Harry."*

"And the leather jock-strap?"

Rogan reached to the floor and picked it up, putting it to Hugo's nose. *"My own, here smell!"*

Hugo laughed, as he smelt them. *"Mmm Eau de Cock and Bollocks, available at all good Gym's men's changing rooms!"*

Rogan's mobile played the sound that informed of an incoming call.

Reaching to take it from his trouser pocket, still on the floor, he realised it wasn't his mobile making the sound alerting him of a caller.

Hugo's mobile was on the bedside table, and it was his with the same ring tone that was calling to be answered.

Rogan picked it up and looked at the screen to see the name of the caller – Alex.

Passing it to Hugo he said. *"It's Viscount Alexander, doesn't he even give you a day off on a Sunday?"*

Hugo looked puzzled as he took the mobile from Rogan.

"Hello, Oh hi, no I can't see you today, I'm busy and I can't chat now, speak soon bye."

"Silly me!" Rogan said sarcastically, realising the name of Alex on the screen, was not Hugo's personal shortened title for Viscount Alexander Ranley.

"And I thought you missed me? Still seeing that rent boy Alex. I thought it was your Viscount boss Alex as you call him."

Hugo didn't want to escalate the situation, after their amended relationship.

"Oh take no notice, he means nothing to me, in fact he's a nuisance, I must block his number so he can't call me."

Rogan was confident that Hugo was back on his hook, but was not going to take any chances of letting his money machine get stolen by anyone else!

"It's okay I know he's just around for a cheap fuck!" Rogan said, as he gave a false kiss to Hugo on the cheek.

"Yes dear, and you're the expensive deluxe fuck!"

The mobile tone sounded again, both Hugo and Rogan reached for their mobiles, this time it was Rogan's, alerting him of an incoming call.

"Hello Sexy!"

Hugo looked at Rogan and frowned, curious of who was calling?

Rogan started to sing into the phone mouthpiece.

"You got passion in your pants, and ain't afraid to show it, you're sexy and you know it, you're sexy and you know it. How's my old mucker?"

Rogan turned to Hugo. *"It's lover boy Eddy."*

"What you been up to?"

"Still fucking about, bit of this, bit of that, dodging and ducking, you know me. Where 'ave you been? Ave't 'eard from you in weeks, fought you might be banged up like me."

"Banged up! What the fuck? Rogan was shocked.

"Turn's out my mates Roller was nicked, I was stopped and arrested whilst driving it. The fuckers fought I was 'im, but I tried to explain 'ow can I be 'im, when 'es already banged up in the nick for attempted robbery!"

Rogan could not stop laughing at Eddy's story.

Hugo started to laugh at Rogan infectious tears of laughter, although he did not know the reason.

Rogan tried to tell Eddy's story.

"It's Eddy, ha, ha, he was nicked by the old bill, ha, ha, ha, for driving his mates car, ha, ha. The police thought he was him, ha ha ha."

"Who? Ha, ha."

"He's mate, ha, ha, ha."

Rogan was naked sitting on the side of the bed, clutching his stomach and crying with laughter.

Eddy was still talking, "I wouldn't mind, but my mate Roderick is black. I ask you, do I look black? Anyway I explained to them its Roderick's Red Roller, not mine, but it took them a fucking week to let me go!"

Rogan roared with laughter again. "Ha, ha, ha, Roderick's Red Roller, ha, ha. Are you sure it didn't belong to Little Red Riding Hood? - I can't talk". He handed his mobile to Hugo. "Here you take the phone ha, ha, ha."

"Hello Eddy, you've sent Rogan into convulsions of laughter, he can't speak. Let's do lunch on me; you free?"

"Yeah! Lovely."

"Meet us at Hunters Kings Rd for three o'clock, they're doing late Sunday Roast and Drag Cabaret.

Hunters

On stage a female impersonator came out as the 1960's film star Bette Davis smoking a cigarette.

She was a raconteur and in-between long drags on the cigarette, told bitchy stories about her old sparring partner fellow film star, the late Joan Crawford.

"They say you should speak good of the dead, she's dead – Good! She's in that big Pepsi Cola bottle in the sky." Referring to her husbands famous soft drink business.

Her next character was another dead camp actress and gay 1930's icon, Queen of double entendres; Mae West.

Focussing on a handsome young man in the audience, she moved to the edge of the stage and directed her comment to him.

"Why don't you come up and see me sometime, all I've got on is the radio."

Her jokes were dated and the young man looked baffled, as he wasn't sure of the dated word 'Radio' in the modern age of technology words Facebook, Instagram, Vimeo, Youtube, which went over his head and the rest of the audience, but laughed anyway.

As he turned his head whilst laughing, his eyes met with Hugo across the dining room, and got up from his chair to go over to the table.

"Alex, what a coincidence!" Hugo said surprised, as earlier he had put him off for them to meet.

Rogan forced a smile. *"Alright Alex, this is my friend Eddy."*

Eddy smiled and without a word, put out his clenched fist to bump.

Hugo looked across to the table Alex had come from.

"Who are you with?"

"His American, says his in the film business. We met at the Queens Head Pub and he invited me here for lunch"

Rogan ears pricked up.

"Films?"

"Yeah porno's."

"Bring him over for a drink."

Rogan was eager to meet him, as he had not made any films for the adult sex industry yet, and had been considering it for some time.

He had heard the money was good, and the more versatile of sexual acts with partners either sex, and the longer staying power to remain hard to perform; the more money was on the table! All of which he was master at.

Alex brought him over to the table.

His hair was a mixture of colours; natural sun kissed golden with blonde tips on light brown hair, bleached by the sunny climate of California.

The top of his hair was long which fell forward as he bent slightly to shake Eddy's hand, who was seated close.

"Hi guys I'm Eddie." He said as he ran both hands through his hair, putting it back in place.

Rogan was captivated with his attractive image.

In his mid 30s he looked fit, but not bulging with too much muscle. Rogan wanted to see more of his body, as his pecs looked firm in a tight white T-shirt, which was hanging over his pale blue jeans.

His tan and gleaming white teeth, made him look like a 'Poster Boy' for a whitening gel?

'What is this stud doing with that little rent a dick-head?' Rogan thought.

"You can't be mate! I'm Eddy!" Eddy said, joking as he claimed possession of his name.

"Eddie with an 'e'?"

"Na, wiv a 'wye', the butch way, but all Eddy's are good looking." Eddy said putting out his fist for a bump greeting. They both laughed at having the same name.

This is all getting very confusing. *"I'm Hugo with an 'aitch'."* Hugo said laughing.

"Confusing? You can talk, I never know, if you are talking about Viscount Alex, or Alex here when you're meeting one of them." Rogan cut across Hugo as he was introducing himself.

"I quite like being called Viscount Alex, sounds good to have a title." Alex piped up.

"You do dear! And it begins with 'P'?" Hugo responded quickly.

"I thought it began with 'T'." Rogan hinted referring to 'Tart' and not Princess, as there was no love lost between them. *"Anyway, I'm Rogan with an 'R'."*

"Yes you arrrre!" Eddie said showing his interest, as he squeezed Rogan's shoulder.

"Sit down, join us for a drink, if you can manage to let go of Rogan's shoulder!" Hugo said, aware of Eddie's lustful look., and lingering squeeze.

"What part of the states are you from?" Rogan asked.

"Hollywood or 'Holly Weird' as it is known."

Alex said you are in films?" Rogan was eager to know more about the sexy American.

"Yes, I'm an actor in x-films."

"I've seen The X-Men film, what part did you play?" Eddy joked.

Everybody around the table laughed at Eddy's quick funny quip.

"Very good man, I've not heard that one before!" Eddie said sarcastically and laughing.

"Pornos." Rogan established Eddie's interpretation.

"You got it!"

"What category of films?" Hugo asked, curious to know more that would get his sex juices flowing and excite him.

"Bodies."

"Bodies?" Rogan repeated.

"Yea, if it has two arms, two legs, a mouth, cock, hole, or a pussy to be filled, and is still alive, I'm your man!"

"So you don't mind what the scenario is?" Rogan dug deeper.

"I'm very adaptable, there is always a role play. I just act out whatever the director wants me to do, to follow the storyline of the script."

"Lately I've been filming for Virtual Reality films."

Everyone around the table looked fascinated.

"It's the latest thing, people buy virtual reality headsets, insert their smart phones, or they can plug in to their computer USB slot and download porn videos to watch in any category. The images appear as 3D and makes the viewer believe the person in the film is performing just for them, which turns them on."

"I'd like some of that, can you introduce me to a production company." Rogan said eagerly.

"I can do better than that, we're shooting a film on Tuesday, and the guy who was supposed to be playing opposite me, has broken his arm, so dropped out. The director was going to call around to some guys tomorrow, to see if they are available, but I will tell him about you and that I think you would be suitable for the part."

Eddie squeezed Rogan's bicep. *"Have you got the rifle that goes with those guns?"*

"Rifle, more like a cannon that can shoot all night long!" Rogan bragged.

Eddie laughed. *"I'm looking forward to you riding with your shotgun!"*

"That's great! What's the pay like."

"Well here's the deal, two thousand for a buyout."

"What's a buyout?"

"It means that's your fee complete, which will be for two films, no matter how many copies they sell."

"That's cool."

"Give me your mobile number, I'll put it in my phone and call you tomorrow morning when I have confirmed with the director."

"Well now we can celebrate with your porno award of 'Best New Comer of The Year', which I can vouch for after last nights ejaculation performance! Lets have a bottle of champagne." Hugo said to show he had first claim on Rogan. Laughing it off, he grabbed the arm of a passing waiter, to order the Champagne.

"Wanna a line sweetheart?" Eddy said, offering cocaine to Alex as he rose up from his chair.

Alex stood up and followed Eddy to the toilets.

A short time later Eddy returned to the table and heard his name being mentioned in conversation between Rogan and Hugo, and mistakenly thought they were talking about him, not realising they were referring to his namesake Eddie.

"Eddie looks like a Celebrity, did you see how everybody turned their heads as he walked around the tables." Rogan said as he placed his hand on Eddie's shoulder with affection.

"Yea most people fink I look like a young sexy Mick Jagger." Eddy said proudly interrupting the conversation.

"More like Mickey Mouse!" Rogan said laughing. *"Anyway we weren't talking about you! We were talking about the American Dream!"*

Hugo was roaring with laughter and added his own quip.

"With that walk, I thought you were Daffy Duck!'

"Alright, alright! I should 'ave known, 'es better looking than me." Eddy said referring to Eddie.

"Ah come on fellas, he's cute." Eddie was quick to compliment Eddy to make him feel better.

V.R. 3D. Studios

"This is Rogan, I told you about." Eddie said introducing him to the director and videographer of the 'Virtual Reality Three Dimensional' studios.

A middle-aged man with long grey hair, tied at the nape of his neck in a ponytail gave Rogan the once-over look.

"Mmm, bit of a hunk? - Nice one Eddie. I'm Casper the director, film producer, and 'Fluffer'. There is a loose script, but we may veer off it occasionally, depending on how your scenes go when you are in action."

"What do you mean?"

"Well it depends on your erect staying power, and not to cum too early. I'd appreciate it if you cum when I say so. If you do shoot too quickly, don't worry though; we can use some creamy shower gel as a stand in. Nobody will ever know the difference, but I would prefer a shot of you actually ejaculating."

"No worries, my dick has been trained!"

Casper and Eddie laughed at Rogan's confidence.

"One thing though, what is a fluffer?"

"That's when I do my fluffing about, to help you get a hard boner."

"As I said, my dick graduated from school with diploma comments. – It doesn't say, 'Try's hard, could do better'. It says, - Stays hard, can't get any better!"

Casper and Eddie both laughed at Rogan's quick off the mark comeback.

A girl in her 20s wearing a short half open pink dressing gown, revealing her breasts, entered the studio from an adjoining door.

A handwritten sign written with a felt tip pen on a piece of paper curling at the corners, marked 'Dressing Room', was Sellotaped to the front of the door.

"Hi I'm Babette, are you the guy whose gonna fuck me!"

"Well I haven't read the script yet, but it will be a pleasure."

"This is not about pleasure, it depends on how big your cock is? I need to see it first before filming I don't do donkey dicks! Drop 'em." She said slightly aggressive.

"So dictorial, I love it!" Rogan said as he unfastened his trousers and pulled down his pants.

Everyone stared at his penis, which had become semi erect due to Babette's command.

"Okay, that should be alright. Last week some guy who had a monster cock almost choked me."

"It's alright for me as well." Eddie said as he tapped it with his fore finger.

"Well whilst we are auditioning, get it out." Rogan said as he gave Eddie's crotch a jiggle.

"Later, you won't be disappointed." Eddie laughed

Rogan laughed. *"Unlike Babette, I've got a deep throat."*

Casper explained the storyline script.

"Rogan, you are playing Babette's lover and her husband comes home early from work, and catches you fucking his wife. He enjoys what he sees, and joins in. You lie back on the bed with your legs up as he fucks you, and at the same time Babette straddles you and sucks your dick. Okay any problems?"

"No, sounds fun, can't wait!"

"Good, then after you can do a VR."

"VR?"

"Virtual Reality it's like 3D, you actually believe you are in the scene."

"Oh yes, Eddie told me about them, sounds good."

"This one will be for the gay market. All you have to do is wank close up to the camera, so the old men think you're doing it just for them!"

Casper handed Rogan a VR headset to put on. *"Here take a look, to get the idea."*

"Wow! It's like she's straddling me, these headsets are fantastic."

"Yea, synchronized sex toys are on the rise! Sex robots are not far away, but for the moment you're still in business!" Casper said laughing.

Babette sat on a sofa whilst Rogan and Eddie went into the dressing room to get ready.

Eddie reappeared naked and climbed on top of Babette who was lying naked on top of a bed in a bedroom set, which was in a corner of the studio. As he started to have intercourse Eddie walked on set, he had brushed his hair back neatly, and was dressed in a suit, shirt and tie, carrying a briefcase and wearing horn rimmed reading glasses to add to his businessman image.

A Clark Kent who would turn into 'Superman'.

After both of his performances, Rogan was paid his £2000 fee.

"Do you wanna come for a drink nothing fancy, just a pub, I'm meeting up with my mate Eddy?" Rogan asked Eddie who had waited around watching Rogan's one-man show.

"No thanks, I'm feeling a bit exhausted after fucking all afternoon."

The Royal Blackmail Plot

Rogan had arranged to meet Eddy at the Warwick pub in Camden Town, the borough where Eddy lived and close to the 'VR 3D Studios' also in Camden.

Eddy was keen to hear how the filming went, as he also fancied becoming a Porn-star.

"Since when did you wear glasses, four eyes? You look like you're from the Mafia Mob!" Rogan said laughing, at Eddy's new image, who was wearing a pair of black thick framed tinted glasses.

"Yeah, I've been 'aving 'eadaches for some time, and fort I'd get me eyes checked out. The optician said I was short sighted and needed glasses."

"Can you see this?" Rogan pulled out a ten-pound note from his wallet, and held it up in front of Eddy.

"Yea it's a tenner."

Rogan put it back in to his wallet, and took another note out as he repeated the same action. *"Can you see this?"*

"Yea it's a twenty pound note."

Rogan put the twenty-pound note back in to his wallet, and repeated his action, but did not really take a note out again? Pretending to hold a note up. *"And can you see this fifty pound note?"*

"No you've got nufink in your hand!"

"I'd take those glasses back mate, you can't see a fifty pound note when it hit's you in the face!"

The two of them laughed.

"Ow did it go today at the VD Studios?"

What are you talking about you berk! They're called VR 3D Studios.

"Its all the same."

"You're nuts! Yea great, easy money, no chatting up to do, had my mouth full most of the time anyway!"

Both laughed.

"Got any punters lined up this week?"

"No, it's gone a bit quiet, I was pleased to get the porno film." Rogan, said as he took a sip of his beer. "It's not as busy as it used to be, suppose it's down to age? I'm getting on for forty, I'm an old man!"

"Shut it!" Eddy snapped and laughed. "Old man at 34! You're still sex on legs, you've always got a party going on in your pants! Besides the bank of Hugo is always open along with his legs!"

"No, he hasn't been too forthcoming recently, we've been arguing a lot he even asked me to go halves the other night, when the bill came for our dinner! I think he holds back with the cash, unless I give him sex. To be honest after three years, I'm getting fed up with having it off with him. He's getting a real old man, and his body is sagging even more."

Eddy repeated Rogan's comment. "Made you go 'alves! Wanker! Wot we need is a big fish, and I know exactly how to catch it!"

Reaching into his jacket pocket he took out his mobile that had a wire attached to it, which was trailing between the buttons on the front of his shirt, around his back and up to his neck and the back of an ear, where it was attached to the side arm of his glasses.

"What the fuck is that!" Rogan was amazed.

Eddy pressed a screen button on his mobile, and turned it around for Rogan to see.

A recorded film with sound, connected by Bluetooth on his mobile, played back of Rogan saying derogatory comments about Hugo, he had said earlier.

("....I give him sex. To be honest I'm getting fed up with having it off with him. He's getting a real old man, and his body is sagging even more.")

"Fuck!" Rogan was shocked and amazed.

Eddy laughed and took his glasses off, and handed them to Rogan, who looked shocked.

"You fought I needed bins! You nutter! Holding up notes for me eye test!"

Rogan laughed as he examined the glasses. *"I don't believe it, James Bond glasses! Oh! I see the cameras are those little pinholes each side of the frame, you would never know? Well I didn't! Where did you get them?"*

"Shop in Soho, would you believe it's actually called 'THE SPY SHOP', I couldn't resist them for a laugh. They had a belt in there as well, wiv a camera built into the buckle, fink I'll go back for that tomorrow."

"What do you want them for?" Rogan asked as he put them on.

"I only got them for fun, but just think, we could film and record someone, get them to say fings, and get some money out of them."

Rogan wearing the glasses lifted them to his brow, and locked eyes with Eddy. *"You mean blackmail!"*

"Yeah."

"Who?"

Eddy had a serious cold expression on his face, - *Hugo!"*

Rogan grabbed Eddy's chin with his hand and gave it a gentle shake, and then placed the palm of his hand on Eddy's cheek as an endearment. *"No! He's not rich enough, if we are going to do this, it's not a fish like you said, we aren't going for a sprat, when we can go for a big fish like a 'Tiger Shark'."*

"Tiger Shark?" Eddy repeated.

"Yes! Viscount Alexander Ranley! We're gonna take the royals to the fucking cleaners!"

Rogan went on to spell out a plan. *"Hugo is still knocking off that rent boy Alex, and when he talks about working in Ranley, he refers to Viscount Alexander by shortening his name to Alex!*

All we have to do is get Hugo to talk about the details of having sex with that fucking little toe-rag, and you know how much he enjoys reliving details about sex with him, trying to

turn me on or make me jealous, and there's never a day
passing that he doesn't mention Alex his boss.

What's in a name?
(Romeo and Juliet) William Shakespeare.

Alex (Alexander) - The Royal
Alex - The Rent Boy
(Although poles apart their names would be used for
ill-gotten gains).

We record him talking about both Alex's, and with a bit of
clever editing we will have video footage of him talking about
having sex with a member of the Royal Family!"
Eddy was still confused of Rogan's plan. *"But 'e 'asn't!"*
"You're not getting it! People will think the 'Alex' he is talking
about, is the Viscount! When really it's the tart with the same
name! It's the same confusion I have when Hugo says he's
meeting Alex; I don't know if he means the Viscount or the
rent-a-dick. Do you remember last week when we were all
pissing ourselves with laughter at Hunters restaurant, talking
about Eddie and you thinking we were talking about you as a
celebrity?"
The penny finally dropped for Eddy. *"Oh yea, I fought you*
were all sending me up."
"Well it's the same."
"You're a fucking genius!"
Who are we going to get the money from, The Viscount? The
Queen?
"No! We go to the National Press, The Sun, Mirror, Mail,
Express, the Times; one of them will pay up! They'll sell
millions of papers with an explosive story like this.
Eddy broke into a broad smile from ear to ear, and rubbed
the palms of his hands together in glee.
"'ow much shall we ask for? A million? Two million?

"No! A million sounds too much, and they'll hold back to think about it. We need them to make a quick decision for a payoff, to get rid of us for an exclusive story. Seven hundred and fifty thousand should set us up nicely."

Eddy took the last gulp of his beer and stood up.

"Where you going?"

"To get us a couple of Sambuca shots to celebrate!"

"Don't spend all your money just yet," Rogan said laughing.

Eddy got the shots and came back to the table.

They both raised their glasses.

"Stand up," Eddy instructed Rogan.

"God save the Queen," Eddy said in a superficial empty mocking gesture, as they clinked their glasses and downed their Sambuca shots in one gulp, and then saluted each other as they burst out laughing.

"I'll definitely get the belt with the built in camera tomorrow for us to use, it will look less suspicious, and 'ee won't ask questions about me bins like you!"

Slowly, Slowly - Catchy Monkey?
      Lord Robert Baden-Powell
      Founder - The Boy Scouts.

I Spy!

Hugo was spread out on his sofa, wearing his kaftan robe as usual. *"Fix me a large whisky while you're up."*

Rogan was selecting some of the dated music tracks from the download list Eddy had loaded onto Hugo's computer two years ago.

"Okay, just a minute, you're going to like this track, I chose it especially with you in mind." The music-track of Shirley Bassey singing 'Big Spender' began to play. Grabbing the neck of the crystal glass decanter of whisky, from the side console table, he poured a treble drink and handed it to Hugo.

"Oh I forgot to get some ice out of the fridge, for the ice bucket. Be a darling and fill it up." Hugo added.

Rogan went to the kitchen and got the ice from the fridge and shouted. *"Ice coming straight up, just like you!"* The sexy remark made Hugo laugh.

As he returned he was singing along with the track playing, and swaying his hips in time to the beat.

Wouldn't you like to have fun, fun, fun?" and thrust his crotch forward, which was at Hugo's eye level, as he was still lying on the sofa, and continued singing. *"I could show you a good time?"*

Hugo laughed at Rogan's singing and seductive behaviour, and stroked Rogan's crotch as he bent over to hand him the drink.

"That's a very-very large whisky, are you trying to get me drunk, so you can have your wicked way?" He said grabbing at Rogan's crotch again.

Rogan did want his wicked way, but not in the way of what Hugo was expecting?

Tonight he and Eddy would get him drunk and stoned on cocaine, knowing that when he was in that state, his loose tongue would waggle as usual, and he would say the words Rogan and Eddy needed to be recorded.

The front door buzzer sounded and Rogan went to open it. Eddy arrived and entered the living room in his usual exuberant manner.

"Allo Ceasar" he said laughing at Hugo sprawled out, looking like a Roman Emperor reclining as he sipped his *'Hanky Panky' cocktail; Gin, sweet vermouth, Fernet Branca, Orange twist.*

"Be careful or I'll send you to the Lions, give me a kiss and I might forgive you.

Eddy gave him a peck on his cheek.

"Thought I'd pop round and see what you two were up to?"

"We were going to have a quite night in, but now you're here that's gone out the window."

"I've got some great gear." Eddy said as he pulled out a wrap of cocaine from his pocket.

"I could do with a pick me up, It's been a long day at work. Alex was in a bad mood and wanted me to go through all of the orders clients have placed from abroad for beech wood candleholders we import from china. They sell like hot cakes. **Alex said he can't get enough.** *Usually that's his job, but he fucked it all up, by mixing all of the reference invoice numbers, and wanted me to sort it out! I couldn't believe it! He left it right till the end of the day.* **He made it really hard for me!** *To sort out."*

Eddy was wearing his Spy belt with the built in camera recorder that he had bought, after going back to the Spy shop. He was pleased that although he had only been in the room for five minutes, he was able to capture Hugo naming Alex and all of his comments, which would be edited out of context.

The comments mixed with intended recordings of Hugo taking pleasure at divulging his sex games with the rent boy of the same name, would be part of the false film footage that would seem as if Hugo is revealing a sexual relationship, incriminating the Viscount a junior Royal.

"Ready for some Okey Cokey?" Eddy said throwing down the wrap of cocaine onto the coffee table. *"You lay out the lines, I'm just going to the loo."* Eddy wanted to check his spy camera was switched on and operating correctly, and while he was in the toilet tested it, by aiming the camera at his penis as he peed into the toilet basin.

As he played back the footage of Hugo's incriminating words to be edited, he broke into a broad smile, as the footage of his penis following, looked even bigger from the downward shot.

Rogan had gone to the kitchen to get a couple of beers from the fridge for Eddy and him, and returned as Eddy left the room.

Hugo was kneeling on the floor, cutting up the cocaine on the glass top coffee table, with his Harrods credit card.

On the table, his prized possession white envelope, from Buckingham Palace, which he kept his wraps of cocaine in, still sat majestically on a silver salver tray.

"I don't know why you need to keep this envelope on show, the post mark is so old, and most of your friends will have seen it by now." Rogan said as an excuse to pick it up and replace it back down, next to the lines of cocaine and Harrods credit card.

"I know, but it still gets a laugh."

Hugo started to sing. *"The King was in the counting house counting out his money; the Queen was in the parlor eating bread and honey. The maid was in the garden hanging out the clothes, and then sneaked off to shove some coke up her nose! Ha, Ha, Ha!"*

The filming on Eddy's Spy camera of the Royal envelope next to the lines of cocaine, would suggest the cocaine was being delivered from Buckingham Palace!

As Eddy came back, Rogan standing behind Hugo, raised his eyebrows and motioned with a nod of his head, to direct Eddy's attention to the envelope placed next to the cocaine.

Eddy caught on immediately and made sure his camera was pointing directly towards Hugo, who was snorting the powder next to the Royal envelope, unaware of the setup.

As the weeks went on, Rogan and Eddy both using their spy belts, used every opportunity to film and record Hugo, Eddy had changed his clear lens spyglasses for a tinted lens sunglasses version, as they would be more acceptable, without any questions being asked relating to his eyesight. Often pumping Hugo to talk in detail about his sex conquests with his regular rent boy Alex, they would be able to splice the film and recordings together, to insinuate there was a heavy sexual relationship between Hugo and the Viscount of the same shortened name.

It was at the 'The Queens Head' pub in Tyron Street just off Kings Rd Chelsea, often patronized by The Queen Mothers courtier William Tallon (Known at Clarence House as 'Backstairs Billy') and Stephen Barry (Valet to Prince Charles) who would both hold court along with Hugo telling young gay studs gathered around, inside royal stories to impress them for their own hopeful gains?
Sitting on stools at the bar, all three took turns in telling their stories.
Billy told an embellished story of the late Queen Mother.
"Whilst waiting to be served her Gin & Tonic, the Queen Mum could hear two gay members of her staff arguing in the hallway outside her sitting room. Impatient at being kept waiting so long she eventually called out "When you two old Queens have finished arguing, this Old Queen wants her Gin."

Stephen then told a story trying to top Billy's anecdotes.
"I was walking the Queen's Corgis around the grounds surrounding Buckingham Palace, and came face to face with the Queen. As protocol does not allow staff to approach the Queen, I turned and took another direction, only to come face to face with her again, so I changed direction, yet coming face

*to face once more! The Queen said, "Will you stop still, I've
been trying to speak with you!"*

Hugo of a similar age and in competition to be the main
attraction would also brag of his Royal and celebrity
associations.
*I'm not saying whom? A young member of the Royal Family
was seen lingering his eyes on an attractive soldier at the
Trooping of the Colour.*
*The Queen Mother told him, "I wouldn't if I was you, they
count them before they go back in!*
The young fit boys loved hearing the stories that made them
laugh, from the three aging Queens, who delivered their
stories with haughty actions and mimicking the Queens
articulate voice pronunciation, Cabaret style.
Hugo enjoyed being surrounded by the young studs, giving
him the opportunity to grope their muscular chests, as he
expressed and delivered the stories punchlines.
Right on cue, the boys would laugh to please Hugo's story
telling vanity, and not particularly for his stories, which they
had often heard before which he repeated when he was
drunk, but mainly for their drinks he would buy.

After the crowd had moved on, Rogan suggested they moved
to a side table, and after a few more drinks Hugo was very
drunk and loose-tongued, as Rogan edged him on to repeat
intimate descriptions of having sex with his regular rent boy
Alex, who often hung out there, looking for punters.
Rogan wanted to capture the erotic stories for his secret
recordings.

"You've heard all of this before," Hugo slurred after his third
whisky.
"Yes but it turns me on." Rogan pumped Hugo for more juicy
information.

*"Okay, hic! (Rogan flicked the ON button hidden in his Spy belt, for the recorder to start). (**CLICK**)*
"One night after I closed Ranley and after all the staff left - hic! Alex turned up, and after a few lines of coke he had brought with, and as no one was around, I sat in a Louis the fourteenth style throne chair as he gave me a blowjob. He loved me looking powerful taking the lead from him. He's Cock mad."

Got it! That'll bump up the price! Rogan thought.
He would be able to splice the recordings with videotape of Hugo snorting cocaine.
The spliced together bogus videotape, showing Hugo talking explicitly of having a sexual relationship with a rent boy named Alex, which had been edited, and unbeknown to Hugo, falsely seem that he was referring to his sexual exploits with Viscount Alexander Ranley, 21st in line to the succession of the throne, would be scandalous and priceless! His close friendship and familiarity in referring to the Viscount by shortening his name to Alex would deceive the editors of leading British newspapers, who would pay handsomely for the scoop of the century!
In other captured recordings, Hugo had divulged; *"In private Viscount Alexander and I are very close, and he let's me call him Alex."* This statement when edited, would cement and point to a sexual relationship.
Over several weeks the two blackmailers set to work on Rogan's laptop iMovie App, splicing the video tapes together, including footage of Hugo snorting Cocaine in his home alongside the Royal envelope, as he talked of his relationships both with the rent boy and the Viscount! Adding to the illusion of intimacy and sexual *'frisson'* between the Viscount and him?

It's in the can – The Coffin is sealed!

The Incriminating Video pieced together!

(Tape Insert reference about Viscount Alexander)
"In private Viscount Alexander and me are very close, and he let's me call him Alex."

(Tape Insert reference about rent boy)
"One night after I closed Ranley and after all the staff left, Alex turned up, and as no one was around and a few lines of coke he had brought with, I sat in a Louis the fourteenth style throne chair as..."

(Tape insert reference to Viscount Alexander)
"he made it really hard for me..."

(Tape insert reference to Rent Boy Alex)
"and gave me a blowjob. Alex loved me looking powerful taking the lead from him."

(Tape reference to Viscount Alexander)
"Alex said he can't get enough..."

(Tape reference to Rent Boy Alex)
"He's cock mad!"

Monday morning 11am, Eddy was at Rogan's flat for business. They were now confident to make a telephone call to the newspapers in order to sell the contents of the explosive information on their videotape.

"Right 'oose first?" Eddy said eagerly.
"Think we should try the Mirror first, then the Sun."
"I fought the Sun was more popular?"
"Yes, but it will be better to negotiate a higher price with the Mirror. If I say to the Mirror, I was going to go to the Sun, but thought I would offer it to the Mirror first. They will want to get one over on the Sun and we can push the price up."
"Good finking Batman!" Eddy said as he slapped Rogan on the back.

Rogan would make the telephone call, as Eddy's cockney accent might not be taken too seriously, and sound suspicious of him being able to be in the company of affluent people.

The operator at the Daily Mirror answered. *"Mirror group, can I help you?"*
"Can I speak to the Editor of the Daily Mirror please?"
"Putting you through sir."
"Editors office can I help you?"
"Hello, I would like to speak to the Editor please."
"Can you tell me to what reference you would like to speak with him?" A woman asked who was intercepting the editor's calls.
"I have a video of someone who is divulging having a gay relationship with a member of the Royal Family."
"Did you say a Royal Gay relationship?"
"Yes!"
"I'll put you through to our Royal correspondent."

"But!" Rogan wanted to speak directly with the editor, but was passed on before he could insist.

"Hello Julian Hammond."

"Hello I've got a videotape of someone divulging having a gay sexual relationship with Viscount Alexander Ranley, are you interested?"

"Viscount Ranley, mmm.. I'm not sure anyone is too interested in a junior member of the Royal Family; it might make a few lines? How much are you looking for?"

"As he is a junior member, I'd be willing to hand over the video for seven hundred and fifty thousand."

"Seven hundred and fifty thousand! The Editor laughed. *"We wouldn't even pay ten thousand if it was a member closer to the Queen, and we would need lots of evidence it was genuine. Try the Sun, they need stories, good luck"* The reporter said being catty about the competition as he hung up.

Eddy looked confused at Rogan hanging up so quickly. *"What did he say, what did he say?"* He repeated.

"I don't think he believed me? He said try the Sun!"

"He'll be sorry!" Eddy said sternly.

"Right next!" Rogan said as he looked down at the Sun's telephone number he had written down on his pad, and dialed it.

"Hello Sun." The operator answered.

"Can I speak to the editor please?"

"Putting you through."

"Hello editors office, can I help you?"

For a moment Rogan thought he misdialed to the Mirror again, as the secretary to the Sun editor answered exactly the same standard sentence.

"I have an exclusive story, and will only speak to the editor!" Rogan said in a commanding voice.

Eddy had his ear next to Rogan's, to listen in of what was being said, and turned towards Rogan to give him a nod of approval at being more forceful.

It worked. *"Just one moment."*

The line went silent and then engaged again.

"Could you tell me what type of story you have?" The secretary quizzed.

"A Royal sex scandal." Rogan said, coming straight to the point.

The line went dead again.

"Hello Robert Porter editor of the sun, who am I speaking to?"

"I'll tell you my name if we have a deal."

Eddy still listening into the conversation turned and gave an approving nod again.

"Okay do you want to tell me a little bit more?"

"I have a videotape of someone very close to Viscount Alexander Ranley, who is talking openly about sex he had with him."

"Is this a woman or man?"

"Man."

"Ah so it's gay sex."

"Yes."

"And what type of sex are we or he talking about? Intercourse, Oral, Bondage?"

"All."

"Did any of this happen in Buckingham Palace?"

"No."

"Okay, I think you should come in, so that I can take a look at it."

"Okay."

"Could you come in tomorrow afternoon about three, I can't make it any sooner as I have to get the paper out."

"Yes that will be okay, where do I come to?"

"I'll pass you over to my secretary, she will give you all the details, see you then!"

After Rogan got the details, he hung up and turned to Eddy.

"I don't like it! He didn't sound that interested, I think we should go for the Viscount himself!"

"But he will know it's not true." Eddy said, worried the plan was going down.

"Doesn't matter, he still won't want any scandal attached to his name, that some people will believe. I think you should call Ranley and ask to speak to the Viscount.

"Why me?" Eddy said puzzled at the change of plan.

"Because they know my voice, as I'm always calling to speak with Hugo."

"How much should I ask him for?"

"A hundred thousand. It's still a lot of money, but not that much to him."

"Only a hundred thousand?"

"Get you! Mr flash, you still owe me fifty quid from last week!"

Before calling Ranley and handing his phone to Eddy, Rogan blocked his mobile number so that it would not appear on their calling screen and be recognized as belonging to him. A woman answered the call, and Eddy asked to speak with Viscount Ranley.

"Just a minute." The woman put Eddy through to the Viscount's office, where his male secretary Paul Laser answered.

Thinking he was talking with the Viscount, Eddy went straight in with his blackmail threat.

"I've got twenty seven video tapes of film and audio recordings of your employee Hugo Walford claiming he has been having sexual relations with you. He has described on tape in explicit detail of you performing oral sex on him and your addiction to cocaine. If you want the tapes, they will cost a hundred thousand pounds or I shall sell them to the press. I will want the money by one o'clock today"

Besides being Viscount Alexander's secretary, Paul was an old friend who had first met Alexander at Kings College Cambridge, and knew him well to be a straight heterosexual, and would not doubt him to be anything else.

Thinking ahead of the situation, he wanted to play for time, to discuss the matter with the Viscount.

"I can't get that amount by one, call me back in half an hour and I'll tell you what time I can make it."

Eddy got angry and tried to be more forceful. *"You fucking better get it today, or I'm going to destroy you in the papers. You've got twenty minutes, I'll be calling you back!"* Eddy hung up.

Paul Laser went straight to the Viscount and told him of the call. At first he laughed, thinking of it to be a practical joke, but Paul assured him of the seriousness of it and said they should inform the police at Scotland Yard immediately, to which the Viscount agreed.

Paul made the telephone call, and was put straight through to the counter terrorist squad and told of the threatening call which was directed at the Viscount. The Commander in charge said both the Mirror and Sun had already informed them of the attempt to sell incriminating videotapes to them, and in such cases the press are duty bound to inform the police of any blackmail threats concerning members of the Royal Family.

He informed Paul that a 'Tap' (Listening in and recording calls on their telephone lines) would be placed immediately, and that he should arrange to meet the blackmailer at a suite in the London Hilton Hotel on Park Lane, for 2.00, which the police would arrange under a bogus code name of Mr Bincourt.

Neither Rogan nor Eddy had indicated in their menacing telephone calls, that there were two of them demanding blackmail, and had always referred in conversation to 'I' as singular.

Unbeknown that there were two blackmailers, the Police Commander assured Paul they would be present to arrest the blackmailer in a clandestine 'Police Sting'!

Paul and the Viscount sat by a desk in Paul's office, waiting for the return call. Paul looked at the wall clock, as it was almost twenty minutes.

He had told Clare who answered all incoming calls, to put the calls asking to speak with the Viscount, straight through to his office without questions.

The phone rang on Paul's desk, *"ave you got it?"* Eddy asked, coming straight to the point.

"Yes, but you can't come here, meet me at the London Hilton Hotel on Park Lane, I shall be in a suite under the name of Bincourt at two o'clock."

"Okay no tricks, I want to see the money before I hand over the tapes". Eddy said lowering his voice, to sound heavy and menacing, trying to sound like the film star Robert De Niro in 'The Godfather', as he immediately hung up.

"We've done it! We've hit the jackpot! Oh my god, we're going to be rich! Eddy was excited and kissed Rogan on the cheek. *"Let's go to Ibiza tomorrow to celebrate!*

The Deal is done!

The Hilton Sting!

As they got out of the taxi that took them to the Hilton Hotel, Rogan walked ahead.

"*Rogan, can you get this?*" Eddy shouted out referring to the taxi fare.

"*Haven't you even got ten quid?*"

"*Don't worry, I'll give it back to you after! Anyway you still owe me for your half for the spy glasses and belt!*"

They both laughed as they walked and entered the hotel. At the reception desk they said they were expected by Mr Bincourt to go up to his suite.

The receptionist rang through to the suite.

"*Yes Mr Bincourt is expecting you, please go up to the sixth floor room 618.*"

The bold pair knocked on the door of the suite, and as it opened Rogan took a step back, as the young man standing in front of them was not the Viscount, and unbeknown to them, was an undercover police officer, an agent provocateur who was in charge of the covert operation.

Eddy also seemed mystified to the man's identity. "*We've come to meet Viscount Alexander Ranley, is this the right suite? Is he here?*"

Not revealing his true identity the Police Officer introduced himself. "*No! I am his assistant, he sent me to do business with you, come in.*"

Rogan and Eddy intrepidly walked in, and sat on a sofa facing the seated assistant they believed was sent by the Viscount.

"*Have you got the hundred thousand, we agreed on?*" Rogan demanded.

"*I need to see the tapes first.*" The assistant replied.

"*And we still need to see the colour of money first.*" Eddy piped up in a stand off.

The assistant lifted a black briefcase by his side from the floor, and placed it onto his lap.

'Snap! Snap!' The gold locks of his black crocodile skin case, sounded like a gun salute fanfare for his presentation, and adding to the drama of presenting the stacked hundred thousand fifty pound bank notes.

Eddy opened a Tablet he was holding and turned the screen toward the agent, and at the same time pressing the play button.

A film begun to play showing Hugo on his knees at a coffee table snorting lines of cocaine and talking of having oral sex with Alex and in the same breath referring to the Viscount. After watching five minutes of the video, the assistant laughed.

"None of this is true! And I can tell it has been spliced together!"

Eddy was angry, snapped the tablet down over the screen and stood up. "Yeah! Well that's wot you fink, wait till the papers get 'old of it! I can see the 'eadlines now, 'Viscount Ranley in line to the 'frone is already a Queen!"

"Okay, okay how many recordings do you have?"

"Twenty seven" Eddy said proudly.

"How did you manage to get that amount?" The assistant quizzed, hoping for more information Eddy's loose tongue would reveal.

"It's taken five weeks, so you're getting them cheap at twenty grand a week for our hard work!"

Suddenly the bedroom door flew open at the same time as the front door. Ten armed policemen from the terrorist unit burst in; dressed in black combat uniform with bulletproof vests, helmets and face shields, whilst ten more were outside standing in the corridor with their firearms at the ready. Pointing their MP5SF rifles at Rogan and Eddy, several of the officers screamed in frightening authoritative voices, as they repeated their commands.

*"Get on the fucking floor! Get on the fucking floor! Get on the fucking floor! Don't move! Don't fucking move! Put your hands on your heads! Now! I said fucking **NOW**!"*

Both Rogan and Eddy threw themselves onto the floor each side of the coffee table that was between them and the assistant, and put their hands behind their heads.

Two police officers leaned over pulled their hands behind their backs, and handcuffed them whilst they were still trembling.

As they were pulled up, one of the police officers questioned them before proceeding to search their pockets.

"Do you have anything in your pockets that may be sharp or harm me?"

The pair replied in unison. *"No." "No."*

After frisking them and searching their pockets, both of their wallets were taken from their inside jacket pockets and handed to the main officer, who had portrayed the Viscounts agent, and who they were now standing in front of.

Opening each in turn, he took out various credit cards and gym membership cards, and read out the names printed on them, as he turned towards Rogan and Eddy in succession.

"Are you Rogan Patrick Ford?"

"Yes." Rogan said sheepishly.

"Are you Edward Greggs?"

"Yea, Yea - Yes." Eddy said still shaking.

A small clear plastic bag containing cocaine fell to the floor from Eddy's wallet.

The undercover officer reached to the floor and picked it up, as he revealed his position.

"I am DC Stephen Riley of the terrorist squad. I am not interested in this, but I am arresting you Rogan Patrick Ford and Edward Greggs on charges of trying to extort money under Section 21 of the theft act 1968 for making unwarranted demands with menaces in order to attain personal gain or project loss on another.

*You do not have to say anything, but it may harm your defence if you do not mention when questioned, something which **you*** *later rely on in court. Anything you do say may be given in evidence. ... You are not obliged to say anything, but anything you do say will be noted and may be used in evidence.*

Eddy looked white with shock, and had urinated, wetting the front of his trousers from fear as the police rushed in.

"We were only joking." Eddy said trying to make light of the serious charges.

DC Riley laughed. *"So were we! My name is not Bincourt but you have - Been Caught!"*

The impregnable Royal firm succeeds.

Sex, Drugs and Video Tapes

Hugo was relaxing at home having a glass of whisky and watching television. A regular TV 'Soap' series was playing, and although he was not a fan, he enjoyed the farcical antics in the storyline that made him chuckle, and forget any problems of the day whilst working at Ranley.

The internal house phone rang right in the middle of a serious scene in the soap, which had him hooked and he was now going to miss. Hugo walked briskly up the hallway where the phone was located. *"What does he want?"* he mumbled referring to Peter the concierge.

He lifted the receiver. *"Hello Peter"*.

"Mr Walford, there are some Police officers here and want to talk with you".

Hugo was puzzled of their visit. *"Yes Peter, please send them up"*.

Anxious and hovering in his hall, Hugo waited for his door buzzer to announce their arrival.

Although expecting it, the sound of the buzzer made Hugo jump.

Opening the door immediately, Hugo with half a smile greeted the two officers, who were wearing suits and not Police uniforms.

"Mr Walford," One of them asked.

"Yes" Hugo replied curiously, as he realized they were not visiting about his next door neighbour Mrs Osband, having a recent bitter argument with him, complaining of his sound system being too loud late at night over the weekend, when Rogan and Eddy had been partying drunk and dancing around. This looked serious?

The officers had wallets in their hands, and opened them to show their warrant identification cards, which bear embossed hologram official stamps and their photos.

"I'm chief agent Alan Collingsworth and my colleague is agent Martin Phillips, we are from the counter terrorist department of MI5".

Hugo was shocked at their titles, and suddenly the embossed letters and number of MI5 was leaping out at him from the cards. He felt his blood sink to his feet, realizing immediately this was of a serious matter to have MI5 calling at his door.

"Please come through to the living room."

The two officers sat on the sofa facing Hugo. "We are from the terrorist squad at Scotland Yard," Agent Collingsworth repeated again, driving home their importance as he broke into a smile to relax Hugo who was still looking shocked.

"This is a major matter, and we would be pleased if you could help us in our enquiries."

Hugo still looked puzzled. "Yes certainly, what is this about Agent Collingsworth?"

"Please call me Alan," He replied as he presented a friendly demeanor to Hugo by giving his first name.

"Are you familiar with Rogan Patrick Ford and Edward Greggs?"

"Rogan Ford, yes, Edward Greggs would he be Eddy?" Hugo guessed.

"Yes of course! You would probably know him as Eddy?"

"What's happened, are they alright, has there been an accident, have they stolen the crown jewels?" Hugo threw in a humorous question, which unbeknown to him at that time, was very near the mark!

Agent Collingsworth continued, "They've both been arrested for attempted blackmail."

Hugo's heart sunk and again his blood drained from his face, giving him a pale complexion.

Agent Phillips saw the shock on Hugo's face, and took over from Alan. "Mr Walford, may I call you Hugo? Hugo nodded.

"My name is Martin, We are here to interview you as a witness and not as a suspect, you may be a victim involving a Royal Blackmail attempt."

As he got up from his chair, Hugo repeated, *"Arrested! Blackmail! Do you mind if I have a drink, can I offer you both one?"*

"Thank-you no, we are on duty."

Hugo poured another whisky for himself, and took a big gulp as he sunk back into his armchair.

"We understand you work at a luxury goods store Ranley in Mayfair, and are very close to the owner Viscount Alexander Ranley."

"Yes."

"How close are you?"

Hugo felt uncomfortable with the line of questioning and wondered where the series of questions were leading too? Slightly nervous Hugo took a sip of his drink, and spoke in a unequivocal way.

"He's my boss! I have the utmost respect for him as a person and not because he is a member of the Royal Family."

"Yes Hugo, I'm sure you do" Alan said assuring Hugo he believed him.

"Are you Gay?" Martin slid in a personal question.

"Yes, its no longer a crime you know!" Hugo quickly came back in defense and slightly annoyed that his sexual preferences were up for question.

"What has my sexual preferences have anything to do with your investigation? I believe ones sexual desires have nothing to do with anyone else, as long as they are not forcing them onto anyone who isn't interested. You know the American author and screen playwright Gore Vidal said, 'There is no such thing as homosexuality, it's what two men do in bed!"

The two officers laughed, *"He's got a point!"* Alan said to Martin.

"I'm sorry I didn't mean to offend you Hugo, but our questions are pertinent to the offence". Martin apologized.

"Well could you please be a little more specific and fill me into the nature of Rogan and Eddy's offence, it sounds pretty serious".

"Yes it is!" Alan's face had turned stony-faced from the friendly smiling face he had at first.

"We have seized tapes and video recordings from Ford and Greggs, of you talking and describing sex acts and sharing drugs between you and Viscount Ranley, along with taking and supplying cocaine to others. The Video Tapes we have in our possession show you clearly cutting and taking cocaine. We are not too concerned about the drugs, but we need to establish your accusations about gay sex acts with Viscount Ranley. You do understand these accusations against the Viscount are explosive to the Queen and the Royal Family!"

"What accusations! Sex acts with Viscount Ranley! I have NEVER had any sexual relations with him!" Hugo was angry at the suggestion and was shouting his denial to the agents, as he moved forward to the edge of his seat.

Calming down and forlorn close to tears, Hugo said softly, *"Are you telling me, they both filmed and recorded me in my home?"*

"Yes I'm afraid so, it seems the covert recordings took place over a five month period."

"Five months!" Hugo was horrified at being deceived and set up.

"We have confiscated twenty seven tapes."

Still in denial, believing he would soon wake up from the continuing nightmare being unraveled, he asked, *"Where were they arrested?"*

"We set a trap, known as a 'Sting' at the London Hilton Hotel." The information brought a smile to Hugo's face. *"Ah yes Rogan would fall for that, spent most of his time wandering around hotel bars looking for rich pickings!"*

"We had the room completely bugged with sound equipment and cameras to record them, and If it's any comfort? You could say we turned the tables on them!"

Martin had taken over the conversation, as Hugo sat dumfounded at the facts being set out before him. For a moment he felt as if he was in the Soap series he had been watching earlier, with a miserable storyline, and if only, very soon would be interrupted by a TV commercial. How nice the irritating TV commercial of a woman singing and dancing around her kitchen, clutching a bottle of Fairy washing-up liquid would now seem for relief!

The two agents suddenly seemed like Rottweiler dogs biting and not letting go until they had answers to their questions.

"We shall be bringing a Police photographer here to photograph the rooms in your flat."

"Why?" Hugo said shaking.

"We need to see if they match up with the video footage we seized".

"When?"

"This evening when we've finished. You've got a beautiful home." Alan added looking around playing the 'Good Cop' as opposed to Martin being the 'Bad Cop' and showing a kindness to Hugo, who was clearly still in a state of shock.

"I imagine lots of your paintings and ornaments come from Ranley?" Alan said delving deeper.

"Yes perks of the job, I get great discounts."

"Does the Viscount come here and socialize with you?"

"No! Alex has never been to my home!" Hugo snapped emphatically.

"Alex? Who's Alex?" Alan played being ignorant.

Hugo was confused by the barrage of questions that were being directed to him, and nervous of his own outburst that revealed his familiarity with the Viscount.

"I mean, I mean, Alexander."

Alan saved Hugo's disclosure for another question. *"I suppose he knows of all your personal purchases from Ranley?"*

The question had a hidden agenda, that Hugo had furnished his home with objects d' art that might have left Ranley through the back door?

Hugo was no fool and caught the drift of the question, as he answered in a very precise clipped tone of voice stating the rules. *"Yes! The Viscount signs off all purchases made by the staff."*

Although Martin had stated Hugo was being questioned as a witness, Hugo felt uneasy at the line of questioning which was suggesting something was a bit more suspicious to his character.

Picking up on Hugo's earlier disclosure of addressing Viscount Alexander by abbreviating his name, Martin took over the questioning. *"As executive manager of Ranley, I assume you have a close relationship with Viscount Ranley, how do you normally address him? Is it always Alex?*

Hugo felt nervous, as Martin was focusing more of his questions on Viscount Ranley, their relationship and the store, and did not understand why the questions had anything to do with Rogan or Eddy, which the agents still had not revealed.

"In public I refer to him as Viscount Alexander Ranley."

"Never Alex?" Martin interrupted.

"Yes I was just about to say, when we are together, I shorten his name to Alex."

Martin picked up on Hugo's admission to their closeness. *"Mmm? Together?"*

"Yes together when we are alone".

Martin raised an eyebrow, *"Alone? Yes I understand,"* and smiled in a knowing acceptance of Hugo's relationship, and reading more into Hugo's answer, that made the hole even deeper that he was digging for himself.

"Why are you asking of what I call him?"

"We have already pointed out to you Hugo, we have video tapes. They do show you clearly referring to Viscount Alexander as Alex, which seems very friendly considering he is a member of the Royal Family. Are you sure there was not more to your relationship?"

Hugo was furious and stood up shouting at the two agents. *"I have told you, I am an employee of Ranley and respect my boss Viscount Alexander Ranley."* He had referred to Alex by his full title so as to distance himself from the familiarity they had built up between them.

"Okay Hugo, please calm down, we just need to be sure of your relationship as the charges against Ford and Greggs depend on the authenticity of video tapes we have seized from them."

Hugo was frustrated "Please just tell me, what this is all about?"

Alan leaned forward, "Ford and Greggs have been charged with intent to obtain money by means of blackmail, concerning either false damaging accusations or information that may be proven true, and in this case, cause a damaging blow to the Monarchy! On the tapes you are seen talking about sexual acts you have had with Alex "

Hugo sat motionless trying to take in the growing horror of the building nightmare of what Alan had just explained to him.

The front door buzzer sounded.

Martin stood up. "That will be the photographer. When we arrived I told your porter, we were expecting him and to send him straight up, I'll let him in."

Hugo just nodded and took another drink of his whisky.

Martin came back into the living room and introduced the photographer who was in his 60s.

"Hugo this is Cyril, 'Mr Happy Snappy' as he is known around MI5." Cyril laughed at Martin's introduction, who was lightening the atmosphere, and then resumed his reason for being there as he pulled out some photos from his case.

Hugo did not show any reaction, as he was still in a state of shock at his world being turned upside down.

Cyril showed one of the photos to Alan. "These have been copied from the video tapes. I've been told by the chief to match them with the photos I take today."

Alan took the photo showing Hugo kneeling and snorting a line of cocaine on a coffee table, and held it out in front of him, as he looked at it and compared it to his view across the living room.

"Yes, that's the coffee table, and the glass naked male torso standing on it is the same from the video".

Cyril reeled off a series of shots from his camera, the whirling sound of the cameras mechanism reeling in Hugo's ears.

"Is that Lalique?" Cyril asked Hugo as he pointed to the figurine.

"Yes!" Hugo replied without looking up.

"Thought so, my wife loves Lalique, she's half French and when she was young visited the Lalique factory in Wingen-sur-Moder France. She still goes on about a glass multi-coloured chandelier she saw there, hinting at me to buy one, but I said to her it would be too ornate in our council flat!" Cyril said laughing.

"Yea, come on Mr interior designer, you've got another photo to take." Alan said as he looked at a second photo, that had also been copied from the tapes.

"Hugo where is your bedroom?"

Hugo looked up, and motioned with his hand to another small hall, leading to his bedroom.

"All we need Cyril is the entrance of the doorway, with the door half open." Alan instructed.

Cyril walked to the bedroom door and pulled it towards him in the half closed position.

"Is that okay," he asked looking back to Alan, who was studying the details in the photo.

"No it's too closed, a bit more open so that we can see the bed." Cyril altered it. "Okay?"

"Perfect!" Alan confirmed the view again of the photo image taken from the secret Videotapes.

Cyril's job done, Alan saw him out of the flat.

Martin was writing down some notes of their conversation with Hugo.

"Okay Hugo, we are leaving now, and will need to interview you again tomorrow at eleven-thirty am. Although there are no charges against you at this moment, I must advise you to have your solicitor present. I know this is a massive shock for you, but I reiterate, it is in your best interest to tell us the truth of your associations with Ford, Greggs and Viscount Alexander

Ranley, this matter is top secret, and with caution under no circumstances are you to discuss it with anyone else! Hope you manage to get some sleep?"

After Hugo saw the Detectives out to the door, he went to his bedroom and screamed as he threw himself onto his bed crying.

Reaching for a framed photo on his bedside table of Rogan standing behind him, with his arms wrapped around and his head resting on Hugo's shoulder, Hugo kissed the photo.

"Rogan! Rogan! What have you done to me? I loved you, gave you everything. I knew you weren't attracted to me for my looks, but you always made me feel good, and now you have made me feel bad, were you lying to me all of the time. I loved you... I loved you."

At eleven thirty the next morning only officer Martin Phillips arrived.

Hugo greeted him at his front door.

"Good morning Hugo, we would like you to make your statement at the station instead of here."

Hugo was taken aback. "You said yesterday you were going to interview me here?"

"Yes, but we now think it best for you to come to the station. Is your solicitor here?"

"Yes." Hugo turned on his heel and walked quickly down the hall to the living room where his solicitor was waiting.

"Samuel! They want me to go to the Police Station, you will come won't you?"

"Of course." Samuel said as he stood up.

Hugo grabbed his jacket and walked with Samuel back up the hallway to the officer and introduced him.

"This is my solicitor Samuel Bloom."

Martin introduced himself as he showed his identity card.

"I have a car waiting for us."

At the station Hugo and his solicitor were shown into an interview room, where they sat alone side by side on bolted down chairs.

The room was stark and empty of any other items, except for a built in recording machine also screwed down onto the bolted down table.

Hugo had never been inside a police stations interview room and commented to his solicitor.

"I don't know why they bolt everything down, I can't imagine anyone wanting to steal the furniture here?"

Samuel gave a slight smile. *"They secure everything, in case some criminal decides to go off on one, and start throwing chairs!"*

A man in his late 50s, with dark skin and grey thinning hair, dressed in a smart black suit suddenly entered.

He smiled and looked friendly at Hugo, as he put out his hand to shake.

"Mr Walford pleased to meet you, under what must be very upsetting circumstances?" He said with a slight eastern accent.

Samuel Bloom took out a card from his inside pocket, which bore his name and the company firm of solicitors he was representing, and handed it to the officer.

"Thank you Mr Bloom. My name is Ari Kapoor I am from MI6 anti-terror for the royal protection squad. MI5 have passed this matter onto us, as it is of National interest and importance concerning the monarchy.

I have gone through all of the notes that MI5 took from you, and twenty seven video footage tapes we recovered after acquisition raids on Ford and Greggs homes, and believe you have been set up as a victim, and in turn they made it sound as if you are saying incriminating remarks of sexual relations with Viscount Alexander Ranley. There is video footage of you taking cocaine, and implying Viscount Alexander has indulged with you on occasions. This will never be mentioned, as it will take us down a different path, so from now on that never happened! Nor will any of the footage of you snorting cocaine be released, that too never happened! It is spurious and without foundation!"

Ari Kapoor of MI6 had just whitewashed the details! By doing this he made it more of a clean-cut case against the two bumbling blackmailers.

"We had Ford and Greggs under surveillance as soon as they had made their demand phone calls to the press, and after the press alerted us."

"How did you know where they were?" Hugo asked.

"We traced both of their mobiles, by the transmitter masts being used for their mobile connections, so we knew exactly where they were. But we needed them to go through with the blackmail demand, to make it stand up in court, and a sting was set."

After being interviewed, and his written statement of associations with Rogan and Eddy, Hugo was told he would be summoned to the Old Bailey Criminal Law Courts in due course, where high profile crimes are tried, and that he would be able to go home without any charges, as he would be a witness for the Crown Prosecution.

The Old Bailey Trial

At the trial held at the Old Bailey, the names of both Viscount Alexander Frederick Ranley and Hugo Peregrine Walford were withheld, only referring to them anonymously as witness 'A' and witness 'B', so that their names would not be known in the public domain and spare them any unwanted publicity that may reflect on the Royal Family.

A screen was erected between Hugo, and the public gallery, so that only the judge, jury, barristers and lawyers would be able to see him, as he was cross-examined.

Viscount Frederick Ranley was not summoned to court, and was allowed to give a short denial of the accusations, as evidence by video link, directly and only to the Judge.

Rogan had been approached by an English businessman and convicted fraudster to represent him, believing he was a Solicitor. He had been involved in legal cases for high-profile notorious defendants worldwide; and had no legal qualifications or registered to work as an advocate in the UK. When the National Press exposed him, Rogan dropped him and got another bona-fide Solicitor and QC.

The defence QC said the police had over reacted, by sending 30 police officers to take part in the capture of his client at the Hilton Hotel, and that the whole operation was farcical. The prosecutor took exception to the claim by the QC of the Police operation, and counter re-acted in naming Rogan as a *'Walter Mitty'* fantasist character.

During the trial Rogan and Eddy said, they had secretly made the video tape recordings, in order to expose and out witness B as being malicious for his made up derogatory stories, against witness A and the Royal Family,.

Rogan made an alarming statement. *"I felt sick at the comments and stories witness B said about the Royals, slagging them off making disparaging remarks."* And added

"He told me he had spiked young men's drinks with the 'date rape' drug rohypnol in order to sexually assault them."

Unusually the judge smiled and there were sniggers from the jury, when Eddy being cross-examined in the court dock claimed. *"I didn't want any money, I just wanted witness A to know how evil Witness B was, so it would be nice if the Royals would take care of me now for helping them!"*

Audio and Visual technology experts, were called to give statements to the authenticity of the dubious video tapes, and verify they had been doctored, by being spliced together to give the impression of incriminating and damaging accusations.

The Crown Prosecution did not believe the claims of Rogan and Eddy, and the plea by both of 'Not Guilty' statements, were not accepted in defence.
In summing up and advising the Jury, the presiding Judge said. *"The defendants Rogan Patrick Ford and Edward Greggs defence are both questionable and unreliable. They had secretly filmed and used audio recording equipment to falsely incriminate an innocent party and make menacing demands of extortion remuneration, for an odious crime and false implications."*

Rogan Ford and Edward Greggs were found guilty and sentenced to five years imprisonment at high security prison Belmarsh.
Due to the secrecy of his name, imposed by the Old Bailey Court Judge, Viscount Alexander Ranley's name was unscathed, and he understood Hugo had not been involved with the farcical blackmail attempt, and was like him, a victim!
He suggested Hugo take three weeks off for a holiday to get over the stressful period, which Hugo did, and took the

opportunity to relax in his home retreat, high in the mountain hills of Marbella.

(The 3-week trial had cost in excess of £1 million.)

Whilst in prison, Rogan was described by the press headline, which had been picked up on by the Court description:
'A 'WALTER MITTY FANTASIST WHO ATTEMPTED A ROYAL BLACKMAIL PLOT, CONTINUES HIS PLAYBOY WAYS.'
Over his bunk bed, he had adorned the walls with colour pages that he had ripped out of magazines, taken from the prison library and stuck with toothpaste.
A red Ferrari sports car, top male model David Gandy wearing a sharp cut navy suit, a Rolex watch, a sexy pose by Beyonce and a white yacht moored in the Monaco marina, were all reminders of the life he craved for, and which led him to being incarcerated at her Majesty's pleasure.

During break time, he played the dashing young Master Spy, as he impressed and entertained other prisoners, whilst swanking around his cell wearing a black silk dressing gown with a gold Chinese dragon motif embroidered on the back, his mother had brought in on a visit, and smoking cheroot cigars he bought from the prison shop canteen.
Amongst his other wall hangings, a torn picture page of a Jeroboam bottle of Bollinger Champagne, which helped him fantasise he was at a cocktail party, as he sipped the illegal 'Hooch' drink, that had fermented after being brewed from fruit, potato, tomato, sugar, and tap water, which was a long way from his Champagne lifestyle.
Inheriting some of Hugo's ways of impressing those who would listen of his encounters with the rich and famous, his prison friends would laugh as he told stories of his escapades with the many who would pay for his sexual services!

The prisoners referred to him as *'Champagne Charlie'*, which *were* two of his individual pleasurable vices on the outside.

Just short of two and a half years, both Rogan and Eddy were released and went their separate ways.

Rogan swore to himself that he would never speak to Eddy again, as he could not forgive him, for trying to put all of the blame on him whilst being cross examined in the court dock, saying; *"It was all Rogan's idea, I didn't wanna do it, I love the Royals."*

They were both put on probation, and electronically tagged, which was fitted to an ankle, and would send regular signals to a receiver unit installed in their home linked to a probation base, for surveillance curfew conditions, which were set to be at home by 7pm daily for 3 months, and expected to attend weekly meetings with their probation officers.

Prison had taken a toll on Rogan's looks and weight. He had not bothered to go regularly to the Prison Gym and although the meals were poorly cooked, he ate as much as he could of greasy chips, crisps, chocolate, biscuits and sugary drinks bought from the canteen shop, giving him an energy kick, but made him over weight.

At 16 stone he hardly looked like he had been starving in Prison.

His usual beauty regime, of using moisturisers and Botox injections every several months had ceased. He had bought a bottle of vegtable olive oil from the canteen, which he used occasionally on his face and now thinning hair.

His finger and toe nails had grown long, as the canteen had run out of nail clippers, and Cheng his Metrosexual Guru at the 'Hero' salon did not do prison visits. Biting his fingernails was his only option until the clippers were back in stock, but getting his foot up to his mouth took more effort.

Gone were his boyish looks as he was now heading towards his forties.

Punters would not be queuing up for him anymore; it was time to make way for younger flesh.

He had lost his rented flat and was broke due to paying his solicitors and barristers fees, and although he did not want to, his only option was to live with his mother again, who had moved from her Shepherds Market Mayfair flat, back to Fulham.

Rich men were far and few, as she too was aging, and not able to compete with the young 'Sugar Daddy Dolls'.

She had stored his clothes, mobile and a few personal items, and as she lived in a one bedroom flat, he had to sleep on a sofa as he used to do, when he was younger, which was a major downfall from the luxurious flat he had been living in. Whilst Lisa was out, Rogan searched her bedroom, looking for something worth to sell, to pay for a trip to Dubai where wealth was King and he would be a Prince.

In prison, a couple of inmates who had been sentenced for running illegal male brothels and laundering money proceeds, told him of many Arab men who would play the field for sex with British men, denying to themselves that they were Gay, and just needed to release their sexual urges before going home to their wives!

Rogan had always thought there to be a fine line between *'Straight and Gay'*, usually two pints of beer!

Over the past years he had heard from some of the other Gigolos and rent boys who told stories, of being flown in private jets to millionaire playgrounds around the world, staying in luxurious hotels, and palaces, given gifts of gold Cartier bracelets, Rolex watches, gold chain and diamond necklaces, designer clothes, money. Everything Rogan had lived for.

There was a bitchy jealous reaction by some of the guys looking for their big catch, to a story going around, of a young cockney builder being given a convertible Saab Cabriolet car, after spending one night with an Arab Prince.

Rogan recalled all of the jealous comments.

"Bet he stole it." "Probably threatened blackmail." "I heard it was taken back, after they had a row."

'Sounds like Eddy?' He thought.

Rogan stared at his face in Lisa's dressing table mirror, and placed his hands on his cheeks pulling them back and then releasing.

"Not much difference. Still got it!" He mumbled, kidding himself.

Rummaging through her Jewellery box on the dressing table, he threw necklaces and bracelets down again, as her jewellery was paste imitations of diamonds and rubies; she would wear with bravado to impress any rich men she was out to catch, and not worth anything to enable him to buy his plane ticket, or even a taxi to the airport!

At the back of her lingerie draw he felt a long hard object, wrapped in a pair of her panties.

'Woops mothers dildo.' He thought, but as he unwrapped the panties a rose gold pen encrusted with diamonds and sapphires, dropped out!

'The bitch! I love you!' He said out loud, realising it was the pen encrusted with real diamonds; she had stolen from Carter Bass when they were on board his yacht 'La Dolce Vita' in Marbella.

Although he knew his mother was a compulsive liar, at the time he believed her when she said, the courier had collected it to be delivered back to Carter.

On his Smart-phone, he went onto the Internet and Googled 'Top Hotels in Dubai'.

Burj Al Arab Jumeirah Hotel was top of the list. *"Wowee! Seven fucking stars!"*

Rogan telephoned the hotel and booked a suite for that evening. He had found Lisa's credit card lying on top of her

dressing table, and gave the account details to the hotel as a hold on the booking.
The hotel would not ask any other questions, as the clientele of Arab Princes often booked a floor of suites for themselves and entourage of staff, and would probably be able to buy the hotel!

After cutting off the electric tagging plastic band from his ankle, he had to move fast, as the action would send a signal to a base unit, and a police patrol car would be sent to his registered address to investigate the interference.
Hurriedly he threw some clothes into a suitcase, hardly bothering to fold them, and grabbed his passport along with Lisa's credit card, in case he needed it.
Although money was tight Rogan was racing against time and with the precious pen in his grip that would be his means to start a new life in Dubai, if he could sell or pawn it?
He took a minicab to a Pawnbroker.

'BENJYS PAWNBROKERS' off Bethnal Green Road in East London, was known to deal in 'Dodgy goods?' No questions asked?

'The Moving finger writes; and having writ, moves on'.
(Whatever one does in one's life, is one's own responsibility and cannot be changed). **Omar Khayam.**

Standing behind a glass security screen, the pawnbroker slid a tray lined with a black velvet pad under a gap of the screen.
Rogan placed the pen on the tray and slid it back for the assistant to inspect.
"That's a beauty, I've not seen one of these before, what make is it?"
"It's a Montblanc Boheme Papillion, I was left it in a will."
Rogan said proudly and with superiority putting on an inflection of upper class speech, making changes in his pitch

that indicated confidence, finality, power and certainty, as if he was used to such extravagant possessions.

He had read books to self teach, on the Art of Conversation and the use of verbal conversation, using speech techniques for his gains.

"I need to Google it for more information."

Rogan started to get anxious, wondering if the pawnbroker would have enough money to pawn or buy it?"

"Okay, I can give you five thousand against it."

"What!" Rogan was shocked at the poultry offer. *"It's worth about a hundred and fifty thousand. It's rose gold, those are diamonds and sapphires embedded!"*

"Yes maybe, but I can't buy it, as I don't have a hundred and fifty thousand on me at the moment!" He joked. *"And nobody is going to be able to afford to buy it that quickly, unless they are a billionaire, and there aren't that many walking up Bethnal Green Road! I will be stuck with it! I can only look at the deal as a loan against it, for a three-month reclaim. The best I can do is five thousand five hundred."*

"In cash?"

"Yes"

"Okay let's do it." Rogan said reluctantly, realising his mother had hung onto it, as it was difficult to sell, and in the hope she would some day get closer to selling it at the retail price. Time was running out, the Police would probably be at his home address by now, and there would be a warrant for him to be re-arrested. Dubai was his next stop.

Lisa arrived home and saw the drawers in her dressing table had been left open. Frantically searching for the pen in her lingerie draw, her heart missed a beat. *"The Bastard!"*

At Heathrow he bought an Airline ticket with British Airways, and telephoned the hotel to say what time he would be arriving, so that their Limo Service could collect him.

A man wearing a chic white double-breasted jacket, with a gold 'J' monogrammed on his breast pocket, and navy trousers, stood by the arrival gate, with a **Burj Al Arab Jumeirah Hotel** name board held in front of him, that had hand written on it; **Mr Ford.** *"Hi I'm Rogan Ford."*

"Hello Sir, I am from your hotel for your collection transfer to Burj Al Arab Jumeirah, let me take your case"
"Thankyou"
They walked outside the airport, where a white Rolls Royce was waiting parked by the exit doors, it's engine gently purring.
Although it was evening, the hot air embraced Rogan top to toe, as if four hairdryers were set to HOT and pointed at him.
"Did you have a good flight Sir?" The hotel porter asked as he lifted Rogan's suitcase and placed it into the trunk.
"Yes, wow it's hot"
The porter laughed as he opened the door for Rogan to get in.
"Hot! It's only twenty-eight centigrade this evening, should be forty-three tomorrow. You'll be nice and cool in here. I've kept the cooling system on for you, and if you open the bar door in the back of my seat there are drinks for your choice and ice."
As the porter closed the door, it made a solid heavy thud that was the sound of expensive quality.
The porter sat in the front with the chauffeur, and Rogan sunk back into the soft cream leather seats, sipping his drink. As they drove past some beggars sitting in the doorways, Rogan thought back to his days in prison and the

small cell where he lay on his bed, closed his eyes, and transported himself to the five star hotels and exclusive shops he had patronised when he was free.

He would imagine himself walking through hotel lobbies, browsing through expensive designer wear in west-end stores and dancing the night away in exclusive London nightclubs.

The beggars were a reminder, of how when all is stripped away, you don't have any place, or acceptance in society.

His wild imagination in prison had carried him through, along with his daily mantra of *'Don't let the Bastards get you'*, and now he was on his way to one of the best hotels in the world!

As he walked into his suite, Rogan was drawn straight to the window, which was floor to ceiling. The panoramic vista was breathtaking, taking in the view of the Arabian Sea.

As he turned, the young bellboy wearing a pale blue uniform, comprising of short waisted fitted jacket adorned with three lines of gold buttons from his shoulders to his waist, epaulets with one holding his white gloves as a sign of perfection, tight trousers and a small pillar box hat bearing the hotels logo 'J' in gold, placed his suitcase on a stand and said in broken English. *"Would you like me to unpack for you Sir?"*

"No thank-you," Rogan smiled and pressed 50 Dirham; (Equivalent to £10) into his hand.

"Thank you Sir, If you need anything during your stay, please ask me, Nightclubs for boys and beautiful girls, or just boys? I know them all. 'IL Paradiso Club' is new and the most beautiful boys go there! I'm usually around the hotels lobby, my name is Jabbad." He said giving a cheeky wink and a cute flashing smile that beamed from his bronzed face.

"Jabbad." Rogan repeated.

"Yes it means good-looking in Arabic."

"Thank you." Rogan laughed at the bellboy's forward remarks, who looked about 18, and thought the tone of his remarks were a come on, offering him sex and probably a

further tip! If anyone was going to be paid for sex it would be himself, after all he had made a career from it!

After a rest and shower, Rogan dressed in a cool white linen shirt and navy linen trousers went to the roof top bar on the 27th floor, where as always he felt comfortable back in his stomping ground and manner.

Sitting on a bar stool he perused the drinks menu.

'Eyes Looking At Heaven', 'Mrs Big' 'Touch Me Not' were listed as Signature Cocktails.

"Mmm? I'll just have a Margarita to get the night started!" He ordered from the barman hovering to take his order.

The barman served the drink and placed dishes of olives, slices of beef, and truffle pommes allumettes along side.

"I didn't order these," Rogan said as he pushed them back towards the barman.

"They come with the first drink sir"

"Thank you"

After a few more drinks of his usual tipple, (whisky with one piece of ice), Rogan was in the mood to catch a Tiger Shark? (His term for a rich punter)

The barman put the drinks bill on a silver salver and placed it in front of Rogan. *"Would you like to sign Sir, it will be put on your room?"*

Rogan gazed at the expensive bill that took his breath away, and calculated in his head.

Forgetting himself he said out loud, *"Wow! 355 Dirham for 3 drinks!"* (Equivalent to 25 pounds a drink)

A handsome young man sitting on a stool at the bar one away from Rogan, turned and reached out his hand, taking hold of the bill Rogan was clutching.

"I'll take care of that."

Rogan broke into a broad smile at the generous gesture from the good-looking stranger.

This was his line! He thought, when he roamed hotel bars looking for rich pickings, often paying for a strangers drink as an icebreaker, and who would end up paying lots more in return for his services.

"Thank-you, but no but really you can't." Rogan half-heartedly pulled back on the bill slip the stranger was holding on to, hoping the young Arabic guy would win their tug of war!

"I insist!"

Rogan was transfixed on the long black eyelashes and big brown eyes of the sexy hunky creature, wearing skinny white jeans and a silk Versace design shirt, bearing the Versace Medusa motif head, surrounded by half naked men with gold crowns and serpents wrapped around their shoulders and body. The first four buttons of the shirt were undone, which revealed his smooth hairless toned chest. His muscular 'V' shape torso and small hips, was obvious he had a strict workout regime.

Putting out his hand to shake and in a charming Arabic accent said. *"I am Prince Aman Fahid Salama, good to meet you,"*

Bingo! A Prince! My ship has come in! Rogan thought with delight. *"My names Rogan Ford, that's very kind of you to buy my drinks."*

"You are a visitor to our country, it is a blessing that you come here."

And it's a blessing I met you! Rogan thought.

On his wrist amongst black leather and gold bangles, the Prince was wearing a gold watch with loose diamonds under the glass face.

Taking hold of the Prince's wrist, Rogan pulled it forward towards him to take a closer look. *"I'm fascinated by your beautiful watch with loose diamonds."*

The Prince demonstrated by shaking his wrist. *"Ha, ha, ha, yes it's a game you have to shake the watch to get the diamonds in the holes to find out what time it is!"*

The time could still be told, as the gold hands moved around the empty holes, but it was a novelty, a very expensive novelty!

222

"I just popped in here to see my friend who is one of the directors of the hotel, but he is busy, so I thought I would take a drink whilst I was here."

Rogan looked at the Prince's drink sitting on the bar.

"Is that orange juice?"

"Yes my father His Excellency Sheik Mahood Bin Salama, does not like me to drink alcohol, although I have a UAE residency permit. He says as Muslims we must set an example. Although I am twenty-seven, he still thinks of me as a child, but I do drink in the nightclubs where everyone else are on clouds. How long have you been here?"

"I've just arrived."

"Wonderful, I will show you Dubai by night, come on."

Rogan downed the last of his drink and jumped off his stool. As they walked outside of the hotel, the hot air hit Rogan again.

"I'm not sure I can take this heat."

"It's even hotter in my bedroom, ha,ha,ha." Aman said laughing as he winked at Rogan.

The two stood on the steps of the hotel, as the doorman turned towards a line of parked cars. Rolls Royce, Lamborghini, Bentley, Ferrari, took their place waiting for their super rich owners.

"They will bring my car." Aman said confidently as the doorman blew several toots on a silver whistle and a wave towards the parking valets, who would drive and deliver the car to clients waiting.

A golden Lamborghini with personalized number plates '5EXY BOY' pulled up in front of them, and as the doors opened horizontally like Aeroplane wings, a parking valet jumped out.

Aman turned to the doorman and the valet handing them several notes of dirham as a tip.

"Jump in"

"This is fabulous!" Rogan enthused as the door above his head automatically closed by Aman pressing a control button.

Sinking back into the tan leather seats that smelt of wealth, and reaching for his seat belt, Rogan noticed the charging bull Lamborghini emblem, embossed and positioned onto the top of the seat, charging over his left shoulder.

The motor gave a sexy powerful roar, as they sped off into the night.

"This is the newest and most exclusive nightclub in Dubai." Aman said as they pulled up outside.

Rogan looked at the sign above the door 'Il PARADISO'. *"Yes this is the nightclub the bell hop boy told me about."*

"Be careful, don't mix with any staff at the hotel, they are out to make money, if they find a stub of a marijuana joint in your room, they will report you to the authorities to get a reward, and you will be arrested!" Aman said motioning a sign, by rolling his thumb along the inside of his fingers like Eddy always did, at the mention of earning some money on the side.

Rogan laughed as he squeezed Aman's shoulder with affection. *'Don't worry, I don't smoke and he was too young for me!"*

Aman pressed his exit button and the door wings raised, allowing them to step out.

Two parking valets walked up to Aman's car, as he carried on walking with Rogan up to the club entrance.

"Good evening Prince Aman" The doorman said, recognising the playboy prince, who pressed several dirham notes into his hand.

Still admiring it, Rogan looked back at the stunning vehicle as it was driven away by the valets.

At a cost of £195,000 for the Lamborghini, it's safe parking needed two valets.

Inside the club, everyone seemed to know Prince Aman; this was his stage as he took the spotlight. It reminded Rogan of his popularity when years ago he was the top dog who frequented Mauies Club in Chelsea London.

Within the inner sanctum of the exclusive VIP section *'Toy Room'*, the Prince and the fallen Playboy were shown to a private booth on an upper tier overlooking the dance floor. The charge for the table including a bottle of 'Ace of Spades' Champagne cost $100.

Rogan was not aware of the cost, which was not printed on any menu, and did not care, as he was there as a guest of Prince Aman Fahid Salama.

Nor did he know that when he got up in the morning, he would be pissing a fortune away!

Being on the upper tier, gave Rogan a sense of superiority, as he was able to look down on the crowd.

Within minutes the Jet-Set of Dubai, with stunning looking girls and handsome hunks, surrounded their table. Some were making small talk comments as an excuse to be seen talking to a Prince, as if they were a personal friend.

"You looked great on the cover of Hello magazine at the Dubai Camel Racing Club races at Al Marmoum, did you win?" Said a giggly girl.

"Yes! My father's camel 'Spike' won 'Gold Cup'!

"I want to know how you got that six pack, your flaunting on the cover of GQ, airbrushing? You didn't have them two weeks ago?" A handsome boy said laughing as he butted in.

He looked like a top model, with long black hair falling over his deep-set smoky brown eyes, and a close cut moustache and beard that outlined his chiseled jaw line and sensuous lips.

"Hard work Udi." Aman said laughing as he lifted his shirt to reveal them to his friend.

"The makeup has worn off!" Udi said laughing as he enjoyed sending up his friend the Prince.

Rogan loved the attention everyone was giving as they buzzed around their table, and although they were trying to further a close relationship with Aman, it was him who was sitting alongside the Prince and drinking his champagne!

"How many magazine covers are you on?" Rogan asked in awe.

"Only three this month, I also made cover on OK!" Aman said laughing. *"Next month I shall be on the cover of 'Oil and Gas Middle East, which will please my father, as I gave a double page spread interview inside, about my directorship of his company."*

Suddenly Aman stood up, and looked down from the balcony to a group of attractive young stylishly dressed girls, seated together in a booth below.

They were all trying to out talk each other, comparing their designer dresses, jewellery, handbags, hair and rich boys with super sports cars they date, and had not noticed one of their friends was looking up to the balcony, and had set her sights on Aman.

Raising his glass of champagne and the bottle as a gesture to join him for a drink, he caught the eye of the beautiful girl with very short blonde hair, which gave her an elf like appearance. She had been looking across at him and Rogan, and lifted her empty glass in a response toast as Aman toasted her, which made her break into a broad smile.

Her top lip, outlined in a burgundy colour lipstick, had no 'Cupids Bow', just a sexy 'O' shaped mouth that begged for oral sex.

Aman motioned her to join him and Rogan.

She stood up still unnoticed by her gossiping friends, and sauntered in a sexy manner across the dance floor and up the staircase, taking every step into the future, to learn more of her invite.

Around her neck a gold pendant with a heart shaped cut diamond, hung just above her cleavage.

Aman reached out, lifting it into the palm of his hand.

Being cheeky and seductive as he stared into her eyes he said, *"I want to steal your heart."* And then kissed her on the lips.

"This is my good friend Rogan, he has just arrived from the UK and knows the Queen."

"I never said that!"

"I never said which one!" Aman joked with a wink.

He was obviously well travelled, hip and familiar with camp banter.

"And what is your name sexy?" Rogan said, as he put his arm around her waist guiding her to sit in the middle of him and Aman.

"Zaynah."

"That's a beautiful name."

"Not only handsome but how clever you are Rogan, her name means exactly that, 'Beautiful."

The sexy young Zaynah sat between the two on the leather sofa, and engaged in conversation with each in turn, and at the same time under the table, placing her hand individually on each of their inside thigh, suggesting a signal for sex.

After another bottle of Champagne, Aman caught the waiter's attention, and pointed at the bottle of Champagne.*"Put it on my account,"* and then turned to Rogan and then Zaynah. *"Come on let's go."*

"But there is still half a bottle of Champagne left! Rogan said as he lifted the bottle.

"Come on, I have plenty more in my apartment."

Zaynah looked over the balcony at her friends who were still gossiping, and still not noticed her departure, so there was no reason to say goodbye.

For a very expensive car, there was not much legroom for Rogan, who sat in the back, allowing Zaynah seated in the front to have the ride of her life, as she watched the view before her arriving at 130 mph.

Aman drove his Lamborghini to the parking bay under his apartment block, where the three got into his private lift. Using his personal key in a security lock to release the lift button, they went straight up to his penthouse.

As the lift door slid back Rogan and Zaynah were amazed at the size of the open plan apartment, and that the lights came on immediately on entering.

A sweeping staircase that had a purple strip light running along the edge of the banister and blue spotlights highlighting the side of each step, spanned from the bottom floor living room to the first and second floor.

"That's a long way up to go to bed." Rogan mused.

"I have another internal lift." Aman replied and clapped his hands that set off his giant 88 inch wall screen that begun to play a video of Madonna singing *'Erotica'* booming out, and changed the lighting to a soft sexy glow, from the table lamps placed on modern metal and glass tables alongside a semi-circle white leather sofa.

Major huge colourful abstract art paintings that were spotlighted, hung on textured silver grey walls.

Aman guided them through the on rolling rooms apartment, to an outside terrace with a large under-lit swimming pool, surrounded in tropical foliage and a rock waterfall flowing into the pool.

Clapping his hands again, another giant video screen outside overlooking the pool switched on, playing the same Madonna video as in the living room.

Rogan was taken aback by the luxury. *"This is paradise! Swimming around whilst Madonna is singing."*

"She can't sing for you by day, the Sun is too bright for the screen, so why don't we all swim now!"

Zaynah laughed, *"Yes! Yes!* And stripped naked before jumping into the pool.

Rogan and Aman looked at each other and grinned as they also stripped off naked, and then ran and jumped, bringing their knees bent up to their chest, as they splash bombed like mischievous schoolboys into the pool, sending sprays of water over the surrounding foliage.

After a short while of splashing each other in fun, Aman pulled himself up onto the side of the pool. His firm shoulders and biceps bulging, as they took the strain of lifting the rest of his body. Both Rogan and Zaynah fixated in delight on his bronzed wet muscular buttocks glistening.

Within minutes he returned clutching a bottle of Champagne and three plastic champagne flutes.

Handing one each he apologized. *"I'm sorry they are plastic, but I have to be careful, if a glass broke into the pool, I would have to drain it completely for safety, meanwhile open your mouths".*

Rogan and Zaynah clinging to the edge of the pool and looking up, at Aman's huge penis, threw their heads back and opened their mouths, as Aman ignored his own safety measures, and put the glass bottle behind his back, and re-entered it through his legs with his semi erect penis and balls resting along the neck, as he poured the champagne into their mouths.

On the giant video screen, a porno film showing an orgy of both sexes began to play.

"I thought you may enjoy this instead of more Madonna?" Aman said as he took a swig of Champagne straight from the bottle.

Rogan climbed out of the pool, his penis shining and ready for action, which he could always turn on by command for clients, but this time he was excited at the thought of having sex with the two beautiful people in the luxurious surroundings.

It had been a long time since he felt this good, almost two and a half years locked up in Belmarsh Prison, enduring cockroaches and mice in his cell, and sleeping on a rubber mattress 2 inches in depth, on a bunk bed, and a pillow filled with a few cotton wool balls, which now seemed like a bad dream.

Having just arrived in Dubai that day, Rogan felt as if his energy was flagging and needed a stronger stimulant than Champagne.

"Have you got anything stronger than Champagne?"

"You'll have to come up to my bedroom to find out." Aman said putting his arm around Rogan's neck in a friendly embrace.

"Me too!" Zaynah joined in.

"Of course! Here take a towel." Aman passed some white towels monogrammed with his initial 'A' in gold thread; he took from a shelving unit at the poolside,

Zayna wrapped hers around her body under her armpits, covering her breasts. As it was a small towel it fell short exposing her shaved crotch?

Rogan did not bother to wrap it around, and just covered his shoulders.

Aman put his arm around Zayna's neck, and led them still semi-naked to the internal golden glass lift, which had gold painted images of three wild horses galloping in the sea, on the glass panels surrounding.

The lift space was small, and the three were forced to squeeze together, with their genitals touching

Rogan's, penis became semi erect, by the closeness of their bodies, and the excitement of being in the confined tight space seemed illicit as previous sexy lift encounters; lusting over Santiago in Milan, Gisiline's Mansion and now with an Arab Prince and sexy elf.

"You're like a wild stallion," Zaynah giggled taking her inspiration from the painted images, as Rogan's penis pressed against her.

Rogan laughed, as he had been compared to a Stallion many times before.

"I'll show you more wild horses in my bedroom." Aman joked.

The lift stopped on the second floor, within Aman's bedroom.

"Come take a line." Aman said leading them to a black marble table, which had a silver bowl containing a mountain of Cocaine and alongside gold metal straws, each with one to six diamonds embedded in the sides.

"Why are there different amounts of diamonds on the straws." Zaynah asked Aman.

"It's just for you to know which straw you are using when you have another line, and you can keep it for next time you come"

"In that case I'll have this one." Zaynah said, Picking up the straw with six diamonds.

Rogan swooped in, and picked the second best valuable straw with five diamonds, in the hope Aman would give it to him as a present too?

Seeing the straws, Rogan thought back to Hugo, who would only use his fake gold colour metal straw to snort, as he thought using a rolled up bank note was unhygienic. It seemed hypocritical considering cocaine can damage your health.

"I didn't think you could get drugs in Dubai." Rogan said after snorting.

"You can't, but I can!" Aman said smugly and laughed.

After several hours of drink and drug fuelled orgy sex, Aman called the night to an end after he had made a phone call.

"I have ordered two cars to take you back to your home and hotel, as I must get up early in the morning."

Rogan walked back into his room at 4.20am, took off his clothes and threw them onto a chair and the floor, before climbing into the King size bed.

He had forgot to turn on the air conditioning, before going down to the bar earlier in the evening, and the burning heat of Dubai surrounded him.

Although he had only pulled an Egyptian cotton sheet across his naked body, it was too hot for him to sleep, causing him to kick it off and lay naked sleeping.

At 12.30pm he awoke and wondered why the chambermaid had not knocked on his door to clean the room.

The DO NOT DISTURB sign was not hanging from the inside doorknob. Curious he opened the door, and was amazed that although he had arrived back drunk he had remembered to hang the sign on the outside door handle.

He picked up the telephone receiver on the bedside table to dial for Room Service.

"Hello could I please order breakfast – Thankyou."

As he replaced the receiver, he noticed alongside a writing jot pad, the gold straw with 5 diamonds.

'Did he give it to me, or did I just take it? That's what Mother said about the pen?' He thought, and broke into a smile.

'Either way I deserved it, I don't come cheap!'

After his shower Rogan walked naked back into the bedroom, and was surprised to see a waiter pushing the breakfast trolley in front of the panoramic window.

The DO NOT DISTURB sign was on the bed where Rogan had thrown it, after he had without thinking, automatically brought it in.

"Whoops! Sorry!" Rogan said grabbing at his shirt on the chair to cover his crotch.

"I did knock Sir."

The waiter smiled and looked down at Rogan's crotch.

"Can I get you anything else?"

Rogan thought the question had an ulterior motive? *'Is everyone here on the make?'*

The waiter held out a small pad and pen. *"Could you please sign sir?"*

Rogan signed, pushed a 10 Dirham note as a tip into his hand, and opened the door for him to leave.

Lifting the silver terrines covering the breakfast dishes, he was salivating at the breakfast banquet before him.

Grilled Halloumi. Honey. Fried Eggs. Green/Black Olives. Grilled Tomatoes. Portobello Mushrooms. Sweet Potato. Smoked Beef. Coconut Croquettes. Smoked Salmon. Toast. Crème Cheese. Spiced Flatbread. Herb Rice and Saffron. Pumpkin Puree and Cardamon. Melon. Various Fruits. Orange Juice and Coffee.

He had the *'Munchies'* from all of the Champagne and drugs the night before, and this was just what he needed.

Later in the day, he took it easy relaxing on a sun lounger by the hotel pool, under a straw umbrella that shielded him from the burning 35centigrade sun.

As he sipped a Campari and orange with a slice of lemon bobbing between the ice cubes, he reflected his thoughts on the previous wild night, and his new friend Prince Aman and his fabulous Lamborghini.

'How lucky is he at 27, good looking, rich and driving a Lamborghini, where did I go wrong?'

After several hours, bored at being alone by the pool amongst old aging tourists, he went to the concierge reception desk.

"I want to hire a sports car."

"Yes sir, I have a brochure 'Super Thrill' for you to select a model, and I will order it for you, all I will need is your driving license."

"What about payment"

"It will be charged to your hotel account Sir."

Rogan flicked through the range of cars in the brochure.

"That one!" Rogan slapped the page and turned the brochure around to show the concierge behind the desk.

"Ah, an Audi R8 sports Super Thrill, that is a beautiful car and very fast, it should be for a hundred and twenty five thousand pounds!" The concierge said laughing. *" I shall call them and see if they have one available?"*

Putting his hand over the mouthpiece of the receiver the concierge asked. *Do you have a preference to colour? They have Silver or Red?"*

"Red" 'If you've got it - flaunt it!' Rogan thought.

The concierge put down the receiver. *"It will be delivered at seven thirty this evening. If you are in your room, I shall call you, otherwise a bellboy will look for you within the hotel perimeter."*

"I shall be in my room, thank-you."

'Staying in a world class hotel pays off.' Rogan thought. *'No credit checks, or checks on previous criminal activities – brilliant!'*

Just as the concierge said, at 7.30 the phone in Rogan's room rang. He picked up the receiver. The voice on the other end was the concierge.

"Mr Ford, your sports car has arrived, please bring your driving license down to confirm your hire – Thank you."

At the concierge desk Rogan met with a representative from *'Super Thrill Sports Car hire'* and signed the paperwork for two weeks hire of the car.

A sense of excitement came over him as he pressed his foot down on the accelerator, and heard the sound of the powerful sexy engine.

As he passed shop windows he glanced to the side, catching the flashing reflection of himself, driving the flame red Audi Sports.

Not knowing where he was going didn't matter, as he was enjoying the prestige of being seen in the sports car.

He made a sharp turn at a high speed, and hit the front offside fender on a street bollard.

"Fuck! Fuck! What's that dong there?" He screamed as he stopped and got out to see what damage had been done.

Running his hand over the fender, which was very badly dented, he hoped of a miraculous intervention miracle of his hand curing the dent to disappear – But he was not God and it didn't!

He got back into the car and sat thinking of what excuse he could say to the car hire Super Thrill.

After a while he got out, purposely leaving the door open, and walked back along the road towards the Jumeirah hotel. Spotting a taxi, he flagged it down to stop and take him back to the hotel.

On the way he concocted a story and rehearsed in his mind, of what to say.

As he arrived at the luxurious opulent hotel, he walked fast up to the concierge, and acted in a distressed state pushing in front of some American tourists checking in.

"Phone the police, the car has been stolen, somebody must have followed me from the hotel? I'm lucky they did not kill me!"

The new arrival Americans looked shocked at Rogan's dramatic entrance and outburst, as they stepped aside.

"Harry did you hear that! I told you it wasn't safe to come to Dubai, we should have gone to Israel, but NO! You wanted to see the Pyramids!" The confused elderly woman tourist said to her husband.

"How many more times have I got to tell you Phyllis, the Pyramids are in Egypt!

"Alright already, to me they are all Arabs and they don't like Jews!

"Don't be silly, Marsha comes here every year and raves about it, she said we would love it here."

"What does she know? She's still living in that run down Condo on the East Side!"

The Concierge focused on Rogan. "I'm sorry to hear this Mr Ford," and hit the button on the top of a gold desk bell, to attract the bellboy who ran forward.

"Get Mr Ford any drink he requires"

"Just water please, this is a terrible shock." Rogan was aware, if the police smelt alcohol on his breath, they might be suspicious.

"Whilst you're at it, get two more, my Harry and I are shvitzing from this heat. Oh, and a slice of lemon in them would be nice and refreshing." The old woman said, leaning over to the bellboy.

"Take a seat Mr Ford, I will telephone Super Thrill Sports Cars on your behalf and let them know the situation." The concierge said with sympathetic concern.

Rogan sat in the Lobby, waiting for the police and going over in his mind of a fabricated story he would tell.

"Mr Ford." Before him stood two very attractive young women police officers wearing the standard uniform, olive green shirt with a red rope band running under the left arm and looped through the left epaulette, olive green trousers and black boots. They were both wearing headscarves due to their Islam religion, finished off with a small trilby style hat in white and olive green, bearing a golden police badge perched on top of their heads and over the scarf.

Rogan stood up. *"Yes thank you for coming, I've had a terrible experience. I went for a pleasure drive in the Audi Sports I had just hired today, to see the dancing water fountains on the Burj Khalifa Lake. I parked in a side road by the Armani Hotel, but must have left the door open, as I am not too familiar with the locking. When the fountain show was over, I went back to the car, but it was gone! I couldn't believe it!"*

A police officer interrupted. *"We have the car."*

"You do! Fantastic! Rogan exuberated.

"It has an offside large dent in the fender, and looks as if someone has crashed it into a bollard? – Pretty bad!"

"How did you find it so quickly?"

"It was parked illegally and towed away. The number plate is registered to Super Thrill Sports Cars. We contacted them and they gave us your details, so were coming to see you here anyway."

"What now" Rogan carried on his act of concern.

"Tomorrow we will gather video footage from the security cameras in the area, and try and trace the driver. For now enjoy the rest of your stay in Dubai – Goodnight."

Rogan went up to his room, and took several miniature whisky bottles out of the mini-bar.

'What am I going to do? What am I going to do?' He kept *repeating in his mind.*

He knew once the police viewed the video security cameras in the area, they would know it was him that crashed the car, and that he had been lying to them.

Fearful, that in Dubai no matter how small, they will lock up a person for any misdemeanor, his mind went into overdrive.

The telephone in his room rang, as he took another swig of neat whisky.

"Mr Ford, my name is Khalifa from Super Thrill Cars, we have been notified by the police and the reception at your hotel, the Audi sports car you hired from us, has been involved in an accident and that they are investigating. We had our own investigators collect the street security videotapes

surrounding the area of the Armani Hotel, who are our associates. Unfortunately it shows you clearly driving when the accident occurred, and you leaving the car on the roadside.

Rogan shouted into the phone. *"That's impossible! I did not crash that car! It was stolen. It must be someone who looks like me?"*

Khalifa ignored Rogan's defense as lies, and continued.
" After inspecting the car, our engineers report shows that not only will the offside fender and door have to be replaced, but also an out of alignment to parts of the engine.
The cost assessment for repairs is seventy-five thousand, sterling." Khalifa came straight to the point. *"How will you be paying?"*
There was a long pause from Rogan.
"Sir?" Khalifa enquired, wondering if they were still connected?

"Seventy-five thousand pounds! Are you fucking mad? For a knock that I DID NOT DO!" Rogan retaliated.

"Mr Ford it would be better if you came down to the lobby, so that we can discuss this face to face."

"I can't, I've just had a call before yours, from a hospital in the UK to tell me my Mother has had a heart attack, and I am waiting for them to call back to tell me how serious it is? I shall have to deal with this in the morning."

Rogan's deathbed excuse went over Khalifa's head, and he became firm and threatening.
"Mr Ford, not only have you smashed our Audi Sports, but you are also a wanted man in the UK. We have already checked with the UK authorities, you leave me no option other than to

report this to the Police, who will probably arrest you and hand you over to the police in the UK."

Rogan threw the receiver down. *"Seventy five thousand! They're having a laugh, fucking conmen!"*

(Karma had taken it's turn, Video footage and recordings that he attempted to use for his own illegal financial gain, had come back to bite him on the bum!)

Remembering his prison mantra, he said repeatedly out loud to boost his confidence in handling the situation.

'Don't let the bastards get you! Don't let the bastards get you!'

They wont! He thought, as he started to throw his clothes and cosmetics into his suitcase as fast as he could.

There were always guests leaving the hotel on his floor. All he had to do would be to catch a bellboy pushing a trolley of cases along the hallway to the lift.

After opening his door several times, he eventually caught one.

"Hey! Could you take my case as well?" He called out to the bellboy who looked back.

Rogan was in luck it was Jabbad.

Jabbad looked back and broke into a full smile. *"Hello Mr Ford, are you leaving already? You've only been here a few days, I wanted to show you the sexy nightclubs."*

"I have a problem with my business and have to leave immediately."

"Okay I take your case to reception." He said in broken English as he lifted Rogan's case and placed it on top of the other guest's suitcases.

"Wait just a minute I will come in the lift with you."

Rogan grabbed his jacket he left on a chair, closed the door and got into the lift with Jabbad and the suitcase trolly.

Jabbad pushed the trolley towards the concierge reception desk and parked it there for the guests checking out. Rogan hung back waiting for his opportunity for the receptionist and concierge to be involved and distracted with the guests checking out bills.

His luck continued as Phyllis and Harry the new American guests were at the desk, pushing their way in front of other guests trying to check out, and causing the distraction he needed for his escape!

"There's a smell coming from the toilet, and Harry hadn't even been in there yet." Phyllis complained to the concierge.

Rogan grabbed his suitcase from the top of the pile, and walked out of the hotel and got into the taxi at the front of the line sitting outside the hotel entrance.

Suddenly Jabbad ran up to the taxi as it begun to move, and banged on the side window. *"Mr Ford, Mr Ford!"*

The taxi stopped and Rogan pressed the button to lower the tinted side window.

"You dropped this in the reception hall." Holding up the gold and diamond cocaine straw Rogan had got from the Prince."

Rogan laughed. *"Keep it or sell it, you'll be able to buy yourself a car."* Jabbad smiled.

"To the airport, drive on fast I'm late for my flight." Rogan instructed the driver.

Turning in his seat, he looked back at Jabbad still smiling and waving goodbye, who had realized Rogan was making a quick get-away!

"You are lucky, I have one seat left." The woman said at the British Airways ticket desk.

"Boarding for London Heathrow at gate K7 is open, please make your way there immediately before it closes."

Rogan thought the Lucky Stars must be in alignment, as everything was falling into place for his getaway.

London

As the plane approached Heathrow, Rogan needed his luck to hold out just a little bit longer, for him to be cleared entry into the UK through passport control, without being stopped as a fugitive and arrested.

As he stood in the long line and gradually got closer to the officer sitting behind a desk, checking travelers passports for entry, he wished Phyllis and Harry who had been staying at the Burj Al Arab Jumeirah Hotel would be his accomplices to divert attention from him again.

Trying to look confidently cool and not nervous, Rogan placed his passport in front of the officer checking. As the officer opened it he sneezed! And took a handkerchief from his pocket to wipe his nose.

"Gesundheit!" Rogan said, pleased of the good omen that had distracted the officer's full attention from his list of wanted criminals, who then handed his passport back for him to walk through into the UK.

Rogan was chuffed. *'Made it!'* He said under his breath.

"Just let me in!"
"Oh you're back!"
Lisa was surprised to see and hear Rogan's voice on the main front door video entry intercom, at the block of flats where she lived.

Impatiently he pressed the intercom buzzer several more times, as at the same time Lisa also pressed the entry button several more times to make sure the door was opening. She often got confused with the three operation buttons 'Sound, Video, Entry', as some of the symbols had worn away, and she was never sure of what button to press for Entry.

Rogan pushed open the heavy entry door painted royal blue with brass fittings. *"Bitch!"* He mumbled to himself.

He never knew the reason of why his mother and father had got divorced, and Lisa would never tell him, which left him to a conclusion, that it was her fault? He had mixed feelings of his love towards her, as although she could be devious, she always stood by him.

Lisa stood at her open front door, waiting for him to arrive from the lift.

As he entered the flat dragging his case on wheels past her, she gave out a mini scream. *"Oh damn you! You ran over my foot! Don't you give your Mother a kiss? Where have you been and where's my pen?"* Lisa fired a barrage of questions.

"You're pen! Don't you mean Carter's? I should've known once you got your hands on it, you weren't going to return it. All that crying in Marbella." Rogan mimicked her voice. *"I must have been drunk, I don't remember, I must return it immediately. Liar!"*

"Don't worry you'll get it back, as long you can pay five and half thousand to Bonnington's Pawn Brokers on Fulham road."

"You pawned it! The Police came here two days ago looking for you, as your electronic monitoring ankle tag reported to the base unit, there was a fault. I told you that once you cut it off, it would send some sort of signal. They said there is a warrant out for you to be rearrested. Where have you been?"

Rogan began shouting. *"I've been in fucking Dubai, I'm not going back to that rat infested Belmarsh prison, I'd rather die!"*

"But why have you come back?"

"A car hire company tried to con me, I had a prang on a hire car and they wanted to get seventy five thousand pounds from me, so I legged it!"

Lisa laughed, *"Ha! Some hope, I'm still trying to get seventy five pounds out of you for the cocaine I paid to your dealer, and what chance have I got in raising five and half thousand to get the pen back?"*

Rogan sarcastically laughed. *"Ha, that's my Mum, she knows every penny! You'll find a way or some rich mug."*

"Well somebody has to keep control."

"Control, that's a laugh, you couldn't even control yourself nicking the pen. Were you going to write to Carter with his pen, and sign it from your Pen Friend! Yea, Yea, here we go, I've not got my shoes off and you're ready to argue. Isn't it enough the pigs are after me again? I'm exhausted and going to bed."

Don't you want something to eat?"

"No I ate on the plane, I'll just have a drink and sandwich."

Lisa stroked his face. *"Okay mummy will bring it in."*

Rogan screwed up his face indicating disapproval, and made a tut sound, by touching his tongue to the roof of his mouth, in response to Lisa's remark at treating him as a child.

No matter what he did, he was still Mummies little boy.

"Not just yet, in about an hour."

Lisa knocked on the door.

"Yea." Rogan called out, giving her permission to walk into his bedroom.

Lisa placed a plate and a glass of orange juice on the bedside table.

"I've made you a nice chicken and salad sandwich, it will give you some energy."

After twenty minutes, Lisa gave a tap on the bedroom door again and entered.

"You've only eaten half of the sandwich, didn't you like it." She said picking up the plate.

"I've had enough."

Lisa turned and went to the door.

Rogan called out. *"Thanks Mum, I do love you."*

"And I love you." Lisa paused, *"Are you sure you don't want the rest of this sandwich?"*

242

Rogan smiled and repeated. *"I've had enough."* Lisa closed the bedroom door.

Rogan got out of his bed and moved a chest of drawers opposite his bed, just enough for him to reach behind and pull part of the skirting away between the wall and the floor, to get to his secret hideaway.

Taking out his stash, of four grams of cocaine, Tramadol, and Diazepan Barbiturates.

He sat back on the bed, and poured a full glass of Champagne he had bought at Dubai Duty Free, into the glass he had drunk the orange from, and then emptied all of the pills from the bottles into a small empty tray he used for loose change. After a few swigs of Champagne and snorting the cocaine, he grabbed a handful of the mixed pills, and swished them down his throat with another gulp of Champagne, and repeated the pill cocktail and coke several more times.

A short while later, the pills began to take effect as he hallucinated, seeing characters from his past.

"Want a line, I've got some great gear." Eddy was saying with his infectious cheeky grin.

"Yea! Yeah!" Rogan replied and leaned over from his bed to the side table, where earlier he had laid out six lines of cocaine.

As he snorted them all at once using a rolled up fifty-pound note, Hugo appeared.

"I told you! Use a metal straw you don't know who handled that note before? It's unhygienic!"

Rogan laughed. *"Hugo you old tart! Always there when I need you."*

Slipping in and out of conciseness, Hugo faded as another image appeared.

"I love my diamond gold straw, thank you."

"Jabbad! Hey! Jabbad sell it, buy a car and have a good time."

A giant of a man stood flexing his muscles.

"Master Spartacus! You beat me with pain on my flesh, which was no match to the pain in my head. I just want it to stop!"

Rogan was delirious...

"I've had enough mum..."

11. 38am MALE FOR–

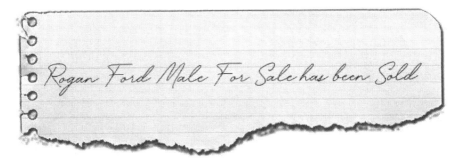

"Rogan... Rogan do you want a cup of tea?" Lisa called out as she knocked on the door.
There was no answer? She entered the bedroom.
Rogan was naked on top of his bed, clutching the empty Champagne bottle to his chest, his eyes closed, his skin pale. Fifty-pound notes and Kleenex tissues scattered over his duvet.

"Rogan! Rogan! Rogan! Aghhh! Lisa screamed as she clutched him on the bed, and cried. *"Wake up! Wake up my little boy, what have you done?*
Kissing him on his cheek, she stroked his head. *"I would have told the police you are a good boy".*

Lisa noticed a screwed up written note in his hand.
She took it to read...

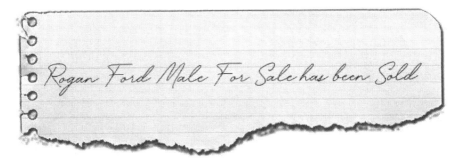

Rogan Ford Male For Sale has been Sold

It was poetic justice that Rogan died surrounded by Champagne, Cocaine, Sex, Money - Retribution just at arms length...

Footnote:

Hugo decided not to go back to work at Ranley, and moved permanently to Marbella, where he dabbled in Antiques and young men!

Lisa got one of her 'Tricks' to loan her the £5,500 she needed to get the hundred and fifty thousand pound 'Montblanc Boheme Papillon' pen out of pawn. She went to Monaco; sold it, and never paid back the loan.

Jabbad did not buy a car with the sale of his gold diamond studded straw. He invested in a new build hotel, and after many years became Managing Director of a Hotel World Franchise.

Eddy was detained and questioned by the police, after acting suspiciously, whilst viewing The Crown Jewels at The Tower Of London.

"I only wanted to try on a bit of Bling!" Was his explanation?

(An attempt to steal them by Colonel Thomas Blood in May 1671 was foiled)